FOR LOVE OF GOD

BOOK 1 OF THE BLESSED BE SERIES

ROBIN REARDON

IAM Books
www.robinreardon.com

FOR LOVE OF GOD
Book 1 of the BLESSED BE series

Cover and formatting by Sweet 'N Spicy Designs
Front cover photograph adapted by Alex Calder
Back cover photograph by Robin Rohrabacher

The events and characters of this book are entirely fictional. Although most of the locations in the story exist, any similarity to events or people, living or dead, is entirely coincidental.

Scriptural references in *For Love Of God* come directly from the *World English Bible*, 2022, available in electronic format through eBooksLib.com and through electronic book retailers. The following information about the *World English Bible* comes from eBible.org: "The *World English Bible* (WEB) is a public domain (no copyright) modern English translation of the *Holy Bible*, based on the American Standard Version of the *Holy Bible* first published in 1901, the *Biblia Hebraica Stutgartenza Old Testament,* and the *Greek Majority Text New Testament.*"

ISBN: 978-1-7340569-4-5

Praise for Robin Reardon's *Trailblazer* series

"Reardon's prose is gorgeous. She always surprises with her originality and her emotional writing. I anxiously await whatever she writes."
— *Amos Lassen Reviews: Best of 2020*

"While I would argue that *On The Precipice* is the most haunting and powerful entry of the series, the entire trilogy is wholly inspirational, fulfilling, and unforgettable."
— *Christopher Verleger, Edge Media Network*

"Robin Reardon invites the reader on a trip that will lead her characters to embrace hard truths about themselves and those they love but also reveal a vast store of courage they never knew they had."
— *Sammy, Diverse Reader*

"I don't give five stars lightly, saving them only for books that I feel are out of the ball park. I adore everything about this series."
— *Cheryl Headford, Love Bytes Reviews*

Many thanks to the Reverend Reid D. Farrell, Jr., my friend, advisor, and guide on this journey into the world of the Episcopal priesthood. The genuine love he feels for God and for all people, tempered by a gentle irreverence for absurdities from any source, made working with him a true pleasure.

From American mythologist, Joseph Campbell (1904-1987):

*"If you can see your path laid out in front of you step by step,
you know it's not your path."*

*"We must let go of the life we have planned so as to accept the
one that is waiting for us."*

"O Lord, you have taught us that without love, whatever we do is worth nothing."

~ The Episcopal Book of Common Prayer, 1979 edition

After 40 years' experience as an ordained Episcopal priest who also happens to be a gay man, I have known any number of Spencer Hills and Donald Raineys—the two main characters in *For Love Of God*—and I can tell you that their struggles are very real and in earnest. Robin Reardon has captured them incredibly well: their thoughts and feelings, their conflicts, and their confusion.

Having lived through the late nineteen seventies and early eighties, when the Episcopal Church was beginning to establish its position on the ordination of gay people, I understand and identify with both of Reardon's main characters. At the time this story takes place, there was no church-wide policy regarding our (gay people's) ordinations. Discussions had begun as had a great deal of controversy throughout the church, and that left gay people in a precarious position with a difficult choice to make.

What do you do if you feel called to the ordained ministry, and you're gay? Do you follow your calling and continue to embrace the faith tradition and the community you have known all your life? If so, you will either deny yourself the joy and fulfillment of a committed same-sex relationship or, worse yet, you will live a clandestine "other life" that can arguably be said to be living a lie. Or do you choose the other option—deny your calling, the calling you believe comes from God—and reject all that you have known of faith tradition and community, and then yearn for it while at the same time mourning the loss? Neither position is healthy mentally, intellectually, physically, or spiritually. Nor is either position what Jesus would have us do.

What did Jesus say? "Love one another as I have loved you." "Abide in my love." "I came that you might have life and have it abundantly." These are not words of exclusion, but of inclusion... not words of rejection and condemnation, but of acceptance and blessing... not words of hatred and division, but words of love, encouragement, and people coming together.

For Love Of God is the first book in Robin Reardon's trilogy, *Blessed Be*. The message she conveys is one of encouragement, not just for the young, but for people of all ages: open up; be who you really are; live honestly and authentically. The character Spencer Hill is only just learning how.

For Love Of God is a story of love and loss, of faith and doubt, of interpersonal relationships and a young man's relationship with himself. Prepare yourself for an inspirational and challenging read.

The Reverend Reid D. Farrell, Jr.
Sarasota, Florida
May 2022

CONTENTS

Note that while reading all three of the Blessed Be books in order will take you on Spencer Hill's journey with him—his first love, his successes and failures, and the maturity he gains along the way—each book can be read and enjoyed individually.

CHAPTER ONE

I shifted my position in the small, wooden, classroom chair. It had been a few years since I was short enough to manage comfort in one of these things. Now, in my first year of divinity school, I was seeing the world from a height of six feet two inches, and this chair was beyond ridiculous for me. I felt ridiculous in it. And it was only the second class of the fall semester. But I was not at the seminary today. I was in a classroom at New School, taking a course in acting.

I felt another jolt. The third one. That was the third time the guy behind me had bumped into this silly chair. Maybe he, too, was very tall and didn't know where to put his legs? I hadn't noticed. But, surely he must realize— And another jolt.

God damn it! This has got to stop!

I turned as much as I could in my cramped position to glare at whoever was in the chair behind mine, this person who kept kicking my chair. My eyes landed on the face of a young man, perhaps my age, perhaps a little older, with the most impossibly long, curly eyelashes I had ever seen. They embellished hazel eyes that were almost green, they had so little brown in them, other than a startling ring of brown around the irises. He had thick, light brown hair long enough to hide his ears.

The words I had planned—*What are you, a six-year-old in an airplane seat?*—never made it outside my head.

One of the eyes winked at me and one side of the mouth lifted in an impish grin.

Torn between wanting to watch that face for its next expression and wishing I could tell the guy off, I turned slowly back in my chair to face the front, where the instructor coached another student in the art of vocal production: projecting, pacing, and dramatic delivery. I'd signed up for this course after Dr. Dunfey, my advisor at General Theological Seminary, had told me my stage presence needed improving if I ever hoped to succeed as a priest. He'd recommended this class in particular.

"Spencer," he'd told me, "you'll never hold a congregation's interest with that monotone. It doesn't even sound like you're interested, yourself."

Mostly, I was doing quite well in my first year at General. But there were two areas that felt like stumbling blocks: my lifeless delivery style; and the fact that I had known for some time I was gay.

By mid-October in this class, I'd had an opportunity to demonstrate my lackluster style. I think "unimpressed" is the best word to describe their response to what they'd heard from me. They'd seemed impressed initially, when each student had described their reason for taking the class, and I'd mentioned my intended vocation. So my intention had impressed them. I, clearly, did not.

Typically the instructor would assign material to some number of students each class, and they'd be on the spot to present at the next class. I paid attention to everyone's presentation, truly wanting to improve my own skills. So I was listening carefully the first time chair-kicking guy took his turn.

His name was Donald Rainey. And instead of the assigned material, he presented something entirely different. His material was from David Bowie's "Space Oddity" song, with Major Tom floating above Earth in a space capsule, out of communication with everything and everyone, getting loopier and loopier.

Donald used just the lyrics from the song, not the music; he didn't sing. When Ground Control was speaking, he turned his back to the class and covered his mouth with his hands, his voice scratchy and distorted. Then he'd turn around and be Major Tom.

Ground Control's script included silly things like telling Tom he's a star, and people want to know what kind of clothes he wears. Tom says he's "floating in a most peculiar way." Then he feels ill and asks that someone tell his wife he loves her. Ground Control's voice grows urgent, telling Tom his circuit's dead, repeating, "Can you hear me, Major Tom?" over and over, while Tom floats, able to control nothing.

I expected that everyone in the class had at least heard the song, even though it was released maybe fifteen years ago, I think in nineteen sixty-nine. But without Bowie's music, just Donald saying the words and portraying Major Tom's dizziness and—even more—his helplessness, the effect left us all silent and stunned.

Perhaps the instructor would have criticized Donald for not presenting the assigned material, except that the portrayal was so… well, transporting.

It was after this class that Donald approached me. As everyone collected their materials and milled about, I turned to lift my jacket off my chair and was surprised to see Donald standing there, looking at me. He was perhaps three inches shorter than I.

"I could help you, y'know."

"I beg your pardon?"

"So very formal, aren't we, Spencer Hill?" He winked at me, and then grinned. "Seriously, though, I admire your intentions. The priesthood, and all. My father was a Lutheran minister." He flung a hand out to the side, a gesture somewhere between flamboyant and dismissive. An edge of facetiousness to his voice, he added, "I'm sure it's how I ended up in acting."

Unsure what to say, I was silent.

He told me, "Dad was quite the orator. Probably where I got my start."

"You're an actor," I said, needlessly. "What have you been in?"

He laughed. "Probably nothing you'd have seen. Mostly off-off Broadway."

I shook my head in confusion, unable to recall what he'd said about his reason for being here. "Why would you take this class? You obviously don't need it."

"I'm auditing." He shrugged one shoulder, as though he knew that wasn't much of an explanation. "You never know where you'll learn something useful. But I'm serious. I could help you."

"And how would you do that?"

"Coaching. One-on-one. You'd almost certainly improve more quickly with personal attention than in a class with fifteen other students."

I could feel myself scowl; it was rather bold of him to assume he'd be a better coach than the instructor. "*Why* would you do that?"

"Like I said, I admire your reason for being here. But, hey," and he lifted his own jacket off a chair, "if you don't want to, no biggie. Just thought I'd offer."

I don't make decisions quickly. Sometimes I don't make them at all and just let things turn out however they will. That day, I watched Donald turn and walk away without a glance back at me.

General Seminary was within walking distance of where I'd grown up, where my mother still lived, so I hadn't moved on-campus. Also, Father had died during my third year at Columbia, so if I had moved out, Mother would have been on her own, forlorn and lonely in the gilded cage of the formally decorated townhouse in the Gramercy Park area of Manhattan.

When I got home the afternoon of Donald Rainey's unsolicited offer of help, Mother was not there, probably at one of her church committee meetings. I'd been unable to get Donald's face, his wink, his smile out of my mind's eye. And I wasn't sure what to make of his offer. Was he gay? Had he picked up that I am? I had been so careful to hide that part of myself from Father when he was still alive, from Mother always, certainly from everyone associated with my family's church, St. Ignatius of Antioch Episcopal, and from the seminary. So if someone who barely knew me had figured it out—well, I'll just say I found the prospect haunting.

As a distraction, I went into the music room to play piano for a while.

I love the piano, the black and white keys, so orderly, so easily distinguishable one from the other, flowing out from the center of the instrument in a pattern that repeats itself in a way that can be relied upon, trusted. But I also loved the music it produced.

My teacher since I was eight years old, Miss Farnsworth, had been happy to have me work on the Bach and Mozart pieces Father had loved. But by the time I was sixteen, already tall and with hands to match, she had another idea.

"Bach and Mozart have taught you discipline and restraint," she told me. "Bach is about voicing and counterpoint, and Mozart is about subtlety and control. They're both about technique. Now, however," and she smiled and gazed at me from under her pale eyebrows. "Look at your hands. Look at the length of the strong fingers."

She held up her right hand, and I placed my left palm against it. She spread her fingers apart, and I followed with mine.

She said, "Keep going. Keep spreading."

By the time I had reached my hand's full spread I had left hers behind in the proverbial dust.

She pulled her hand away and grinned at me. "Do you know what you can do that many pianists cannot?" I shook my head. "Chopin. Many pianists play his music with smaller hands than yours, but you will be able to do true justice to it, which requires a hand-spread larger than most people have. And Spencer?" She waited until she was sure she had my attention. "You are a very expressive musician. You will be able to make it sing."

I'd started with some of the less ambitious pieces—a waltz, a nocturne—but I'd loved the music and had moved quickly toward the Barcarolle in F-Sharp Major, which I was playing that day, after Donald's Major Tom presentation.

I didn't know Mother had come home. I was at the piano, and—facing the keyboard—I couldn't see the door to the hall very well. I executed the long, liquid runs that lead to the final cadence as well as I'd ever done. My fingers lingered on the smooth, cool surface of the keys before I released them from the final chord. And I heard a slight sound, almost but not quite a sigh.

I turned and saw Mother standing in the doorway, watching me. I wasn't surprised that she'd been listening. I knew she loved to hear me play, as had Father (though his comments had been along the lines of "Good job on that Mozart sonata, Spencer. You're no Vladimir Ashkenazy, but—not bad"). No; what surprised me was the look on Mother's face.

Tears stood in her eyes, making them glisten even in the late October afternoon light that barely lit the room through the floor-to-ceiling windows. Her face was soft, though; these were not tears of grief or pain. And she glowed.

I saw delight. I saw joy. I saw the kind of rapture that might even be called euphoria.

It was a remarkably pretty face, still almost as pretty as in the photos I'd seen of her as a young woman, after she'd left the path she'd been on toward the convent so she could marry my father. Perhaps that beauty had been part of what had tempted him away from his calling as a Catholic priest, away from being any kind of priest, leaving cassock and altar behind.

Pretty as she was, though, I couldn't recall ever seeing on that face the kind of emotion I saw as the final notes of the barcarolle faded in the room.

She covered her mouth with a hand briefly, and when she dropped it the joy was gone. She smiled with her mouth, not with her eyes. The soft, tender look had been replaced by the pleasant, neutral face she'd typically worn while Father had been alive.

She didn't speak before she turned and walked away, but it was almost as though she'd said, "Lovely, dear. Your father will be home any minute. Perhaps some Mozart now?"

I spent the next couple of days searching through every theater announcement I could find, scouring the information for the name Donald Rainey.

I found it.

So Saturday evening I stood outside an obscure theater in the Union Square area of town, in a short line of people waiting to buy tickets for a production of Shakespeare's *A Midsummer Night's Dream*. The actor playing Puck was Donald Rainey.

I sat as far from the stage as I could, which in that small house wasn't terribly far. No one sat to my right, but on my left was a woman who reminded me, somewhat disconcertingly, of my mother.

Watching the characters cavort about for our entertainment, I felt myself reminded of high school, and it wasn't because I sat beside someone who could have been my mother. No; I found myself glad of the jacket I had worn. Bunched in my lap, it enabled me to be certain I hid what was happening.

I was getting an erection.

It started as Puck talked about the practical jokes he would play on people: being a crab in a gossip's bowl of soup, only to come frighteningly to life; pretending to be a three-legged stool only to slip away as someone attempted to sit.

Obviously, these statements were not erotic. It was Puck himself. Every look, every gesture he made seemed rife with carnality. Oh, hell; rife with *sex*. Though I had known I was gay for a few years, I had never acted on it. I'd been as chaste as if I'd taken a vow.

When Puck left the stage at the end of that scene, a silent sigh of relief left my body. And yet, once he was gone from the stage, I found it hard to concentrate on the conflict between Helena and Demetrius or on anything else, until Puck reappeared.

It was tantalizing.

As the play wore on, I waited for each of Puck's appearances. I knew the play; I didn't need to follow every character to know what was going on. So it would seem like forever until Puck appeared again.

Such a wonderfully silly play. Or so I had found it in the past. There was Flute. Snout. Bottom. Cobweb. Peaseblossom. Moth. Mustardseed. All delightfully ridiculous characters. But there was only one I wanted to see. Hear. Feel.

I barely caught any of his words. Something warm expanded within me, and my head buzzed in a way that nearly blocked out sound. I knew Puck was fated to sprinkle a magic love potion on the wrong man, because he mistook him for another. The actors playing Demetrius and Lysander looked nothing alike, and I wondered if it had been the director's intention to demonstrate that Puck cared so little for human foibles that he couldn't tell the two apart.

I watched intently as Puck tiptoed up to the sleeping Lysander, Donald's body absurdly contorted to exaggerate—or even ridicule—his need to be quiet. And when he was about to release the magic dust, he turned toward the audience with the most devilish grin on his face, and in a sudden thrust of his arm a handful of sparkles flew away from the stage.

As his hand, now open, was lifted high over his shoulder, he looked out at the audience. And he looked directly at me. His head tilted to the side just for an instant, and then he was back in his role again, releasing sprinkles from his other hand over Lysander.

Did he actually see me? It felt like torture not to know, not to be sure.

Once the scripted mistake was done, the unintended consequences troubled Puck not at all. His comment: "Lord, what fools these mortals be!"

I left the theater quickly, during the audience's final enthusiastic applause. I walked toward home at a determined pace, head down, barely aware of the chilly night air. But I didn't want to *be* home. I couldn't respond reasonably to reasonable questions from Mother about the play, about whether I had enjoyed it, about how it compared to other productions I'd seen. So I headed for that small, intimate oasis known as Gramercy Park.

In most cases, strolling through a Manhattan park at night is inadvisable. But as a resident of Gramercy Park East, I had a key to the locked gate. I used it.

Nowhere in New York City is it ever truly dark at night, unless one wanders deep into Central Park, or ventures into the inner tangles of Inwood Hill Park at the north end of the island.

So I was able to walk easily into Gramercy Park, find a bench, and sit staring at the statue of Edwin Thomas Booth. His fame is a little overshadowed by John Wilkes Booth, his younger brother and the assassin of Abraham Lincoln.

ET, as I like to refer to him, stands forever, having just risen from one of those open-backed, bucket-seat chairs one often sees depicted in affluent homes from sixteenth century Europe. There's a pelt of some kind draped across the seat.

ET wears a tunic with a hem above his knees, and a shawl is draped low across his chest. ET's right hand leans gently on the side of the chair, his left hand near his throat, head bowed just slightly as if in deep thought, or contemplating something of significance he is about to say.

Regarding him that night, I was struck by the similarity between ET's fame and the fame that Donald, it seemed, pursued: that of an actor. In fact, as anyone looking at this statue might guess, ET's specialty was Shakespeare's work, though he preferred the dramatic to the comedic, the tragic hero to the fool.

Fool.

Suddenly I was no longer looking at the statue. I was not thinking of Donald. All my attention was on scenes inside my head as they tumbled one over the other:

Father chastising me when my middle school peers, hearing of my intention even at that young age to go into the priesthood, called me "Stuffy shorts" and worse;

Father responding to my wailed "I feel like a fool!" by saying, "Be a fool for God, Spencer. Be a fool for Christ;"

Father's rigid disappointment when anything I had done—from school grades to a stray dinner comment—caused his displeasure, casting me yet again in the figurative role of the fool.

And, finally, there was Puck's accusation, his condemnation of foolish "mortals."

A fool. I would *not* be a fool! Not for Puck, not for Father, not even for God. I would be a priest, humble unto my role, but not a fool.

And—as I nearly said aloud—I would not submit myself to Donald's guidance. I would rely on the instructor to do his job, and I would play my part and learn.

It was a good feeling, that resolve. But it didn't survive past that night.

CHAPTER TWO

The class was held once each week, and I spent the remainder of the time before the next class struggling with myself—a useless pursuit, I have come to realize. Analyzing a situation, considering pros and cons, that's one thing. But one cannot win a wrestling match with oneself.

I tried to be honest with myself about why Donald's offer was so tempting. Was it his proven acting ability? His evident personal charm? His self-confidence, a quality I'd always found seductive in others? Or was the commitment to improve myself, the intention to satisfy Dr. Dunfey, what motivated me?

But if I'm honest, the most troubling aspect of Donald's offer was the realization that I was attracted to him—more so than ever after seeing him as Puck—and that he might very well be attracted to me. Else, why had he singled me out? There were others in the class who would benefit from personal attention, and his stated reason for approaching me was not very convincing.

And there had been the chair kicking. It hadn't occurred to me at the time, but after consideration, his behavior seemed to resemble that of a ten-year-old boy, wanting the attention of the pretty girl who sat in front of him in class. The boy might pull the girl's hair. He might drop his pencil on the floor beside her and grin oddly at her as he bent to retrieve it.

He might kick her chair.

I was now convinced Donald was gay. What I didn't know was whether he'd guessed that I, too, was gay, and whether he merely wanted to connect on that basis or because he was attracted to me.

I wasn't entirely sure what effect coming out would have on my candidacy as a priest. I knew there were gay priests, but I didn't know whether they had identified themselves in any formal way. Certainly, they were not all out, except perhaps to each other. So what if I started some kind of relationship with another man—Donald Rainey, for example—and then were discovered? Would it have been better if I had confessed to Dr. Dunfey about my orientation before something like that could happen? Because what if the truth were never discovered, and there had been no need to confess?

And was it a confession? Was it the sin it was called in the Bible? Or was it a fact of nature?

It was a fact of *my* nature. Of that much, I was certain, despite my complete lack of experience in the realm of relationships.

I'm not sure what pushed me into my final decision to accept Donald's offer. All I know is that I couldn't get his face out of my mind.

"Fabulous!" was Donald's excited response when I gave him my permission to take me under his proverbial wing. "When do we start?"

"Well, I—" *When do we start?* Why was he asking me? I had expected he had a plan. Maybe this was the time for me to stop going with the flow, to take some initiative. I glanced around at the other students, chatting and meandering as they made their way out of the room at the end of class. I couldn't have said why, but it seemed advisable not to advertise the special attention I'd be getting, special attention from someone whom other students had possibly recognized as gay.

No one was watching us, of course. I asked, "Do you have time now?"

"I do. Shall we just wait until everyone leaves? I think this room will be empty for a while. We can stay right here."

He busied himself pulling a few things out of his backpack. As he set one small book after another onto a desk top, I read the titles. I saw *Equus. Sleuth. California Suite.* Clearly, he had come prepared. He had anticipated me.

"I saw your performance Saturday night."

He looked up from the copy of *Sleuth* in his hand. "Yes." Not a question. His tone didn't seem to be asking for more than I'd said.

"You saw me in the audience?"

"I did. Listen, I think we'll start with this one." He handed me *Sleuth.* "It's the only one I have two copies of at the moment. Plus it should give you lots of practice talking to people about the Bible."

"It—what?"

"You know, like in the Book of Job, where Job asks God why he's being treated so badly, and God says something about a goat." He looked at me like he thought I should know what he was talking about. Something in his expression pulled at me in a way I couldn't have described. It was as though he needed, almost desperately needed, to be understood.

"You mean, when God spoke from the whirlwind?"

"Exactly! People who believe in God are always asking why. Why is God punishing them? Why do bad things happen to good people? Why, why, why. But there's no answer. Or if there is, it doesn't seem to have anything to do with the question. So it's hard to be sure it actually is an answer."

As Donald talked, his face seemed to shine with some kind of light that came from inside him. He stopped for breath, or perhaps to see if I was following his logic, and into the silence I laughed.

I laughed so hard I had to sit back down into the cramped little classroom chair. In all my days, listening to Father, and the priests at my church, and anyone else who talked about God, never had I heard anything simultaneously so absurd and so full of truth.

I'm not given to laughing. Growing up in the formal, even slightly severe environment of Father's home, I'd wanted for nothing. Or, that is, nothing I knew was missing. But mirth…. If someone like Donald had entered that home, he'd have seen that mirth was conspicuous in its absence.

Donald watched me, grinning, evidently amused at my paroxysms. As I wiped my eyes, he said, "If you like that, you might like the way I see this play."

He waited until I said, "And how is that?"

"Seems to me it's just this side of allegory—the play is not really an allegory, by the way—maybe metaphor would be a better word? Anyway, it calls to the relationship between mankind and God." He waited again.

"Details, please."

He sat down in the chair beside mine. "Right from the start, the character Andrew Wyke—who writes crime and mystery novels, you know, like the Bible—is kind of patting himself on the back about his writing. Sounds a lot like the Old Testament God, who was kind of childish. You know, petulant. Mercurial. Demanding of praise. Unreasonable, often, and very fond of tantrums. If he were human, one might call him a cockalorum. And the further into the play we go, the more Andrew seems like that."

"You're calling God a cockalorum?"

He ignored me. "The author, Anthony Shaffer—by the way, the twin brother of Peter Shaffer, author of *Equus*—places the Egyptian game of Senet in the first scene. It's probably the oldest game known to man. It represents the journey of the soul to the afterlife. And having it in the play at this point is the technique of foreshadowing."

"You mean, someone's going to die?"

He hesitated for just a second. "You don't know the play?" When I shook my head, a smile spread across his face, and he handed me a copy of the script. "Fabulous. Then for now, you play the part of Milo."

I accepted the script, not quite willing to dig myself any deeper into the hole of the uninitiated, of the newbie.

Donald said, "Another time, we'll swap roles. While we're reading today, don't worry so much about acting. Instead, think about the characters. Who is Milo Tilden? Who is Andrew Wyke? Who are they to each other, aside from the obvious, the superficial? Next time we meet, you can tell me your thoughts about them. Are you on board?"

I lied. "Sounds simple enough."

Donald gave me a look I couldn't interpret and then he walked to the front of the room and sat at the instructor's desk. A glance at the start of Act One of the script told me Andrew was alone in the opening scene, so I stayed where I was. And Donald began to read. In nearly a monotone, he read aloud the scene description, and then he began to speak as Andrew Wyke.

At first I followed along in the script, but Donald's acting was so engaging that I kept looking up at him. It was just lucky that I saw my cue in time.

Donald had said not to worry about acting, but he'd done such a good job playing Wyke that it was hard to resist.

We read, and we read, and Donald intoned the stage direction bits almost like a priest might intone the lesson in a church service.

I lost track of time and didn't even glance at my watch until my character, mocking Wyke's work, said something facetious about how the police are stupid and crimes are always solved by the amateur sleuth.

"Yes!" Donald said, out of character, and not reading the script. "This is the crux, isn't it? This is the thing upon which the story turns. And Shaffer just lets it go by, almost a throwaway line."

He laughed at my puzzled look and then asked, "What does the word 'amateur' mean?"

What was he getting at? "Not professional. It might also mean not doing something especially well."

"Ah, but what is the etymology?"

I thought for a few seconds. "Love?"

"Love!" he nearly shouted, his eyes wide. "Yes! And by that meaning, an amateur in something—sleuthing, acting, sports, music—is doing it because they love it."

"So… who is sleuthing here?"

He snapped his script shut. "You know, I think that's enough for today. Don't you? It's getting dark, and I'm hungry. Dinner?"

I was torn between two impulses. One was to protest, the way a therapy patient might protest when the therapist, in the midst of some breakthrough, says, "That's our time for today." I wanted more. The other impulse was to jump at the implied invitation to have dinner with Donald. But, as I've said already, I am not an impulsive creature.

I chose a middle ground. "Shall I read forward in the script on my own, then?"

He shrugged. "If you like, though that might spoil the surprises Milo and Andrew have in store for each other."

'Well… but real actors would already know."

"They would. And you're right. Yes, read ahead. And next

time I'll expect you to engage more of your acting abilities." As he put his belongings together, he said, "Where shall we go?"

"Go?"

"Oh. Sorry. I thought dinner together was afoot." Was there a slight hesitation? Some uncharacteristic uncertainty?

It became my decision after all. "I see. Well, um," *Think fast, Spencer*. "I'd just need to let my mother know not to expect me."

We located a pay phone in the main lobby of the building. Mother was surprised.

"Really? You won't be home for dinner?"

I tried to read her tone. Or, rather, I tried not to hear it, not to be affected by the undertones of hurt disappointment. "I'm having dinner with someone from class. I'll tell you all about it when I get home."

It was the most I could offer her, and she had never been one to push her own agenda. No one living with Father would have done so without repercussions. He was no tyrant, but he was definitive. Decisive. And, in case there was any doubt, always right.

I glanced at my watch. "It's early enough we should still be able to get a good table." I mentioned a couple of restaurants I knew of, and Donald's face registered something I couldn't quite interpret.

"Well, shit, Spencer. I was just thinking we'd grab a burger and a brew. I'm a starving actor, you know." He waited long enough for that to sink into my brain and then suggested a more budget-friendly place "right around the corner."

As we waited for our order to be filled, I asked something that had come to me during our short walk.

"I'm looking forward to finding out what these surprises are that you referred to. But I'm not entirely clear how something like *Sleuth* or any other play is going to help me become a more effective preacher." Donald looked a little surprised, so I added, "I mean, beyond pacing, that sort of thing."

"Well.... If I'm going to be specific, I'm going to have to give away those surprises. But you'll have to know, anyway. And that's kind of part of it."

I waited, confused, watching his face as different thoughts passed behind his eyes.

"See," he said, "as a priest, you'll already know the scriptures better than most, or maybe any, of your parishioners. Yet you need to help them understand how this stuff that was written yea lo these many centuries ago applies to their lives. Yeah?"

He waited until I nodded.

"Great. So, just like it's an actor's job to help the audience see into the deeper meanings of a play like *Sleuth,* you'll need to know how to unpack God's Word in a way that makes it relevant and real. To do that, you'll need to see inside the scripture, and you'll also need to see inside of *them.*"

He sat back to let our waiter set plates before us.

"And," he continued, "I get the sense you aren't very good at that. Yet."

"You—what?"

He shrugged. "Am I wrong?"

He was not. But it felt like an accusation, one to which I did not want to admit. I heard a little belligerence in my tone when I said, "Is that all?"

He lifted a long French fry and pointed it at me. It bent over, and he laughed. "No. Far from it. Okay, so here's the thing. Andrew knows Milo is fucking his wife."

A few fries disappeared into his mouth, which he didn't entirely dispense with before continuing.

"He wants that to stop; Marguerite is his, even though we're not convinced he actually loves her, and he doesn't like to share. But he lies to Milo, saying he'll be happy to have her out of his life. He also knows his wife is used to having money, something Milo does not have. Andrew has disdain for most other people. Make that all other people. He fancies himself clever beyond words. He invites Milo for a visit to his big house for a chat. Getting the picture?"

I didn't know what Donald wanted me to get. "Why would Andrew want to chat with a man who was cuckolding him? Surely, it wouldn't be merely to say he didn't care."

Donald laughed. "Exactly! And really, he didn't want to chat. He wanted to trap Milo into a situation that would force him out of the picture. And he wanted to do it through deception. Game-playing. A game that Milo wouldn't even know was a game until he had lost."

Donald took a bite of his burger, and ketchup dripped onto the plate. He nodded, eyes closed, enjoying the flavor. When he could speak, he said, "Ain't no fun if you don't make a mess."

I used my knife and fork to cut a triangular piece of my burger, making sure I had corresponding pieces of top and bottom bun, and I dipped the section into a pile of ketchup I had pooled onto one side of my plate. Even as I did so, even as I lifted the bloodied triangle with my fork, even as one part of me knew I was silently correcting Donald's table manners, I felt like a stiff-necked prig and couldn't stop myself saying, "If you say so."

"I do. But to each his own. Now, the game Andrew plays is this: He makes Milo see that he will need money if he's to keep Marguerite happy. And he's dreamed up this scheme whereby Milo steals some insured jewelry. Milo is supposed to sell the jewelry so he'll have money to mollify Marguerite, and Andrew will collect the insurance and live on to enjoy his mistress."

I watched Donald's boyish face as he took another bite of burger and ate a couple of fries before continuing. Clearly my implied chastisement had no effect on him.

"Mr. Rainey?" The young man's voice startled me. He spoke from behind me and moved to Donald's left.

He was fairly short, with tousled dark hair curling almost coquettishly around his pretty face, which had an eager expression. He held what appeared to be a well-worn program from some production, probably a play. Donald looked at the program, then at the young man's face, and smiled. "You carry this around with you, do you?"

"Everywhere." His admiration was so unabashed as to be almost bold. "And I'd do almost anything if you would agree to sign it." He held the program and a cheap pen toward Donald. The word presumptive flashed through my brain. "To Michael."

He watched as Donald scribbled, ignoring me as completely as if I were an unfortunate piece of sculpture, any acknowledgement of which would be rude.

Donald completed his scribble and handed program and pen back to Michael. "There you are."

As Michael reclaimed his items, his hand lingered on Donald's for what I felt was a blatantly transparent amount of time.

"You were so wonderful," Michael gushed. "I simply don't know what to say."

"Whenever that happens to me, I find that 'goodbye' works as well as anything else." Donald gave Michael one last smile and turned back to me. Michael, who either didn't know or didn't want to know that he had been dismissed, stood there for several seconds before disappearing.

Donald, seemingly unaffected by this attractive young man's admiration, said, "Where was I? Oh, yes. What actually happens is that once Milo agrees and gets in over his head, Andrew pulls the rug out from under him and says, essentially, 'Gotcha!' Because now it looks as though Milo broke into the house, beat up Andrew, and was trying to abscond with the loot. This is when Andrew reaches for a gun and shoots. He fires two shots around the room, and then shoots Milo."

Wrists resting on the edge of the table, Donald watched me carefully.

For some reason, I wanted to appear unimpressed with his description of the plot, which didn't seem to hold any lessons for me. I also wanted to silently dismiss the gushes of the young groupie. If I'm honest, I also felt something akin to jealousy, unreasonable as that would have been. I decided to follow Donald's lead and ignore the interruption. My voice flat, I asked, "So Milo dies?"

"Ha!" Donald nearly shouted, causing a couple of people at nearby tables to glance at him. "That's what we're supposed to think! But it's only the end of Act One."

"It sounds like it should be the end of the play."

"Doesn't it just? But Act Two includes yet another game. A few days later a detective, someone for whom Andrew would feel nothing but disdain, shows up." Donald waved a fry in the air before consuming it. "I won't go into details here, except to say that this detective, named Doppler, talks Andrew into a corner and pretty much forces him to admit what happened. But Andrew insists the third bullet was a blank, and that Milo fainted but didn't die. Doppler insists that Milo is missing. Andrew grows more and more anxious, then terrified, believing that he'll be arrested for murder, until finally he guesses that Doppler is really Milo in disguise. Andrew can dish it out, as the expression goes, but he can't take it. And he's so into the game aspect that he doesn't believe Milo about the police arriving momentarily. So, pissed off royally at having been tricked, he kills Milo. For real, this time. And the police arrive. The end. Curtain drop."

The last of Donald's burger disappeared, leaving a trail of greasy red substance all over his plate. My meal was gone, plate empty but for a few fries. I looked at his face, which was nearly glowing with self-satisfaction.

"Maybe I'm being dense," I said into the gap between us, "but I don't see what you're getting at."

He nodded. "I'm not surprised. But, see, this is what I mean by understanding not just the words but also the characters. Do you remember when we were reading earlier, and Milo picked up a game piece? Andrew had a board of Senet set up."

"Yes, but that really *was* just a game."

If it's possible for someone to chortle, that's what Donald did. "Remember, Senet represents the journey of the ka, the soul, to the afterlife. Shaffer is playing a game on us, but he gives us a clue."

"But Andrew doesn't really kill Milo during their game."

"He doesn't kill Milo during his *own* game. Milo merely *appears* to die. So, to tie this to religion, Milo is like Jesus. Wyke, someone who fancies himself superior to others, more clever than others, goes through the motions of killing Milo. But —behold! Milo is resurrected. And at first Andrew, representing mankind here, doesn't recognize him. So Milo gives him a kind of test. Plays a game on Andrew. And Andrew, who can't 'take it,' who can't stand not to be on top, as it were, freaks out and does something that's going to get him sent to someplace he *really* doesn't want to go. To a kind of hell. His own lack of self-examination, his conviction that he is above it all, is his downfall. He didn't figure things out. He's no sleuth. All his writing of crime novels didn't save him."

"All right, I follow you, but it's an imperfect representation. Jesus can't actually be killed. He really *doesn't* die."

Donald let out an exasperated breath. "This isn't intended to be a morality play. It's not an allegory. And if you're honest, you have to agree that even scripture is imperfect. It contradicts itself over and over."

I made a sound that I hoped would be interpreted as disdain. He was right, but I wasn't going to give him the satisfaction of saying so.

"The point, Father Hill, is that we're always playing games. People always play games. We might be trying to avoid admitting that our behavior matters. We might want to lord it over the loser. We might want to validate our own feelings of superiority by fooling someone else. But in the end? In the end the game is real. So is it still a game?"

We stared at each other, the air between us nearly crackling with words that were unspoken because our brains couldn't land on anything that represented what we were thinking. At least, that's how it felt to me.

I needed time to think about this. I needed to read the whole play myself and see if Donald was lending it importance it did not really have. My tone edged with sarcasm, I said, "My, what human mysteries must *Equus* reveal."

Donald clapped his hands a few times. "Oh, just you wait. Just you wait."

I paid for dinner—compensation for his time and expertise. Outside, a gentle snow had just begun, tiny specks of white drifting down and disappearing as they landed. Hands in the pockets of his thin jacket, shrugging a little against the cold evening, Donald asked, "What are you doing this weekend?"

From inside the warmth of my camel hair winter coat, I answered without thinking. "The usual. Studying. Seminary classwork."

"Wanna have a go at *Sleuth* again?"

I did a quick calculation in my head. Would I have time to read the thing all the way through by then? I decided I would. What I couldn't decide so quickly was whether to meet with Donald again so soon. His enthusiasm was infectious, and I had enjoyed watching his face light up as he'd explained what he saw as hidden meanings within the play—which was precisely why I hesitated. Was I falling for him?

"Sure," I said, avoiding my own question. "Where?"

He handed me a slip of paper with a phone number on it.

"There's a practice room in the theater where you saw me as Puck. I can get us in there. If we're lucky, we might even be able to use the stage, but I can't promise that. Let's meet at the stage door Saturday around, say, two?"

That sounded harmless enough, which meant it didn't sound like a date.

But that's when things changed. Suddenly I could understand how Milo must have been profoundly shocked when Andrew shot him. Because that's when Donald, smiling his Puck-ish smile, took hold of my coat lapels, reached his face up to mine, and kissed me.

It was not a long kiss. It was not a quick kiss. He left his lips on mine just long enough for something in my brain to explode.

And then he was gone.

CHAPTER THREE

I stood where I was, my brain full of turmoil and empty of thoughts, as Donald's huddled figure disappeared, gradually obscured by other pedestrians and bits of white fluff. The only sound was the panicked thumping of the frightened creature temporarily in residence where my heart should have been. Someone bumped me as they passed, and we both apologized. Shaken out of my trance, I headed toward home.

I had promised Mother I would tell her about my day, my evening. I'd essentially promised to give her a reason why I had suddenly decided not to be with her for dinner. I was always with her for dinner. What the fuck was I going to tell her?

How I wished I could be as oblivious to—or as uncaring about—the world's opinion as Donald seemed! Did it come with the trade? Did actors have to be unmoved by both the approbation and condemnation of others so that playing a part, whether hero or fool, was possible?

My own world, so stilted, so formal, so subsumed by an almost desperate need to be seen as reserved, felt like so many shades of grey beside Donald's world of vibrant colors and mercurial emotions. Was I so much a creature of the grey world that I couldn't indulge in—well, in indulgence?

If I were to allow a lively, colorful spirit into my life, would my own world shatter? Puck was not kind to the "mortals" he encountered. He dismissed them, ridiculed them. But Donald had kissed me. If I let him into my world, would my world survive? Would I?

At home, in what felt like slow motion that went by entirely too fast, I hung my coat up. I could see that the kitchen was nearly dark, with just the light over the stove on. Mother must be in the living room, I figured, where several lights were on. I was right.

She sat in her usual place, a floor lamp behind her upholstered chair lighting the pages of a book, a glass of watered brandy on the pedestal table to her right.

She glanced up as I entered the room, an unconvincing smile on her face. "Hello, dear. Did you have pleasant dinner?"

"I did, yes. I, uh, a classmate and I spent a little extra time working on an assignment, and then we went to a place nearby." I took a breath and waited. She waited. I added, "I'm sorry I couldn't give you more notice about missing dinner here."

She nodded slightly. "Apology accepted. You have your own life, Spencer. But yes, a little more notice would have been nice." And she looked back at her book. I was dismissed.

I never put much stock in dreams. I saw them as the brain's way of trying to combine many disparate threads into a pattern that could not possibly make sense, could not represent anything worth teasing apart for understanding. I tried to treat the dream I had that night in the same manner. That is, I tried to dismiss it.

It wasn't really a dream. It was more an excerpt of a scene from a really bad play. It took place in the car of a train, moving very fast (no tunnel; sometimes a train is only a train, right?). It wasn't a standard contemporary train; it was more like the trains one sees in scenes from England or Europe several decades ago, where there are separate compartments. I was alone in mine, looking out the window, though all I could see was a blur. I turned my head toward the door of the compartment, and across from me, where he hadn't been seconds before, was Donald.

In the way of dreams I knew it was Donald, although it didn't really look like him. He looked more like Puck, half naked, with bits of leaves and twigs in his long brown hair. His smile was lascivious.

I closed my eyes, and when I opened them again he was very close beside me, and he had placed his hand between my thighs. Instantly I was throbbing, and then I was writhing, and then we were both naked. He held my jaw with one hand and thrust his tongue into my mouth, his other hand kneading, squeezing tighter and tighter until I thought my balls would burst.

The door flew open. It was the conductor. His face was the face of my father. Donald was gone, as though he had never been there, but the look on Father's face told me he had seen me at last, seen the part of me I had worked hard to keep from him.

He knew I was gay.

I sat bolt upright in bed, my breathing ragged and fast.

Had he known? Had Father known all along, or at least as long as I had known?

A voice in my head, coming from the lingering effects of the dream, said, *That's why he couldn't love you.*

Saturday morning I stayed in bed until I was sure Mother had finished her breakfast and had left the house. I knew she had another church committee meeting this morning, and I wanted to avoid her asking me what my plans were for the day. More than once, I had considered using the number Donald had given me, which I assumed was his number, to say I wasn't going to be able to make it. But I wasn't quite sure why I would do that. I also couldn't have said why I would not.

It had snowed during the night. Not a lot, but enough to brighten the city streets. I sat at the kitchen table over a pot of coffee and some toast, arguing with myself yet again whether to meet with Donald as we had planned. I had finished reading *Sleuth,* and I hated to admit that Donald's interpretation was a reasonable one. Not only that, but his point about what I needed to do also made sense.

Donald knew his craft. He knew that the words on the page of a script were a sheer curtain, constructed not to hide meaning but to enhance it. One's experience of meaning is deeper if one finds it oneself. So the role of the stage actor is to show the audience the curtain, pulling it aside just a little at those junctures where an attentive audience would be able to glean relevance, to detect—no, to feel—the connection between their life and the lives of others.

This is also the job of the priest. It will be my job to help people see relevance, not just between themselves and scripture, not just between themselves and Jesus, but also between themselves and each other. And it will be deeper, more meaningful, for them if they see it for themselves.

If Donald could help me develop that skill, it would be not for my benefit, but for the benefit of my future parishioners. So I should go.

Except for that dream. Except that I was now sure I wanted Donald in the carnal sense. So was he a Greek bearing gifts? Or, in language closer to my life, was he a messenger from Satan? After all, both Satan and Saint can quote scripture equally well.

"Ahhhhhh!"

My own voice in the silence startled me. I rose so quickly the chair almost went over backward, and I nearly threw my used dishes into the sink. I turned to move out of the kitchen when I ran into something that was almost a physical barrier, it was so undeniable. I turned back to the sink, rinsed my dishes, and placed them carefully in the dishwasher.

There was homework to be done for school, but I knew I could not focus on it yet. Instead I went to the piano and played a few of the most bombastic pieces of music I knew.

I left a note for Mother saying I didn't know whether I'd be home for dinner and not to count on me. I grabbed my school backpack and my copy of *Sleuth* and left the house before I expected her to return.

~

The library at General wasn't as crowded as it usually is on Saturdays. Perhaps the snow had tempted students to enjoy the brightness out of doors. I sat at a long, library reading table where I could see out the wall of windows that overlooked the close, the open center of campus, where the whitened ground was made whiter every so often by flakes drifting lazily down and settling onto it.

Before one o'clock I'd done all the work I could manage. On the walk to the theater where I'd meet Donald, I stopped for lunch at a sandwich shop, a place Father would never have patronized. My meal disappeared very quickly; I felt a strange kind of hunger that food seemed barely to diminish rather than to satisfy.

The marquee on the front of the theater announced a play for the evening, one I didn't know, by a playwright I didn't recognize. I rounded the building's corner to the stage door, deliberately ten minutes late, and even so, Donald was not there. It was another seven minutes before he came hurrying around the corner, nearly colliding with two men who had just come out of the building. He slipped on the snowy sidewalk and went down.

One of the men bent to help him up. As he brushed melting snow off himself, he muttered, "Oh, my. I guess it's been a while since I inhabited a body."

I tried not to laugh, but the two men near him were practically guffawing. Donald seemed not to react. He said, "Thank you so much," and walked toward me as though nothing had happened.

He stopped in front of me. "Ready to be Andrew?"

"What?"

"I'm Milo today."

"But—"

He jerked his head slightly toward the door. "Come on in."

I followed, asking, "They just leave the door unlocked?"

Donald's voice came to me from over his shoulder. "It's a risk, but there's a play tonight, and people will be coming and going."

He led the way along one hallway and then another, finally turning into a small room on his right. As I entered, he shut the door behind me.

Feeling anxious, not quite knowing what to expect, I set my backpack down and draped my coat over one of the three metal folding chairs. I had actually practiced Milo's part a little, expecting to pick up where we'd stopped a few days ago. But Donald had other ideas.

"If it's okay with you," he opened, "I'll read the stage direction, like I did last time. Then you pick up where Andrew comes in."

"But I was Milo last time."

The expression on his face seemed to say, "And?"

"And," I added, "why aren't we starting where we left off? Why go back to the beginning?"

"So you can play Andrew, of course." He smiled at what must have been a confused look on my face. "You need to be able to experience what's going on from both perspectives. Also, you've heard the material before, so you should be able to inject some acting into it."

Fine. "I only wish I had known."

"Why?"

"Well… so I could be prepared."

He gave me a mocking glance from under his eyebrows and opened his script. "I know you've read the whole thing. And this way I can give you a few acting pointers as we read. I didn't do that last time. Shall we begin?"

I couldn't have said whether the absurdity of Donald's comment on the sidewalk had infected us, or perhaps it was my own nervousness at being alone in a closed room with the only man who had ever kissed me, but we were unable to take our work seriously. Almost every time he stopped me to offer coaching, as we resumed we both flubbed our lines so badly that we laughed almost as much as we spoke. Mostly it wasn't especially funny. It's just that we were, as they say, in a mood.

As Andrew, I asked Milo, "How are you settling in at the Laundry Cottage?"

Donald, as Milo, didn't miss a beat, and he spoke over my "Sorry; I meant Landry."

The next mistake was mine again, with the phrase "'… normal reaction of noble minds.' I mean, recreation."

Donald lowered his script. "I kind of like your version better. It makes more sense." We went on with our lines until the same phrase was in one of his lines: "Noble minds are the normal reaction of detective story writers."

"You mean recreation."

"No, I don't." He smiled and began to laugh, and then I laughed, and it was a minute or so before we could continue.

A few lines later, instead of watch maker, Donald/Milo said, "He was a wife maker…." He looked at me, his face contorted with the attempt to avoid exploding with laughter. He cleared his throat a few times before he went on. Then he stopped. Off script, he asked, "Cairngorms and Minehead. Are those real places?"

"Well," I said as myself, "you know the English. Chances are they don't pronounce them the way they're spelled."

A little further along I stumbled over "hebdomadal."

Donald shook his head. "What the hell is that, anyway?"

"It means something that occurs every seven days."

I was stopped short a few lines later at the word "coelacanth." I glanced at Donald. "Did I even say that right?"

More laughter. It seemed to me that we were beyond taking this exercise seriously at this point, just managing to read our lines between giggles. Until I read, "The thot plickens."

I sat down and wiped laughter tears from my eyes. "I don't know what's going on. We can't do anything right."

"Maybe it's time to try something else."

"Like what?"

"Stand up."

I stood, and he moved close to me. I tried to step back, but the chair was right behind me.

"Spencer." He waited.

"Yes?"

"Kiss me."

My ears buzzed. The room seemed to shrink. I both wanted and didn't want to look anywhere other than his eyes, so they were all I saw. *Maybe,* I thought, *if I wait long enough and don't do anything, he'll back away.*

But he waited. And waited. I heard my own sudden intake of breath, and then something pulled my head down and forward, and I kissed him. Lightly. Barely, even. And I pulled back.

His eyes stayed on mine, waiting as though nothing had happened, until I leaned toward him again. This time he took my face in both hands and pressed our mouths together, kissing me in a way I'd never been kissed, a kiss like my dream version of Puck had given me.

I closed my eyes, and the word *Yes!* echoed through my entire being. Guided by something other than my mind, my hands traveled down Donald's back to his ass and pulled him as close to me as I could get him. If my brain had been operating I'm sure I would have realized that he felt my erection as firmly as I felt his.

Panting slightly, Donald pulled away from me. He smiled. "Would you like to see where this would go?"

I shook my head in confusion. Why had he ended this embrace, this excitement, this aching ecstasy?

He picked up my coat and handed it to me and put on his own. I stood there, still muddle-headed with longing, and he handed me my backpack. He took my hand and led the way back out of the theater, back to the slippery sidewalk, over to Fourteenth Street, down Third Avenue to Eighth Street, where he turned left onto the section called St. Mark's Place.

We walked all this way without a word, and because he wasn't telling me where we were going, I could tell myself that it wasn't where I really knew it was: that is, we were going to where he lived. I could pretend I didn't know what would happen when we got there. I used these pretenses to quell the near-panic I felt.

In my mind I saw the face of that train conductor, my father, scowling his profound disapproval at me, at my very nature. A hot fury rose in me at the man who had never convinced me he loved me but who would deny me love from a source he couldn't understand.

Under my breath, inaudible to Donald over the noise of the city, I rasped, "Fuck you."

Donald stopped at an obscure doorway between a head shop (bongs and associated paraphernalia in the display window) and a clothing store that evidently catered to the sort of people who wear a lot of black leather, and pulled out a key ring. He pushed the door open, I followed him in, and the door shut with a thud behind me, an audible punctuation to a decision I hadn't actually made but was allowing to be made.

We climbed two sets of somewhat grimy stairs to a heavy door painted dark red with three locks on it. Donald opened one after another, and as he turned the knob and pushed, a slight scraping sound came from within the room on the other side of the door.

I had to enter with the door still slightly ajar. The mechanism inside, which prevented the door opening all the way, baffled me. I watched as Donald shut the door and slid a long, metal bar into place, with its opposite end braced in a metal plate embedded in the floor.

"What on earth?" I asked.

"Later." His coat was already on the floor, and he made short work of mine, backpack thudding as it landed.

I expected him to kiss me again. I wanted him to kiss me again. But instead he undressed himself, so I followed his lead as well as I could, undoing shirt buttons with quivering hands.

Donald took one of my hands in his. "You're shaking." He looked up at my face. I tried and failed to hide the anxiety that was entangled with desire. "You're a virgin!"

He dropped my hand and pulled away from me, his jeans around his ankles, his penis pointing at me from a mass of brown curls.

I wanted to deny it, to say I just wasn't very experienced. Maybe I could lie and say I was a virgin with men but not with women. I tried to speak but couldn't.

He bent over and pulled his jeans back on, tucking himself in tenderly, the erection already starting to grow flaccid. He turned his back to me, a hand running through his hair and clinging to his scalp as if that could bring forth an explanation. He raised his bare arm, and I watched the muscle definition change, admiring it, wanting it—at least from a safe distance.

I found my voice. "Does this mean—"

He didn't let me finish. Wheeling around to face me he said, "My god, man! How old are you? You made it all the way through college intact? Did you take some kind of vow, or something?"

Anger and relief vied for supremacy in my chest—anger at being rejected for purity, relief that maybe I wouldn't be having sex today for the first time in my life. I watched Donald's face as I refastened the few buttons I'd managed to undo. And I let anger win. "I didn't realize a résumé was necessary. I hope your next candidate meets your requirements more completely."

"No, wait. That's not—I mean, look." His shoulders raised and then dropped as he exhaled a long breath. "Are you even sure you want to do this? With a man, I mean? Because I'm not sure I wanna be the one to bring someone over."

"Over?"

He waved a hand, an exasperated gesture. "To gay. From straight, or from assuming you're straight."

"I do not assume that I'm straight. I'm quite sure I'm gay."

Holy Mother of God. I had never said those words aloud to anyone, ever.

"Yeah, I'm quite sure you are, too, or else things wouldn't have gone this far." He grabbed at his hair again and then dropped his hand. "Look, here's the thing. I've seen what happens when friends of mine, gay friends, fall for a virgin, or maybe for a guy who's been with women. The—I'll call him a newbie—the newbie will either hate what he has to accept about himself and hate the guy who showed him, or he and the guy who showed him will fall in love. But Spencer, the first time a gay man has sex with a man, he has sex for the first time, despite anything that might have gone before. And at our age, with sex being so high on the priority list, the newbie soon realizes that he's a kid in a candy shop, and he can't stop himself. He wants to taste everything."

"And you think that's me?"

"I… I don't want to show a man how to love a man and then have to watch him go off and do it without me."

That hit hard. *Love?* My tone bordering on sarcastic, I said, "Is that where you want this to go? You think we'll fall in love with each other?" Was he crazy? I just met him. Well, practically.

There were exactly two wooden chairs in the apartment, which seemed to be more or less all one room. Donald sat in one and, this time, grabbed his head in both hands. I sat in the other and waited. Maybe a minute went by before he dropped his hands and let them dangle between his knees. His face looked a little ragged, as though revealing an exhaustion that went deep.

He let out a long breath. "I was involved with someone. Before I met him, I was—well, let's just say I was very active. He had been as well, but in the eight months we were together I don't think either of us slept with anyone else. Maybe we were both afraid of the plague, but I don't think that was the reason we—"

"Plague?"

He blinked, almost startled. "The gay plague. You know, AIDS." The blank look I know I had on my face seemed to anger him. "Seriously, Spencer? How cloistered have you been? You don't know there's a plague spreading through our ranks, sickening people? *Killing* people? My god, man!" He shook his head twice, and his voice grew louder. "The government doesn't give a fuck. The medical establishment doesn't give a fuck, except for a few brave souls who care more about helping people than everyone else. Because, you know, it's just 'the gays.'"

He stood. I don't know why, but I stayed in my chair. Perhaps I was intimidated by Donald at that moment.

"Jonathan died. He fucking died, Spencer. He died of a cancer that raged through his body after his immune system was destroyed. He got so sick—" Donald's voice had started to crack, and he turned so I couldn't see his face. I heard him take a couple of ragged breaths, and it occurred to me to say I was sorry, but that seemed profoundly inadequate.

Donald turned back to face me. "I watched him fade and sicken. I saw how the lesions multiplied until they nearly covered his body. I saw the nurses in the hospital try to make someone else go into his room so they wouldn't be exposed. Finally they wouldn't even let me see him anymore. You know, 'family only.' But do you think *they* were there?"

He didn't even try to disguise the tears that filled his eyes and ran down his face. "He died all alone in a room empty of anything he cared about and anyone he cared about." Donald's breath caught, and he lost control of a couple of sobs. "And I—" Another long breath. He lifted his arms out from his sides and dropped them again. "I don't understand why I didn't get sick, too. I've gone for testing, like, four times since he died. Seven months ago now. And I haven't been with anyone since."

I couldn't take my eyes off his face. A tightening in my throat and in my chest told me I was feeling at least a little of his pain.

His voice changed, nearly to a whisper. "You were to have been my first since Jonathan." He glared at me, his eyes still watering, and I nearly squirmed. "I don't know whether I could love you, Spencer. I don't know whether you could love me. But I will tell you this. I don't think I'll ever again sleep with any man I know I couldn't love."

I stood and moved quickly toward him, not knowing whether he would want the embrace I needed to give him. But he didn't move. We wrapped our arms around each other, and his head dropped onto my shoulder. I held him as his shoulders shook, his breath catching in sobs he tried and mostly failed to control. It was heaven to feel his bare skin and it was hell because I shouldn't be feeling good when he was in such despair. We stood like that for a few minutes until the sobbing lessened.

Across the room, under the only window, was a bed that

looked barely big enough for both of us. I released my arms, took his hand, and led him to it.

We lay down, and as I held him to my body, relishing the physicality, I listened to his breathing until it slowed to the rhythm of someone dosing. And I allowed my thoughts to range where they would.

Had I heard of AIDS? Of course I had. I didn't understand it very well, but because it didn't have relevance to my life, understanding didn't seem to matter very much. I didn't think I'd ever heard of it referred to as the gay plague, though now that the term had been spoken out loud I would never forget it.

Donald had been sure I was gay. Well, yeah, I suppose that had been evident since the night he had kissed me, right out in public. He thought maybe he could love me, maybe I could love him. The angel on one shoulder said, *How wonderful!* My other shoulder's inhabitant had a different opinion. *Are you kidding me with this? You're just getting started. Don't tie yourself down. You'll want lots of men!* This thought was so much like what Donald had said, about what happens when a gay man shows another gay man his true nature, that I cringed. But then I shook myself mentally. No, that's not me. I'm not looking for a wild and crazy sex life.

So, I said to myself, *Self, how far do you want this to go? Is Donald someone you could love?* The answer to that question came so fast I nearly spoke it aloud: *How the fuck do I know?*

I must have shifted my position, because Donald took a sharp breath in and lifted his head a little. He dropped it again, against my shoulder. "You're still here."

"I am."

"I didn't drive you away."

"You tried."

He chuckled. "I sorta did, didn't I?" Slowly he sat up and looked down at me, his face a little blotchy, his eyes half closed.

"I gave you some time to think. Maybe not deliberately. Do you know what you want?"

"I want you." I don't know whose voice said those words. It couldn't have been mine. And yet the words were true.

He shifted his position so that his knees were on opposite sides of my hips. Propping himself up with his arms, he lowered his face until it was very close to mine.

"Are you sure?"

I could already feel my breathing quicken. "I am."

He brought his lips so close to mine that they barely touched. I felt his tongue caress the tender flesh just inside my mouth, and then I felt my erection as it tried to escape from the captivity of my jeans, of my inhibitions, of my fears, of my father's disdain. I let it strain. Donald would know what to do. I would make myself wait for him.

Donald pulled away just far enough so that he could undo those buttons on my shirt that had already been unbuttoned once. This time they would stay unbuttoned for much longer.

With my chest fully exposed, Donald kissed my neck, ran his tongue along my collarbone, left trails of moisture that cooled as the heat of his mouth left them. With one hand he pinched a nipple, hard As he continued to kiss his way down to my jeans, I heard myself moan.

I don't know how he removed his jeans, or mine, or what happened to anyone's underwear. But suddenly we were both naked.

I wish I could remember everything that happened after that. I know that I wanted—needed—to touch Donald everywhere at once. I had never before felt an urgency like it.

Remember…. I remember the feel of his warm mouth pulling on my dick. The feel of his hand gently kneading my tender balls. His insistent finger pressing and releasing and pressing again in that strip of flesh behind my balls. I think I remember an animal cry that came out of me when I finally released everything into the flesh of Donald's hand.

I felt completely overwhelmed. I will never understand why all of this felt familiar to me. Or maybe it just felt natural.

I admit, it was more of an effort when the tables were turned. I loved the feel of Donald's dick in my hand—the firmness, the heat, the life—and I almost didn't mind teasing it with my tongue. But when I tried to take it into my mouth, I nearly gagged. I had to pull away. And I heard Donald chuckle.

"Don't try to take me all at once," he said. "You're not practiced enough. Yet." He reached for a tube of something, and I realized he had used it on me toward the end. "Here. Just use your hand for now."

With some lube on my hand, I quite enjoyed working him into a bit of a frenzy. Imitating what he had done, I lubed my other hand and poked gently behind his balls, then harder, and all at once I felt a finger disappear inside him.

"Ah!" Donald nearly shouted. "Yes! Please!"

I had sent a finger into his anus.

I wasn't sure what to do. I was pretty sure what he wanted me to do, but could I do it? Could I bring myself to pump a finger in and out of—well, that place?

Don't be stupid, Spencer. You knew something like this would be part of what happened.

Telling myself that didn't help a lot, but it helped just enough. Finally I left my finger inside and wriggled it around, nearly stretching the skin around it. Donald groaned. And that helped.

I pulled and pushed on his dick and I thrust in and out of his ass. Faster. And faster. Donald started to whine, and I realized he was holding his breath. His back arched, his neck arched, his ribs thrust themselves upward as his belly contracted and released. Suddenly my hand on his dick had a lot more than lube on it. Donald had made barely any sound at all as he had come. But his body spoke for him. It shook almost violently for about two seconds and then went completely limp. He could almost have been unconscious. Or dead.

Glad that his eyes were closed, I took advantage of his afterglow to grab my underwear and jeans, find the bathroom, and wash my hands. I had to pass in front of the door where that long metal bar was wedged. When I returned, Donald was watching me, a faint smile on his lips.

"You done good, Newbie," he said. "I don't think I can call you that anymore."

CHAPTER FOUR

Donald sat up as I got closer to the bed. He asked, "How do you feel?"

My brain was empty. I shook my head.

"You got nothing, eh? Well…. Are you confused? Are you elated? Are you grossed out? Are you wondering what else we might do? Are you sorry we did this at all? Are you—"

I chuckled. "Stop already. I don't know. I probably won't know for a couple of days." I sat at the foot of the bed, not realizing at the time that it was as far from Donald as I could be and still sit down; using a chair at this point could have seemed distant, and I didn't yet know if that's what I wanted to express.

He tilted his head. "Really? Your processing is that slow?"

"It's that thorough."

"Of course. I'm sorry. Everyone has their own way of figuring things out."

"Change of subject. Can you tell me now about that weird bar contraption at the door?"

"Sure." He sat up and wrapped his arms around his knees. I could see his genitals. "It's called a police bar. Don't know why. If someone tried to get in by coming through the door, that bar would hold against almost any onslaught. I suppose it's possible someone could pick that lock if they picked the other ones, but it helps me sleep at night. This neighborhood's not bad, but Alphabet City isn't far away, and crime increases as you move closer to the East River."

"Alphabet City?"

He shrugged. "You live here. You haven't heard of avenues A through D referred to that way?"

"Don't think so."

He got off the bed and retrieved his underwear. When he sat down again, he was very close to me. "I know you're feeling a little weird right now."

"Let's call it ambivalent."

"Sure. Okay. Anyway, I want you to know that I'd love to see you again. If you decide you don't feel the same way, I'll understand. I knew that was a risk before we… you know."

I didn't know what I wanted any next steps to be, so I just nodded. "So I'll see you in class next week?"

He seemed to need a second to take that in, and it sounded to me as though his tone hid disappointment, or pain. "Sure. And we'll be just classmates." He watched my face carefully as he said, "And if you want to stop the coaching sessions, that's fine. In fact, I'll assume for now that they're in hiatus unless you let me know otherwise."

I nodded again. He was making me decide something very important. I wondered whether he already knew that deciding things was something I generally avoided.

We kissed at the open door as I was leaving. I initiated it, but still it felt odd. I couldn't have said why.

～

There was no way I could sit across the dinner table from Mother after what I'd done. I stopped at a small French bistro on the way home and sat alone, staring at whatever was in front of me without seeing any of it. The place wasn't busy, so I sat there long after my meal, nearly finishing a whole bottle of Bordeaux.

At home I greeted Mother but escaped immediately to the study, mumbling something about homework. She looked sad and lonely, but I couldn't risk her seeing that I was troubled by something I would never talk to her about.

I did manage to do a little homework, but I kept nodding off. Finally I gave up and went to bed, not knowing how well I'd sleep.

Around six o'clock the next morning I opened my eyes, and the reality of what I had done—what Donald and I had done—nearly sent me tumbling onto the floor. I sat on the edge of the mattress, elbows on knees, head in hands, and whispered into the silent room: "You had sex with a man." I wasn't chilly, but I began to shiver. I tied my bathrobe as tightly as I could about myself, hugged my ribcage, and paced the room, shaking my head in a sort of daze.

I whispered again. "You told him you *want* him, for Christ's sake! What the hell were you thinking?"

I sat down once more, rubbed my face, and fell sideways onto the bed. What was it Donald had said? That I'd hate what I realized about myself? That I'd hate him, too? Was he right?

I'd known I was gay. But today, I was prepared to admit that there was a veritable chasm between knowing something and acting upon it. "Realizing" is a word we use without usually understanding that it means to make something real. Donald had made my homosexuality real.

All the voices I'd managed to quell after I had become convinced of my true nature came crashing into my brain, stones thrown at the infidel. The voices spied my weakness, and they shouted. "Sick!" "Twisted!" "Perverted!" "Unnatural!"

These ugly words were bad enough. But the worst was "DAMNED!"

I reached for a pillow and covered my face with it so I could do some shouting of my own: "Stop!" and then a wordless cry, half growl, half howl. My entire body clenched in painful spasms and I wanted to retch. I began to cough, and my mouth filled with liquid from the wrong direction. I hurled myself into my bathroom and spat repeatedly into the toilet, shaking violently. I felt disassociated from myself with no way into my own head.

I crawled into a corner on the tiled floor and pulled my knees up to my chest, arms around my legs, like a little boy who'd been scolded very severely. Dispassionately, as if from a distance, I watched myself sit there and whimper. After a time something like a half-dream state overtook me. I leaned against the wall.

With a painful jerk a leg muscle tensed and threw me sideways, causing my head to strike the wall. I gasped, stood as quickly as I could, and threw myself back into bed again. On my side, peeking out from the covers at the clock, I saw that it was six thirty. Breakfast, if I sat with Mother this morning, was at eight, and that would be followed by church. Ninety minutes until I had to face her, until I had to pretend everything was normal, until the guilt of my lie of omission—not telling her I was gay, never a serious problem until today—might make it impossible for me to speak to her. And would it be possible for me to be in church, feeling as I did?

A shivering that began in my belly gradually caused spasms in my arms and legs. I clenched my jaw to stop my teeth chattering. When I clenched my eyes shut, Donald's face—the face of the man whose dick I had milked, whose mouth I had tasted, whose ass I had penetrated—seemed painted on the insides of my eyelids. I turned violently in the bed to face another direction. Any other direction. The shivering stopped.

Did I hate Donald? Or did I hate that he'd shown me something about myself, something I'd prefer not to admit, and was he guilty by association?

Was I ashamed of the passion I'd felt? Was I horrified that I could feel about a man the way I had felt about Donald yesterday? If so, was I not really gay?

I shook my head from side to side, refusing to focus on this thought. But even as dazed as I was, I understood the difference between refusing to focus on the idea and actually denying it. My body began to shiver again. Shudder, really. It seemed to want to intervene, to give me something to focus on other than the cause of my distress.

Forcing myself to be calm, I went over as much as I could remember of the previous afternoon. One thing in particular kept throwing itself into the front of my mind: It had felt natural. There had been a sense of deep familiarity, almost as though someone I didn't quite recognize had possessed me. No, wait; it was more like a stranger I did recognize.

If there was hatred here, was it for Donald or for that stranger —the stranger within myself?

I took several deep breaths, letting the air out slowly, and I began to feel calmer. But that left an opening for my feelings. As though Donald were behind me right here in my bed, I felt his arm move over my rib cage, hand curling sweetly around my penis. In my mind, his soft hair caressed me where his head rested against my back. His knees nestled forward into the backs of mine. And the soft lumps of his genitals pressed against my ass.

A kind of sob escaped me. He was not really there. And I wanted him to be.

Bloody hell.

~

I stood a long time in a hot shower, the water washing away all traces of Donald. But it couldn't wash away what I felt. Any of it. Horror. Passion. Revulsion. Desire. Fear. Longing.

Most importantly, being with Donald had left me feeling apart from God. That was the worst.

Brushing my teeth, I avoided looking at myself in the mirror. My own eyes would accuse me, rightfully, of cowardice, of fear of being who I was, of transferring negative feelings to that sweet man who'd awakened these feelings. I didn't know what to do with these feelings. It almost didn't matter whether I wanted Donald or not. I didn't want myself.

Before leaving the bathroom I forced myself to look into that mirror, and I made a decision. I decided what I would do about Donald.

I dressed, sat down with Mother and had a polite conversation over breakfast, and then we went together to worship God.

But that was no escape. Ironically, or so it seemed to me, I struggled in vain to pay attention to the sermon or to fit the words of hymns to music I knew by heart. I was obsessed with carnality. Instead of feeling the shame that had come to me earlier that morning, my mind's eye recreated images of the source of the passion I had felt. That is, I saw Donald. I was used to being haunted by his face. Now, I was haunted by his body.

He was shorter than I was, and slender but not skinny, with muscle definition but no bulk—nothing special, really. And yet, as my imagination pictured his chest, I could almost feel my hand move over the nearly-flat, nearly-hairless surface, teasing his nipples, stroking slowly up to his neck. My lips reached for his Adam's apple, a symbol, perhaps even a celebration, of his masculinity. I caressed his thighs, not pausing at the crotch but moving up to the lines of muscle, hidden beneath skin, that point from the hip bones down to the genitals, following those lines with my fingers down to where that masculinity—promised by the throat and the chest and the hips and the muscular thighs—was realized.

So here I was, in the house of God, in the kind of environment where one day I hoped to bring God's Word to worshipers, and I was thrilling to the sexually charged image of a man. Could there be a greater separation between me and God?

This had to stop.

When I walked into my acting class the next week, I was prepared. I had a note, folded and tucked into a pocket of my backpack, for Donald. I had written it after Mother and I had returned home after church on Sunday, and I hadn't looked at it once since then. It read: "You were right. I can't do this. Thanks for understanding." It was signed, "Newbie."

Donald was already at his usual chair behind mine, standing beside it, searching through his backpack for something. As I got close, he looked up.

I couldn't have said what I would have expected to read on his face. No, that's wrong. I just didn't want to see it. I expected he would seem happy, glad to see me, looking forward to more time together. I expected that would be hard for me to take, given that my note would crush his hopes. I was sure I'd move to a different chair rather than force him to sit behind me after the pain my note would cause him.

But that's not what I saw. Instead, there was a wariness, almost a cringing, as though bracing himself for a physical blow. Had he predicted my reaction? He hadn't sat down. Had he felt so sure of my decision before he even knew it that he was poised and ready to move away from me?

I froze. And then I set my backpack beside my chair, nodded once to Donald, and sat down.

Coward, I yelled inwardly at myself. *You coward! You would have given him the note only if he wasn't prepared for it? But he anticipated you, so now you have to do the opposite?*

I was barely aware that Donald had settled into the chair behind me. And I confess I didn't hear much of what was said in class that day. I spent the time wrestling with myself. Again.

I could still feel how wonderful, how natural it had felt to kiss Donald, to have him kiss me, to have him do to me what he did. But then I had to face how—not uncomfortable, exactly, let's say how ambiguous I felt when it was my turn to pleasure him.

Was I gay? Yes.

Was I comfortable with that? Not exactly.

Did I want someone to love, someone to love me? Yes.

So….

Was I always going to be alone, my face pressed up against the glass between me and the place where love waited? Was I afraid or unwilling to go in?

Whatever the answer to that last question was, this waffling —this struggle—was not fair to Donald.

As soon as class was over, I stood quickly and set my note onto the arm of his chair. He didn't look at it. He looked at me, his face projecting a combination of disappointment and pain. I turned and left.

That Friday afternoon, Dr. Dunfey called me into his office. This was the man who had encouraged me to do something about my delivery style. So, in a certain way, this was the man who'd caused Donald to come into my life.

More than once I had wondered whether Dr. Harlan Dunfey had been assigned as my advisor because he was a good two inches taller than me. I was accustomed to people thinking I'm a little arrogant, and perhaps his height was seen as a way to keep me humble.

In other ways, his appearance was unremarkable: pale skin dotted with freckles or age spots; thinning, light brown hair gradually disappearing from his forehead; pale blue eyes, wide-set and often appearing to be focused on nothing.

But he was formidable. He was possibly the most intelligent person I would ever meet—so intelligent that he had frequently let me go on about something, convinced I was right, expressing myself with the bravado that I believed proved my point, only to nod slowly and say something that sliced clean through the logic on which I had founded my position. But I'm no slouch, either, so I learned quickly that I must tread lightly, not say too much all at once, and be sure he was with me before I stated any conclusions.

He was also one of the most Christ-like individuals I had ever known. Even as he sliced through my premises, he was kind and soft-spoken, and he always found something to praise. He asked about my personal life and listened with genuine interest, or sincere concern, or whatever else was the most compassionate position he could take.

When he left word to come see him, I was never sure whether it would be a pleasant visit or a critical one, but there was always some pleasure in it. That Friday, it could have been either.

"Spencer," he greeted me from behind his desk. He was smiling, but that signified nothing other than his typical demeanor. "Sit down, won't you?"

I sat in one of the two heavy, highly polished wooden chairs, facing him across his desk.

He asked, "How are you?"

I had learned that he was not expecting me to say, "Fine, thank you. And you?" No; he wanted to know.

Despite my rebuff of Donald, all week I had been tempted to

let my secret out, to confess—if that was the correct attitude—to Dr. Dunfey who I was, and what I had done. Here was my chance. Did I take it?

No.

Instead, I said, "Very well, actually. I feel as though I've made some progress in my acting class." Not a lie, really; between the class instructor and Donald, I felt I was getting a clear picture of what I needed to do.

"That's one thing I wanted to talk to you about, as it happens. Did you see me sneak into your Intro to Preaching class?"

I blinked, surprised. "No. I didn't."

"Good. I didn't want you to see me." He smiled again and leaned back a little in his chair. "You were very good."

I'm sure I blushed. Certainly, I was gratified. The assignment had been a ten-minute sermon, and I had incorporated as much as I could of what I had learned in class. And what I had learned from Donald.

"Thank you, sir. The acting class I'm taking off-campus has helped me improve. I'm glad you recommended it."

"So am I, my son. And the other reason I wanted to speak with you is related. I want to offer you an opportunity that will not only challenge you in terms of your presentation skills, but will also give you a chance to be seen, a chance few of your peers will ever have." He stopped.

Doing my best to ignore the odd feeling growing in my stomach, I said, "I'm intrigued."

"You're probably aware that we're putting on a show for the seminary and close family, in December."

I nodded. "*Everyman*. The morality play."

"Yes." He leaned forward, arms folded on the desk. "The man who was to play the part of Death has decided the life of a priest is not for him, and he has left us."

I was not sure I liked where this was going. I said nothing.

"And I thought of you." He held up a hand as though to ward

off a protest from me. "Death is an imposing character. He must be taken very seriously, and he must be convincing. Your height, your deep voice, and your recent training have encouraged me to recommend you for the part."

I reminded myself to breathe. "Are others auditioning?"

"As far as I know, no one else has come forward. If you're willing, I'll send you right now to Dr. Baird, the play's director. I hope you don't mind that I've spoken to him already, and he's waiting for you in the auditorium."

There was no way out of this. As much as Dr. Dunfey made this sound like an option, I knew it was not. It was one of those things one is expected to accept with grace, rather as if one were assigned a parish in a place where one decidedly did not want to live. One could appeal, to be sure, but one had better have a good reason. And I had no reason at all to decline this offer, which was how Dr. Dunfey saw it—how anyone, really, would see it.

I bowed my head slowly, accepting my fate. "I appreciate your confidence in me."

Dr. Dunfey beamed. "I will look forward to the performance."

I made my way to the auditorium, doubting that I had it in me to play this part. I was never shy, but I had always been reserved. But—perhaps that's what they wanted from Death.

Dr. Baird, a short, lively man with a full head of dark hair, white streaks shot through it along both sides looking almost like angel wings, sat on the stage, legs dangling.

"Ah! Spencer, my boy. Excellent. Dunfey thinks you're just the man for this job." He scrambled to his feet. "Willing to see if he's right?"

I couldn't help smiling. Dr. Baird's enthusiasm and good humor were contagious. I mounted the stage, and he handed me a script. It seemed as though the decision about giving me the part had already been made.

"Have you seen the play before, Spencer?"

"Yes, though it was a few years ago. I'll read through the whole of it on my own."

"You do that. For now, let's just try it out a little, yes? Let's begin after humans are called into existence, told to keep their eyes on the final reckoning, beware of sin, blah blah blah. Then God complains that humans are growing more sinful by the hour and an accounting is imminent, beginning with death. That's you. Death. So I, God, summon you."

Dr. Baird cleared his throat and began to read, his voice carrying—I was certain—all the way to the back of the hall and beyond. I could not hope to achieve the theatrics he accomplished so apparently effortlessly as he told me about the pilgrimage man must make, and why. But watching him, listening to him, inspired me to try.

I rose to my full height, aiming at an additional inch or two, and promised to be outright cruel in my search for anyone not living according to God's law.

In his normal voice, which was still animated, he said, "Very good! With a little practice, you'll scare the living daylights out of the audience. Let's keep going."

In spite of my misgivings, I began to enjoy myself. When we came to the end of my part, I felt a little disappointed; there was a good deal more to the play. I almost wished I'd been given a larger part.

Walking home after my audition, I felt the urge to tell Donald, not that I had any reason to think he'd be happy for me. We were still in hiatus on *Sleuth*, and that seemed unlikely to change.

I didn't go straight home. Instead I went to the main library and checked out a copy of *Equus*, the play by Peter Shaffer, twin brother to the author of *Sleuth*. I'd avoided seeing the play, knowing much of the plot hangs on an act of the most horrible violence a central character perpetrates on horses. I couldn't imagine why Donald would imply that it had anything to do with the relationship between God and man.

There weren't many people in the periodical room, so I read quite a bit of the script in there and became so engrossed that I barely got home in time for dinner.

Having decided a relationship with Donald was not in my future, I realized that my preoccupation with him, and my absences from some meals, made me feel as though I had pulled back from my mother. It had not been intentional. Mostly, I think, it was that I didn't want to burden her with the truth about who I was.

Or was that just an excuse?

No. It was not. I did not want to pull away from her. She and I had always been on an island together, surrounded by the forceful tides of her husband, my father. Without using words, we knew we understood each other and our situation. And I truly believed telling her I was gay would destroy the bond that had survived Father's death.

So I wanted—needed—to be home in time for dinner. And I think Mother needed that, too.

"Oh, Spencer! That's wonderful," she said when I told her I would play Death. "I know that play well." This time her smile showed all over her face. "But—will I be allowed to see it?"

"Of course! It's for the seminary and close family, I was told."

With a look that was almost coy, not a typical look for Mother, she asked, "Do you suppose I could help you rehearse?"

My surprise at this suggestion must have shown on my own face. She dropped her eyes to her plate. "I understand I might not be good enough."

Coming to my senses, I said, "I think you'd be great, actually. Let's plan on that."

The next look on her face melted my heart.

After the meal I was tempted to retreat to my room for more of *Equus*. But instead I sat with Mother in the living room, each of us engrossed in our individual reading, until I made some involuntary, startled sound. The character Alan Strang, a severely troubled youth, had just driven metal spikes into the eyes of several horses.

"What is it, dear?" Mother set her open book down in her lap.

"It's...." I couldn't bring myself to say the words. "I'm reading *Equus*." I knew she would remember that we had discussed seeing it.

"Oh, dear Lord. Whatever for?"

I closed the script and set it aside. "I haven't told you very much about my class, have I?"

Her tone was sweet, but I heard a gentle accusation in it. "No."

I nodded and moved to a chair nearer hers. "Dr. Dunfey suggested I take it." She nodded, no doubt remembering that he had. "One of the other students is an actor. His father is a minister, so we got to talking. And he offered to help me outside of class, to coach me in ways that would help specifically with sermon delivery."

I gauged her expression. There was no change that I could see.

"So we met a couple of times to work on material he selected. We started with *Sleuth*."

I told her how surprisingly well that particular play demonstrated an aspect of man's relationship to God, and how delivering it intelligently and sympathetically could help an audience to see that as well. And then I lied to Mother.

"He's just been given a big role in a play, so he doesn't have time to work with me right now. But he suggested I read

Equus for a different understanding of what religion can mean."

"Horse blinding, Spencer? What has that to do with God?" Yes, indeed; she remembered why we hadn't seen it.

I nodded again. "Good question. But I'm seeing that it's not the specifics that matter. They're symptoms." She looked at me skeptically. "Tell you what. When I've finished reading it, I'll tell you if I see what I think my friend wanted me to see."

She sighed. "I suppose, really, everything we do has to do with our relationship with God. I'll be curious to know how this terrible deed fits into it."

Mother smiled, a genuine smile, which I took to mean that she was happy to have me talk to her about what I was thinking. I confess it made me happy, too.

I finished reading *Equus* Saturday morning. As usual, Mother was out. I was glad of the alone time to sort through my thoughts. My feelings. My epiphany.

For that's what it was: an epiphany.

I don't know that I'd say scales fell from my eyes. It was more like my eyesight had been barely good enough for me to see what was right in front of me. Somehow, the blinding of horses had the opposite effect on me: I saw something very important for the first time.

The character Alan Strang seems to have had a passionate (in every sense of the word) relationship with horses and with Jesus. With God. With God as Equus. If that sounds confusing, well… Strang was confused. And he seems to have confused the hell out of his psychiatrist, Martin Dysart, who was thrown into confusion about his own role in life and his own relationship with religion in general and God in particular.

Dysart had questions like, could religious passion be good? If not, was it the fault of religion or the religious? Could Dysart lead young Strang out of the darkness of his twisted creed and into the light? But where was the light? It did not seem to lie in the direction of the accepted standards of Dysart's career. Must Dysart, in his latent passion as a kind of Christ figure, sacrifice the esteem and the gratification of his career in order to save Strang? And was reclamation for Strang even possible?

During the standard Discernment process I had gone through before being accepted at General, I had been asked more than once why I wanted to enter God's service. My answers had been rooted in my upbringing, which had been barely on the secular side of ecclesiastical. I felt at home with God, I'd said. I wanted to help others experience the inner peace and hopeful reunion that comes from faith, I'd said.

What hit me about *Equus* was that Dysart's career was not directly related to religion or to God. But he struggled to see how it could be otherwise, so his work with the God-obsessed Strang aroused in him a jealous fervor—an unrequited desperation for passion which, if he reached for it, and whether he achieved it or not, would bring the rest of his life tumbling down.

I was in the enviable position of having none of Strang's misguided passion while possessing a distinctly God-centered life goal. Unlike Dysart, I had nothing to lose and everything to gain by choosing a life of religious passion.

I had finally—at last!—heard a calling, the Calling that is so essential for anyone living the life of a religious leader. I would unite passion and God and help others do the same.

I compared the empty phrases (as they now seemed to me) I had spouted during Discernment to the Calling I was now certain would be mine. One word arose in my mind about my past assertions: Bullshit.

CHAPTER FIVE

The next week, during which Donald and I sat as far away from each other in class as we could, I met the other actors for the *Everyman* production. And I learned that the others had been working on it for two weeks already.

Most of the parts weren't in every scene, and any actor not in the current scene was expected to play the role of an audience member.

There were very few women at General; the seminary had changed its policy to include women not quite a decade ago. One of the current female students, Tegan Langley, had been asked to play Good Deeds.

Tegan was a petite blond with a heart-shaped face that would have been almost too precious if she hadn't also been blessed with a typical English nose. Think Princess Diana, and you wouldn't be far off, except that Tegan's hair was long and parted in the middle without bangs. There was something timeless about her, as though she could have modeled as an angel for Botticelli.

If her appearance weren't charming enough, she had a delightful, almost indistinguishable English accent. I couldn't help watching her, whether she was on stage reading her part or observing from the audience. At one point our eyes met, and she looked away very quickly.

I made the mistake of describing her to Mother over dinner that evening.

"She sounds delightful," was Mother's first comment, followed fairly closely by, "Perhaps I could meet her sometime," and accompanied by the kind of smile any young person might correctly interpret as the beginnings of an expectation relating to marriage and children. I changed the topic quickly.

Although I was loathe to get Mother's hopes or expectations up, I couldn't help fixating on Tegan. And she made it easy. As our little troupe continued to work on *Everyman*, it seemed natural, when she and I were audience members, to sit together. She had a musical giggle, and a sweetness about her made her seem more innocent than she was likely to be.

By the second week of rehearsals, I suspected that Tegan and I looked like a couple. I had been giving a lot of thought to the idea—often put forth by people who deny the reality of homosexuality—that before Tegan, perhaps I had just never met the right woman. When Donald and I had started avoiding each other in acting class, I had felt guilty about previously leading him on, and I was disgusted at what I had done. But after I had spent enough time in rehearsal with Tegan, and enough time thinking about her generally, I could almost completely dismiss thoughts of Donald. This realization emboldened me to ask Tegan out for dinner.

My boldness faded somewhat after its initial thrust, so that it wasn't until the final week of rehearsals that I carried out my plan.

As we were leaving rehearsal that Thursday evening, I took

care to make it seem unremarkable that Tegan and I were walking out at the same time. I slowed my pace as we left the building, and she slowed with me. There were still a few other students around us, so I stopped; I wasn't sure why, but I didn't want to be overheard, perhaps in case of rejection.

"I've been meaning to ask you about something," I opened, keeping track of how far away the others were getting. She looked up at me, her expression sweet, open, ready to listen to whatever I said. "I, uh," (I had never done this, but I'd practiced hard for at least three days), "There's a restaurant I've always enjoyed that I'm hoping I could introduce you to."

She didn't speak immediately, so I added, "Of course, you might already know it." I named the place. "Tomorrow night, perhaps?"

This time I waited. I knew I should stop talking.

A slow smile spread across her face, and she tilted her head charmingly. "Why, Spencer, are you asking me out on a date?"

I told myself to smile. I told myself to be calm. I told myself to draw on everything I had been learning about acting. It might be fair to say I assumed a role that wasn't entirely mine.

"You know," I said, doing my best to insert subtle confidence into my deep voice, "I do believe I am." I wanted to ask if she was accepting my offer, but I had also cautioned myself to avoid arrogance. I had to leave it up to her, now. It wasn't easy, and I hoped the calm appearance I was working so hard to maintain did not reveal the inner turmoil I felt.

"Tomorrow night won't work, I'm afraid."

A sharp pang shot through my chest. "Ah," I said, and then was at a total loss. I stood there, my face frozen in a grin, feeling like an idiot, trying to remember how I had practiced for this possibility.

"But if Saturday evening is good for you, I could say yes to that."

"Oh! Well. Um, yes. By all means." *Now what? What do I*

do now?

"Would you like my telephone number?"

We exchanged numbers, and I walked home, chiding myself the whole way. She was obviously more practiced at this dating thing than I was. Of course, that was a low bar; I'd never dated anyone. But even as I criticized my performance, I was keenly aware of a quivering feeling that I felt throughout my body.

Here were those butterflies I'd heard so much about! Here was that static energy that comes from anticipating being with someone you liked, someone you wanted to like you, someone you wanted to spend much more time with! Were these signs that I had, perhaps, found the "right" woman, or at least a candidate? Was I not really gay after all?

Mother was ecstatic at the news that I had a date. I almost didn't tell her, but that didn't seem fair. And she did her best not to gush, not to make me feel any more self-conscious than I already did.

I didn't think about Donald at all that night.

Well, not more than once or twice.

I considered hiring Mother's favorite car service for Saturday evening, but that felt not only ostentatious but also a little presumptive for a first date. The restaurant I'd chosen was impressive enough. I decided to rely on my excellent record for hailing cabs, which was easy for me as a tall man with a big voice. It was the right choice.

I had worried about conversational topics for my dinner with Tegan. I shouldn't have. Tegan was easily amused and delightful to watch.

"Oh, my goodness! I have to try this soup. Did you see it?"

I looked at her rather than at my menu. She was dressed in a high-collared, blue velvet dress with slightly puffy shoulders. The color enhanced her blue eyes, and the cameo pin at her throat—a carved ivory image on a dark blue background—might have seemed old-fashioned on someone else, but on her it was perfect. She wore her hair up in an artful sweep, soft tendrils escaping apparently at random.

I shook my head and smiled.

"Cream of chestnut with wild mushrooms. So seasonal, don't you think?"

"Indeed. I'll have that as well."

As soon as our order was placed, Tegan sipped her water and then said, "Something tells me you're musical, Spencer. Do you sing? Or play an instrument?"

"Both, as it happens." I described briefly my membership in the exclusive choir I'd been in during my high school years at Loyola. "But what I love best is piano."

"Really? Why, especially?"

The waiter brought our wine, and I had a moment of brilliance. "Tegan, would you like to taste the wine to see if it's acceptable?"

"How evolved of you! I'd love to."

I hoped that was a compliment.

She was impressed when, wine poured and waiter gone, I told her of my love for Chopin's music. She glanced at my right hand, curled around the step of my wine glass. She held her left hand toward it.

"Let's see."

Rather automatically I gave her my hand, and she examined it with her fingers, toying with mine, testing the size of mine against hers, and finally setting my hand palm up on the table. I watched as she ran her forefinger in circles on my skin, so lightly that I felt shivers travel from my hand to my groin. I wondered if she was fully aware of the effect she was having on me. One glance up at her face told me the answer to that was a definite Yes.

She pulled away and gently swirled the wine in her glass, her eyes watching mine.

My head spun. The contrast between the sweet innocent she could appear to be and the sultry temptress on display right now both delighted and confused me. When I reminded myself that this woman was in training to be a priest, the confusion increased. But then the memory of how I had behaved in Donald's tiny apartment made me sit back in my chair and examine the table settings.

At that moment two people arrived to serve our soup. The first waiter placed a large white, wide-rimmed bowl in front of each of us, an artfully arranged pyramid of sautéed mushrooms in the center. The other waiter, holding what looked like a silver-plated pitcher, poured creamy, pale brown liquid around the pyramids. A sprinkle of some herb—parsley, I guessed—completed the presentation.

Tegan clapped her hands together once, lightly. "How wonderful! Aren't you glad you ordered this, too?"

"I'll let you know when I've tasted it." She sat still, watching while I raised a spoonful of the soup and inserted it into my mouth.

She laughed softly. "Based on your expression, I'm going to say it tastes delicious."

The meal proceeded like this, with excellent dishes providing a gustatory foundation for Tegan's sparkling conversation. At one point, I realized that one reason it sparkled was because of the way she got me talking about myself. I wasn't just droning on. No; she made me sound interesting. Even maybe a little fascinating.

While we waited for dessert, a glass of Armagnac each, she asked, "Do you enjoy plays, Spencer?"

I felt one side of my mouth lift in a half-smile. "You know, so many people would have asked whether I'd seen any good ones lately." She seemed almost not to have heard me. So I said, "As a matter of fact, I do. And I'm about to complete a course in acting methodology." I took a sip of Armagnac and waited.

"Whatever for?"

"To improve my delivery. Sermons, and all that."

Her head shook slowly. "But I've seen you in rehearsals. You're actually quite good."

I lifted a shoulder and dropped it. "As I said, I've nearly finished the course."

She laughed obligingly. "And did you work on specific material during this class?"

Of course, she would certainly have known we had; she was giving me a chance to show off a little. Again. But I didn't want to talk about the class material.

"I've been working on two plays in particular, each written by one of two brothers, twins in fact. *Sleuth*, by Anthony Shaffer, and *Equus*, by his brother Peter."

Her eyes widened. "I know that play. *Equus*, I mean."

Suddenly a plate was before me, a ramekin on it containing my favorite dessert: creme brûlée. Tegan had declared it boring when I'd placed the order, but I thought this restaurant made it better than any other place I'd tried it. Bright raspberries and mint sprigs decorated the plate around the ramekin. Tegan's choice, which *I* thought was boring, was chocolate mousse.

We sampled our food in silence, savoring the flavors. Then she said, "Mine's better."

I chuckled. "No way."

She waved her spoon in the air and said, "Anyway, back to *Equus*. What do you think of it?"

"Oh, well…. Where to begin?" I sifted through my perceptions, trying to land on one comment.

Tegan was more prepared. "I found the frustration of Dr.

Dysart to be rather self-involved. I mean, didn't it seem to you as though he was all about his own role in a patient's recovery?"

"I—but it was his job. To help people recover, I mean. Recover from emotional states they needed to leave behind."

"Yes, but I'm talking about the way he's portrayed. You agree that he saw himself as some kind of Christ figure, yes?"

"I think he found himself going in that direction. I'm not sure it was ever intentional."

"Interesting." She paused as if thinking, and then said, "And as a man, what can you tell me about the stimulation a naked Alan Strang would have felt riding a horse bareback?"

I blinked as something in my crotch gave a kind of twitch at the thought of that stimulation. I sat back in my chair, doing my best to appear as though I were not completely nonplussed by her question, and feeling grateful for the fairly dim lighting of the restaurant.

"Never having done anything like that, all I can tell you is that it would probably have been extremely stimulating."

"Would he have ejaculated, do you think?"

I gave a kind of snort, which I hoped camouflaged my embarrassment. "I'm not sure that young man needed physical stimulation in order to do that. And I do think the script leaves little doubt that he did. You didn't pick up on that?"

"He saw Equus as a God figure, and yet he came all over it. Does that strike you as depraved?"

"It strikes me as profoundly misplaced passion."

Her spoon made a quiet clinking sound as it reached for the last bits of chocolate. Tegan placed the spoon into her mouth, upside down, and watched my face as she pulled the silver utensil out again, slowly.

She placed both elbows onto the table, rested her chin on her interwoven fingers, and gazed at me. "Do you want to know my favorite part?"

I stayed where I was, pressed against the chair back. I shrugged as if to say, *If you insist.*

"It was when he blinded the horses."

I shifted uncomfortably in my chair. *Who was this woman? Why had she embarked on this thread of conversation? Was she obsessed with sex? With blood? With torture? And if torture, was it really the horses', or was it mine as well?*

"Spencer, you look a little terrified. Aren't you going to ask me why that's my favorite part?"

"Fine. Why?"

"It's because they had seen what he had done in the loft. With Jill Mason. Or, rather, what he had tried to do. Don't you see?" She dropped her hands onto the table. "He was ashamed that he had wanted to transfer his passion for God, Equus, to a mere human female. And he couldn't tolerate the judgement."

She seemed to be waiting for me to say something. So I said, "And this is your favorite part?"

It was Tegan's turn to sit back in her chair, and as she did, two people arrived to remove our dessert dishes. I hadn't quite finished mine, but I had lost the desire for it.

The main waiter asked, "Is there anything else I can bring you?"

I was about to assure him there was not, as I was now anxious to leave. But Tegan said, "I'd love a glass of the moscato grappa."

I made a mental note never to take a first date anywhere that would keep me there longer than I might want to stay.

As the waiter retreated, Tegan picked up where I'd left off. "Yes. It makes me wonder whether it's likely, or even possible, for ordained men to fall victim to the same kind of misplaced passion, just not for horses."

I scowled, I'm sure of it. I decided to meet fire with fire. "So you think priests—sorry, male priests—might flagellate themselves into orgasm? You think that ceremonial robes cover secret erections?"

"Do they?"

Her glass of grappa appeared.

"Where on earth do you get that impression? What must you think of us? What must you think of men?"

She sipped from her glass and set it down, fingers still lightly gripping the stem. "I'm just being realistic."

I shook my head slowly. "I don't understand. You think we confuse a passion for Christ with a passion for sex? Or maybe you think men have no control over our physical reactions."

"So you admit men react physically to religious passion?"

I felt my back stiffen. "I admit no such thing. And, by the way, there's plenty of writing about nuns who masturbate to thoughts of God or Jesus."

She actually laughed. "I'm sorry, Spencer. I seem to have caused you to be hot under your proverbial collar. Not to be punny."

"Punny?"

"Collar. As in ecclesiastical."

I scowled, not for the first time that evening. Saying *Not to be punny* was cover for *Wasn't that a clever pun?* I said, "I find puns tiresome."

She leaned a little forward, eyes down, the fingers of both hands resting on opposite sides of her small, stemmed glass. When she looked up, she said, "I apologize, Spencer. I've offended you. I've done my usual stupid thing when I'm nervous."

"What's that?"

"Poked a hornet's nest." She let out a long breath through her nose, shook her head. She closed her eyes. When she opened them I saw a combination of chagrin and pain. "And that was the wrong thing to say, as well. What I mean is that I find an area that might make someone uncomfortable, and I aim right at it."

I gave that some space. "Why are you nervous?"

Her smile was almost demure. "I want you to like me."

I laughed. I couldn't help it. "Sorry; not laughing at you. Laughing at this oh, so typical human behavior of sabotaging that which we most want."

We sat quietly for a moment, eyes on each other. Then she said, "I don't see any sabotage on your part. You're not nervous?"

I opened my mouth, expecting to say something helpful, something to put her at ease, something to establish common ground. But with a shock that made me spontaneously lift a foot off the floor and plant it again quickly, I realized that despite the nervousness I had felt when I was asking her out, and despite the butterflies I had felt after that, I had been too busy arranging the evening and worrying about conversational topics to feel anxious in advance of the meeting. And once the evening had begun, and Tegan and I were in each other's company, I never felt nervous. I was going to have to examine this mystery later. For now, I just wanted to make her feel comfortable.

"Of course."

"But no sabotage?"

I shrugged. "Maybe not this time. Don't give up on me."

I had the cab wait while I walked Tegan to the door of her apartment building in Chelsea; like me, she didn't live on campus. She turned to me at the outer door, her face sweetly tilted up toward mine.

"Good night, Spencer. I really enjoyed the dinner, even if I wasn't on my best behavior. Hope I didn't spoil anything."

I shook my head. "You spoiled nothing." It might have been a lie.

I hesitated—couldn't have said why—before bending

forward to reach her mouth with mine. Instead of the gentle, soft meeting of lips I had in mind, she opened her mouth for a deeper, penetrating embrace of tongues. I nearly pulled back in surprise, but I caught myself in time.

～

I lay in bed that night, reliving the evening, bewildered by more than one aspect of the date. Every time I sent my thoughts to the odd way Tegan's conversation over dinner had prodded me, they snapped back to my reaction to her kiss as if on a strong elastic band. Finally, I had to admit the truth.

I had not enjoyed the kiss. If I were honest, I hadn't really wanted a kiss. It was expected. That was all.

If she had taken my lead and allowed the kiss to be sweet, even innocent, I knew I would not be feeling this sense of—God —of revulsion.

My sheets, tangled with my tortured squirming, were a physical representation of my emotional state.

If it's possible to shout and whisper at the same time, that's what I did. "Fuck!" I brought my fist down hard onto the mattress beside me.

Into the darkness, my voice a true whisper now, I pleaded with—well, I'm not sure with what or with whom. With myself perhaps. "Why did she do that?" My eyes stared at the pale grayness of the ceiling.

When Donald had kissed me the first time, standing on a sidewalk with snowflakes drifting around us, it had been soft and light. When we'd kissed the second time, in the theater practice room, it had still been soft and light. And then, gently, he had teased my lips with his tongue. He hadn't thrust himself into me the way Tegan had done. He had made me want more, and when he'd given me more, I had been ready for it.

I sighed into the air above me. What was I supposed to make

of this? If Tegan had kissed me lightly, would I want more passion the next time I saw her? Conversely, if Donald had kissed me passionately the first time, would I have felt the revulsion I'd felt with Tegan's forceful kiss?

Was Tegan the problem? Or was I?

In an effort to make my mind focus on something else, I imagined playing the piano. It didn't matter what piece; I chose a Mozart sonata.

The distraction was a good one. Or, it would have been, if I had chosen a different composer. My imagination hadn't progressed beyond the second statement of the main theme when a play, also by Peter Shaffer, was suddenly front and center in my mind: *Amadeus*.

Shaffer's narrator for the career of Wolfgang Amadeus Mozart was Antonio Salieri, a composer with a keen appreciation for the beauty of Mozart's music. Salieri was competent enough to understand Mozart's genius and also to know that his own talent—that his very best efforts—paled in comparison, despite his relative success on the European music scene.

So, like Dysart in *Equus*, Salieri knew greatness when he saw it, but he also knew he could not achieve anything like it. In both cases, the shortcomings these men saw in themselves drove them at least a little mad.

I wondered what Shaffer would have made of me: a man who appreciated women, who admired them, who wanted to want them the way most men wanted them, but a man whose admirable intention and desperate aspiration would be thwarted by something within himself that he could not change, regardless of how clear the necessary change was.

Dysart and Salieri were, in a way, "wannabes."

Would that be my fate as well?

I had to try to avoid it.

CHAPTER SIX

For the next several days, right through the remaining *Everyman* rehearsal and the two performances just before Christmas, I felt like someone other than myself. According to audiences—including Mother, who came to both shows—I did very well. Of course, acting is, in a sense, being someone else.

After a few meaningful looks from Tegan during this time, which met with an answering smile but no more from me, I steeled myself, determined to move the relationship along after the shows were over. I called to mind some trite expressions for the effort: step up to the plate; take the bull by the horns; bite the bullet. Would fortune favor the bold? There was only one way to find out.

After the second and final performance, a Saturday night, there was a small cast party. Mother stopped in long enough to congratulate Dr. Baird, and I introduced her to Tegan.

Tegan was as high on adrenaline as anyone who's just had a

great (if short) run of a performance, but when she took Mother's hand she was a model of decorum.

"Spencer has told me about you, Tegan, but he didn't tell me how lovely and how talented you are. And you're going to be a priest?"

Tegan laughed charmingly and, I suspect, used her faint British accent to its full advantage. "I am, yes. I'm so looking forward to bringing a woman's insight and sensibilities to the vocation."

Mother nodded and smiled; I couldn't tell whether she thought this would be good thing, or whether her upbringing in Catholicism would make her unable to see it that way. But whichever way her thoughts went, she obviously liked Tegan and even gave her a quick hug before heading home.

During the party, Tegan was often at my side. I fetched her drinks; I sometimes let my hand touch the small of her back; once or twice I put my arm across her shoulders.

It was all very deliberate, very calculated, as though I were still in a play, taking the role of a man who wanted to behave this way, who hoped that the gentle attentions he paid a woman would endear him to her romantically. And I found that when I took this approach, that is, as an actor, it was more manageable, less disturbing, and less likely to bring on guilt from what was possibly nothing more than leading her on.

If there had been anyone in the cast or crew who had not previously thought of Tegan and me as a couple, it seems unlikely they left the party with any doubts.

After the party, as I walked her the short distance home to her building, we chatted about our impressions from the performance. I hadn't noticed the first time I'd been here that it had appeared rather shabby, at least by the standards of my own home. Of course, I would not hold that against Tegan; whether she had money or not was irrelevant to me.

This time I let her ascend the front steps ahead of me so I

could be far enough away to avoid another thrusting kiss. She turned toward me at the door, looking just slightly surprised.

"I'd like to see you again," I said. "Perhaps a concert?"

She tilted her head, looking as though she wanted to say something but changed her mind. "I'd like that. I'll be leaving for England on the twenty-fourth, though, and I won't be back until the third of January."

I stared at her blankly for a second, and then I laughed. "We had a whole evening together over dinner, and neither of us asked the other about family."

"Even so, we found a lot to talk about." She smiled knowingly. Then, "I'll be visiting with my father in St. Albans. It's not far outside of London. Father is retired now, but he taught for many years at the Heathlands School for the Deaf."

"The deaf? That's interesting."

Tegan made several quick motions with her hands. "That's sign language to say my mother was deaf."

"You mother has passed?"

"Six years ago. I have a brother who lives nearby, so Father isn't alone. He has two grandchildren to keep him busy. What about you?"

"No siblings. Father passed a few years ago. I live with Mother for now, not a long walk from here. It didn't seem to make sense to board at General when home is so close."

"Does your mother work?"

"No. She's got a large house to keep up, though. Father taught philosophy at New York University."

"Oh! Isn't Dr. Friedman-Kien a professor there?"

"I—um, I don't know. Why?"

"He identified a new form of cancer that led to a break-through in identifying AIDS."

Here was AIDS again. My mind flashed back to the tortured look on Donald's face as he'd told me about Jonathan.

I was at a loss for appropriate words, so I said, "Well, have a happy Christmas, and I'll call when you're back."

"Happy Christmas?" She laughed. "Was that for my benefit?"

It took me a few seconds to realize what she was asking. I shook my head. "I don't know why we always said that at home. But maybe I should just say yes to you and get the credit."

She gave me the sort of smile that invites a kiss, but I stepped down to the sidewalk and said, "See you next year." I turned without waiting for a response and walked toward home.

Mother had gone to bed by the time I got home.

I sat in Father's chair with a glass of scotch at my side, the room dark except for the floor lamp beside me, contemplating the evening. At one point, I sat up suddenly.

Tegan had referred to her father as "Father." As had I. Very few people I knew did that. And then there was the "Happy Christmas."

It almost seemed as though Heaven were showing me things Tegan and I had in common, gently urging me to deepen the relationship.

Lying in bed, I was just about to drift off when it occurred to me that an Episcopal priest could do a lot worse for a wife than someone who knew sign language. And only the next day did I realize that I had assumed that of course, my wife would follow me to my assigned parish. Tegan wanted her own.

Christmas in my childhood home had never been a joyful time. Yes, we had a tree. Yes, there were presents, and a festive meal. We would go, Father and Mother and I, to church for midnight mass and carol singing. We would come home late and each open one present, which was very meaningful to me because Father always insisted we would receive only two presents each. This meant I had one from him and one from Mother; Mother had one from me and one from Father, and so on. So on Christmas morning, although there had been a stocking for me until I was thirteen, there was only one gift left to open.

Gift opening acquired the same stern atmosphere as everything else Father dictated. I've often wondered whether there would have been more energy, more joy, more celebration if I'd had at least one sibling, or if Father's dampening influence would have prevailed regardless.

After he died, however, Mother and I began to indulge ourselves. We bought as many gifts for each other as we wanted, and Mother would even buy something for herself. She would wait, however, until after Christmas day, and battle through the throngs of people pursuing after-Christmas sales. I suppose she was reluctant to allow herself too much luxury.

The Christmas after my acting debut in *Everyman*, after midnight mass at St. Ignatius with Mother, it was a delightful chore to select one gift to open before retiring. In the morning, we opened our remaining gifts with only slightly muted abandon. Mother sighed happily as she gazed over the colorful carnage we had made, wrapping papers having disgorged their secrets, bright ribbons and bows no longer pretending to be functional.

She smiled at me. "Happy Christmas, Spencer."

"Happy Christmas, Mother."

I never asked why my family had always said "happy," as I'd said to Tegan, instead of "merry." Perhaps it was related to the fervor with which Father had thrown himself into his adopted religion, which had its roots in England. There, you're more likely to be wished a happy Christmas than a merry one.

Over breakfast Mother revealed to me her plan for tomorrow, the day when she would shop for herself.

"Please come with me Spencer, won't you?"

"Where are you going?"

"It's a little shop on East Fifty-Seventh. I've had my eye on a coat in the window for over a month now." She almost giggled. "I went by two days ago to be sure it was still there."

I knew the smaller shops were less likely to offer major discounts. Although money was never in short supply, Mother was accustomed to denying herself. This time, at last, she would allow herself an indulgence.

I grinned. "Of course I will."

We set out on our shopping trip right after breakfast the next day. I hailed a cab and sat beside Mother for the drive uptown, silently thrilled that she seemed so excited about our errand.

"I would describe this coat to you," she said, arms around her ribs as if to hold herself in, "but I couldn't do it justice."

"Fur?"

"Not exactly. You know how I feel about killing animals just for their skins."

I did. She had often said that as long as we consume animal meat, we shouldn't waste the skin. But she would never wear the fur of any animal killed just for its beauty.

Not exactly. Was it leather, I wondered? I stifled a chuckle at the thought of Mother in a black leather jacket.

I paid the driver and opened the cab door for my smiling mother. But as soon as we stood before the shop window, her mood plummeted.

"Oh, no! It's gone!"

I opened the shop door. "Let's go see."

It was a little larger inside than it appeared from the street, but it was still a small shop. There were several women inside, although the store had been open only about fifteen minutes.

Mother stood, looking helpless and worried.

I said, "Can you tell me enough about this coat that I could help look for it on a sale rack, or something?"

"It's green. Dark green."

I placed a hand on the small of her back and we moved forward, careful to avoid other shoppers and racks of dresses and displays of handbags. It wasn't until we were almost to the back of the shop that I spotted something large and dark green, hiding on a rack with other coats.

I pointed. "Is that it?"

Mother doesn't often move quickly. This time, she dashed. She grabbed the thick green thing, hugged it to herself, and turned a shining face toward me.

I laughed. "Excellent. So? Try it on!"

The three-way mirror was in high demand. Mother wouldn't even put the coat on until the two women admiring themselves in front of her had moved away. I stood near her to be sure no one tried to shift her aside.

Mother thrust her handbag at me to hold while she shrugged into the coat, not waiting for me to help her on with it.

"Not exactly" had been correct. It was fur, but it was lambskin. Mother loved lamb. So, philosophically, she could wear this coat.

Sueded green dropped from the shoulders down nearly to the floor, while soft, darker green pile seemed to embrace her throat and then to cascade alongside the front edges of the suede. There were two fasteners, large buttons of horn on one side, encircled by large suede loops on the other. The sleeves folded up into cuffs that revealed more of the soft pile.

Mother stood transfixed. Her only movement was to slowly caress the fur around her throat. It was a large coat, but it seemed like a good size for her. At any rate, she could wear it. I stopped myself asking how much it cost. It didn't matter.

"You look absolutely gorgeous," I told her. And she did.

Mother wore the coat out of the store, and I carried a dark maroon bag containing the coat she had put on at home. She turned to me as we stood on the sidewalk.

"Do you mind walking for bit, Spencer? I feel like showing off a little."

I laughed. "Let's do that. Where would you like to gloat?"

She giggled. "Can we walk over to Fifth Avenue and go up to the park?"

"I'm at your disposal. Lead the way."

She seemed to float rather than walk the short distance to Fifth Avenue, where we turned north toward Central Park. Mother kept walking until we were somewhere near Sixty-First Street, where she stopped and gazed around happily. I was about to lead her to where a crosswalk would help us through the traffic so we could cross the avenue when she thrust her arm out, pointing.

There was a child, a young girl, across the two lanes of Fifth Avenue. She was alone, crying, obviously lost. She began to move into the busy street.

It happened so quickly, and yet it moved so slowly. Mother eluded my impotent grasp and charged into the traffic to get to the child.

I cried out as the bus, unable to avoid the green lambskin coat that would have protected my mother from the cold, screeched—too late—to a stop.

I can't describe details of the aftermath. What remains in my mind is a collection of bits and pieces: the lifeless body; the bloodied lamb, the metaphorical sacrifice of my selfless Mother;

the wailing of sirens; the weeping that wouldn't stop which I only dimly recognized as my own; the heavy, haunted silence of the home I no longer shared with anyone.

St. Ignatius Episcopal is a lovely church with dedicated clergy and—mostly, as far as I could tell—sincere parishioners. It's not as grand as, say, St. Mary's, but it always seemed to me as though Mother was comfortable there. In that more intimate environment, she had seemed to thrive, and (I suspect) would have felt overwhelmed at St. Mary's. Father's funeral had been well-attended, with many people dressed in mourning black and appearing duly somber. Few had wept.

At Mother's funeral, the crowd was smaller, but the mourners were doing just that: mourning. She had never been a conspicuous church member, but she had been quietly and reliably involved in the church's charitable efforts. Her gentleness, her childlike openness, and her genuine concern for others had endeared her to those who knew her.

The priest used the reason for Mother's death as a symbol for her life.

"Theresa Hill," he intoned, and paused to gaze at the congregation. "Theresa Hill was a woman of God. And by that, I mean she was a woman of Jesus. For Jesus is about love. And that word describes Theresa Hill better than any other I can think of. The very manner of her death speaks to this."

He paused briefly and surveyed the people before him. "Theresa saw a child about to walk onto a busy street. She thought of nothing but the danger to the child. Before her son Spencer could stop her, she charged into the traffic to get to the child, directly into the path of a city bus."

I couldn't breathe. I had managed to hold my own tears to this point, but when the priest, evidently overcome with emotion, paused again, holding my breath was the only way to prevent a gasping sob, much like those I heard around me.

As distressed as I was at Mother's death, I was also furious with her for her thoughtlessness. Who would do that? What responsible adult would dash directly into multiple lanes of city traffic? Who would not know—know!—that they would be struck down before they could ever help that child? The priest thought he knew.

"Why did she do it?" he continued. "Did she truly think she could reach the child and pull her to safety? Or," and here he gazed around again, "did she know in her heart that if she were to see the child struck and killed, if she had to watch that happen before her eyes, she would not be able to live with that image?"

He bowed his head and was silent for several seconds.

"The child survived. She was reunited with her frantic parents. And Theresa…. Theresa Hill died for love. And because of love, she is now with the source of all Love. She now lives in spirit, within that Peace that passes all understanding."

My thoughts tumbled, matched in their chaos by my emotions. If the priest was right, if Mother had known she couldn't live with the sight of a child mowed down by traffic, why was it she had no thought for me, having to watch that same fate fall upon my own mother?

If she had died for love, it was a love tarnished by selfishness. Had she loved me? I had no doubt of that. Had she loved me more than she loved her own subjugation? Perhaps not.

I had been with Mother to visit Father's grave, in Green-Wood Cemetery in Brooklyn, several times. It's a lovely piece of land, and the cemetery supports artistic efforts and even has a birding program. I was grateful for the beauty and for the familiarity I felt for the place—aspects that hadn't mattered to me for Father's burial but which were calming and even comforting for Mother's.

Not many people attended the burial, so far away from the church. I was glad for this; I'd already had more than my share of solicitous, well-meaning people fixing soulful eyes on me as they expressed their sympathy.

As though it might protect her from cold the way it had not protected her from death, I had her buried in her lambskin coat.

CHAPTER SEVEN

The nightmares started a few days after the funeral.

It was guilt, I'm certain, that fueled them. Even as I told myself I had not been to blame, as I reminded myself yet again that I couldn't have anticipated and could not have been prepared for an intelligent, city-bred woman charging heedlessly into oncoming traffic, it felt as though her demise was something I had to atone for.

Most of the dreams had nothing to do with Mother. Not directly, anyway. The one that tormented me more often than the others had to do with a dog. We'd never had a dog. I don't know where the image came from.

The dog was missing. It had to be found, for reasons the dream didn't make clear. It had no name. I don't even know whether it was male or female. Somehow I knew it was a fairly large dog, and it had curly brown hair. So I knew what I was looking for, but I never actually saw it.

I waded through nasty ponds, struggling through unseen vegetation that clung tenaciously to my feet and legs. I moved over high, grassy hills, trying desperately to run and failing. I lost my way in dense, dark forests, the trees seeming to move around to confound me and prevent me from escaping.

This dream would end at the same place each time: the lawn in the center of General Theological Seminary. I would find myself there suddenly, having followed no identifiable route to get there, and I would see my advisor, Dr. Dunfey, dressed in a black cassock and waiting for me. Only somehow I knew that it wasn't Dr. Dunfey. It was Dr. Dysart, from *Equus*.

I'd stand before him, knowing he had something to tell me. And each time, as though I'd never heard it before, he'd say:

"What you seek is not here."

And each time I would wake up, curled into fetal position, weeping.

Eventually I connected the dog's image to something it had in common with Mother: curly brown hair. But why would anyone tell me that the dog, or my mother, was not at General?

I did my best to look forward to Tegan's return. Whether my lukewarm enthusiasm was the aftermath of Mother's death or my own lack of conviction that I could have a full relationship with a woman, I couldn't have said. But I had promised Tegan a concert, and a concert she should have.

On the third Saturday in January, I took Tegan to see a concert in Avery Fisher Hall at Lincoln Center, an extremely impressive venue.

We went for a quick bite at an Austrian pastry shop after the concert, a place Mother and I would sometimes sneak out to without telling Father about our indulgence. I should have chosen a different place.

Tegan kept the conversation going with stories about her visit to England, talking about taking her nieces to a museum (their review was "Yuck") and a live demonstration of dressage (deemed by the nieces as "the best *ever*!"). I gathered she and her father were quite close, based on the way she spoke of him.

We sat across a small table from each other, pastries and coffee in front of us. At one point, Tegan set her fork down.

"You're very quiet tonight, Spencer. Is something wrong?"

So she had noticed. Of course she had. But evidently she hadn't heard anything from me that would help her understand.

I sat back and took a deep, steadying breath. "I don't want to say much about it, but—" Another breath. "My mother died the day after Christmas. A road accident."

Tegan sat up straight. "Oh, Spencer!" She shook her head rapidly once or twice, more at herself than anything else. "Sorry. I won't ask you anything." She held a hand toward me, and I took it reflexively. "Soon I hope you'll be able to tell me more. For now, just know how much my heart goes out to you."

She squeezed my hand gently and released it. Hands in her lap now, she gazed down at the table for several seconds while I fought to maintain composure. Then she looked up and said, "It was very brave of you to attend this concert tonight."

"I had made a promise."

She nodded. "And it could have been fulfilled later. If I had known, I would have suggested waiting."

"No; she would want me to go forward." She would want me to go forward with Tegan. But that would have been too much to say aloud. "Tell me more about your nieces. Your enjoyment of them makes me feel better."

And it almost did.

I had the cab wait at Tegan's door as I walked up the steps with her. She turned toward me, and I was almost desperate to avoid a kiss. But all she did was put her arms around me. I held her as well, and we hugged firmly before she released me.

"Good night, Spencer. I hope we can see each other again when you feel more like yourself."

"Yes. I'm sure we will. Good night."

~

We did see each other again, of course, at General. But I didn't contact Tegan again for a couple of weeks.

One Saturday in mid-February, I sat at one of the long, wooden tables in General's library, close to the large windows that overlook the close. Today's sun had that brightness that promises a change of season without delivering it. Shadows threw themselves in sharp contrast to the frozen ground, nearly devoid of snow.

I had spent a lot of time here lately, in the library. Home was still haunted, and being there held the threat of depression, something I've always suspected was just over some thin line from my usual emotional state. In that empty house, Depression hovered somewhere near the ceiling, and only when I played the piano could I forget that it watched me.

My classes were not going well. My concentration was not up to my usual standard, I was falling asleep in classes, and my grades were sliding in the wrong direction. My attempt to bolster my studies by spending time here in the library was too often thwarted by my tendency to gaze around, either at other people, at the close, or at the grain of the wooden table in front of me. And, too often, I dozed.

I wasn't quite dozing one February afternoon when I heard a familiar voice.

"Spencer?"

I looked up. It was Tegan. I had seen her here a few times, but she had respectfully kept her distance, apparently waiting for me to be ready to reconnect. Perhaps she had lost patience.

"I hope I'm not intruding. It's just that you look—well, you look sad."

I gave her a smile that could only be called "wan." She took it as at least not a rejection, if not an outright invitation.

She slid into a seat across from me. "What subject are you working on today?"

I closed the notebook before me. "Nothing that seems to hold my interest."

She nodded as though she understood. "Listen, I have an idea. Why don't we forget studies for the afternoon, and just go on a long walk? Have you been outside in the last hour or so? It's almost warm!"

I closed my eyes for a few seconds, opened them on Tegan's pretty face, and said, "That's the best idea I've heard in a while."

We dropped our backpacks off at Tegan's apartment, which was much nicer inside than the building indicated, and we took the subway up to Seventy-second Street and walked along the Hudson River to the boat basin.

There was a chilly breeze blowing on us as we walked, but still the sun felt warm. We talked little, avoiding by silent agreement anything to do with classes. Tegan never asked, "What are you thinking about?" or "How are you doing?" Most of our conversation was based on people and things we noticed and pointed out to each other.

Once or twice during the afternoon it occurred to me how few people I'd met who could not only carry on an intelligent, interesting conversation when appropriate, but also maintain a comfortable silence for long periods of time.

We settled close together onto one of the benches over-looking the river, gloved hands snuggled deep into our coat pockets for warmth. Sometimes I gazed out across the water toward New Jersey. Sometimes I closed my eyes and turned my face toward the sun as it gradually lowered itself into the south-western sky.

I was the one who broke the silence.

"I'd like to tell you what happened to Mother."

A second went by. Then, softly, "I'd like to hear it."

I made sure I felt calm and took a deep breath just to be sure. "I'd gone with her to pick up a coat she'd had her eye on for weeks. Dark green, lambskin suede on the outside and soft pile inside. It was the day after Christmas. We were on the upper East side, on Fifth Avenue just above Sixtieth Street, and she wore her new coat. Across the street, on the sidewalk outside Central Park, there was a little girl. She was crying, looking around, obviously lost."

I paused here, and I felt Tegan's body stiffen.

"It looked like the girl might be about to step into the street. Mother pointed and then ran into the street to get to her." Another deep breath. "A city bus hit her."

Tegan did not utter any condolences. She didn't tell me how sorry she was. There were no assurances that Mother was "with God now." She said nothing. But less than a minute after I stopped speaking, I heard a very quiet snuffle, and I knew that if I looked at Tegan, I would see tears on her face.

We sat there, silent, staring out across the water, for another few minutes, before Tegan pulled a tissue from her pocket and blew her nose. Then she removed the glove from the hand closer to me, inserted it into my pocket, and wrapped her fingers around my wrist.

On the way back to Tegan's apartment, she suggested we make dinner together. "I owe you a dinner, anyway."

It felt natural, at least in standard societal terms, to accept, so

I did, trying my best to ignore the shivery misgivings that ran through me.

We stopped at a grocer near Tegan's apartment, selecting enough to make a casual meal out of spaghetti and meatballs with side salads.

She adopted a facetious tone and said, "I have a bottle of wine that would be good with this. An amusing little thing, cheap but drinkable."

I didn't know a lot about cooking, but Tegan gave me tasks I could manage. We worked to music that, to my ears, fell somewhere between classical and jazz.

"What are we listening to?"

"Isn't it fun? That's Jean-Pierre Rampal on flute. Claude Bolling is on piano, and Marcel Sabiani plays drums. Bassist Max Hediger joins them on some of the cuts."

This gentle yet lively music, and Tegan's ease in her tiny kitchen, changed everything about the day. I felt lighter, more fluid, and almost happy.

Dinner conversation ranged from cuisine to wine to music. The longer we talked, the more it seemed that we had in common. She claimed not to be a pianist in any way, but when I told her of my love for Chopin, she said, "I remember."

Ah, yes; I had mentioned it over our first dinner together. And she had stroked my hand seductively. I gave her a quick glance; was she going to do something like that again? And, come to think of it, why had I come alone with her to her apartment? *Was I mad?*

Her smile was fond, not sensual. "You look worried, Spencer. But I know now that you aren't the sort of man who moves quickly into things."

She stood and removed our empty plates. "Don't get up," she told me. "The kitchen is too small."

I watched her as she moved easily from table to kitchen, organizing the used dishes so they took up as little room as possible.

"I have some almond biscotti to go with coffee. How does that sound?"

"Perfect." I sat where I was and allowed her to wait on me as I followed her movements with my eyes. She was efficient without being stiff, lithe but not sultry.

Before placing anything else on the table, Tegan changed the music to a collection of Fauré's art songs, sung by a baritone I didn't recognize. Then, with coffee and cookies before us, Tegan began a new topic.

"Where do you live, Spencer?"

I sipped my coffee. "About half an hour's walk east of General." I was a little reluctant to mention the address; it was rather an expensive part of town. But I didn't fool Tegan.

"Are you near Gramercy Park?"

"Yes. Very."

"Do you have a key to the park?" Her tone was enthusiastic.

"Yes. Would you, um, would you like to see it?"

"Very much! I know it's hardly a secret garden, but it sort of has that feel to it." She dipped the end of a biscotti into her coffee. "Is it the house you grew up in?"

"Yes. Feels pretty empty, now. Just the cleaning crew comes in once a week. We used to have someone come in and prepare Sunday dinners when Father was still alive."

"How long do you think you'll stay there?"

I bit a cookie to stall for time. "I haven't given it any thought."

"You could sell it and board at General, if there's a room open."

I felt my neck stiffen. It was true the house was depressing, but it was home, and the idea of packing up or selling off the things that had been important to me all my life was more than unappealing. It nearly took my breath away. I didn't speak.

Tegan did. "I'm sorry. I can tell I've gone too far. I'm not trying to arrange your life for you, Spencer. Please, pretend I didn't say anything."

I stood. "Let me help you clear, at least, before I leave."

She didn't protest again that the kitchen was too small, and as a result we nearly bumped into each other a few times. If we'd been in some kind of romantic comedy show, there would have been sparks. At one point, we were face to face, not more than an inch or two between our bodies, and our eyes met. If there were a right moment to kiss this woman, it was then. The thought occurred. And my stomach lurched, just a little. I smiled nervously and moved away.

I left without exchanging any touch other than the shaking of hands. Tegan's expression gave me the distinct impression she was disappointed, or sad, or confused, or maybe all three.

Two cabs passed me, but I didn't hail them. I needed to walk. I needed to think. And the most prominent thought, one that got stuck in my head, was that Tegan didn't deserve the kind of man I was. She deserved a man who could give her all of himself. And I was by far less than convinced I could be that man. I resolved to leave her alone, to let her remain open to exploring other relationships.

Monday, Tegan sat beside me in our medieval church history class. I had hoped she would feel discouraged enough to keep her distance, but—no.

"I love this class," she told me by way of greeting. The she leaned close, and in a low, almost conspiratorial voice, she said, "You know, sometimes I wonder if I was a monk in a former life.

Maybe one of those Irish monks who lived in stone huts and survived on bread and water."

That got my attention. "A former life?"

She laughed and then shrugged. "Why not?"

My mind went to the kinds of sexual mischief in which reclusive monks are believed to have indulged. It seemed unlikely Tegan's picture of these cloistered men was the same as mine. Mercifully, the instructor entered the room and called the class to attention.

Later, as the class ended, Tegan said, "I'm thinking we might get together to study medieval churches. What do you think?"

"Um, thanks for the suggestion. I find I study best on my own, though."

She smiled faintly and finished collecting her things. I waited for her to leave, wracking my brain to come up with a way to convince her to look elsewhere for companionship, preferably a way that preserved her dignity and didn't require harshness on my part. Nothing suggested itself.

For several days, I did my best to avoid Tegan. I told myself it was for her sake, and I truly believed it was. I knew it would be beyond unfair for me to continue to lead her on, just so that I could see whether a straight lifestyle with her was possible. At the same time, it seemed as though God had put us in each other's paths. But I couldn't see why.

My prayers during this period were intense. If in fact God had sent Tegan into my life, what was the lesson? Donald's comment about Job getting an answer that mentioned a goat came to me.

I wasn't sure where my prayers were going. I couldn't precisely remember the last time it had felt to me as though I had sent prayers anywhere other than the ether, but I felt sure that

God and I had had no meaningful connection since he'd taken Mother.

One thing that felt clear to me was that God would not want me to go forward with Tegan, or with any woman, into a marriage that would be essentially a sham. It would be cruel to her and a torment for me.

Surely, though, God was not pointing me toward finding a man to be my partner.

Was He?

Something was. Because no matter how hard I tried not to think of Donald, he kept creeping into my thoughts. And into my feelings. His face would startle me at odd moments. I might even feel his lips on mine. The memory of how it had felt when my penis was in his mouth—the warmth, the moisture, the pressure, the way his tongue rubbed against the tip....

All the passion I wanted to feel for Tegan went instead to the image of Donald. Although the reasons were different, I was convinced I couldn't have either of them.

My thoughts danced around and around the third option that was right in front of me, an option I wanted to pretend didn't exist.

Chastity.

Chastity was not required of Episcopal priests, even gay ones, I knew. But I couldn't shake how disgusted I had felt after being with Donald—that what I'd done had separated me from God. I couldn't tell whether that feeling was coming from me or from God, but it didn't matter. Tegan had pointed out to me something about *Equus* I had somehow overlooked: Alan Strang had blinded the horses because he did not want Equus to see what he had attempted with a young woman. But it was Alan's shame, not the condemnation of the god Equus, that drove him to that horrible act.

So whether it was my shame or God's condemnation was not

the point. The point was that acting on my nature made me feel apart from God.

There is an idea in the Christian community that to live life as though one had a pebble in one's shoe is to have a constant reminder to keep God foremost. One person's pebble is not necessarily the same as another person's. What was true for all was that it's not easy, it's not convenient, and often it actually hurts. But my life as a priest should be a life about God, not a life about myself.

So maybe what God wanted me to see was that chastity would be the pebble in my shoe.

One night, sitting in Father's chair, the now-default glass of scotch beside me and, again, the only light coming from a floor lamp, I think I stopped breathing to ponder these questions. Something in me didn't want to breathe again until I had landed on the right answer. And the right answer, the one that a normal man would arrive at, would have been that I would want Tegan.

I clenched my eyes shut, holding the breath in, refusing to release myself back into life until I got the answer I was sure I should want.

Tears squeezed their way from under my tight eyelids, and my lungs forced out a desperate gasp.

The right answer would not come.

The true answer was that I would never want Tegan the way I had wanted Donald. Nothing about her would ever inspire that aching ecstasy Donald had made me feel. Could I live a life of apparent contentment with a woman like Tegan taking my name and my ring and sharing my home? Possibly. But as for sharing my bed....

I both hated Tegan and felt immensely grateful to her—grateful for helping me acknowledge the true version of myself, and hatred for the exact same reason. How ironic; wasn't that what Donald had said I might feel about him?

A verse from the book of Hebrews, 4:12, came to me: "For

the Word of God is living, and active, and sharper than any double-edged sword, and piercing even to the dividing of soul and spirit, of both joints and marrow, and is able to discern the thoughts and intentions of the heart."

Tegan was that double-edged sword, and God had sent her to me.

CHAPTER EIGHT

Classes had felt different in many ways after Mother's death. And after I gave up on the idea of having Tegan in my life, everything felt even more depressing. The worst times were eating breakfast alone at home, coming home after school to an empty house, and going to bed at night. It was difficult to get to sleep, and the nightmares made success unappealing. I took to staying up very late, playing piano; music took me to a place where I didn't feel guilt or responsibility or obligation.

I was sure that at least some of my instructors noticed me dozing in class. My eyes just would not stay open. My grades suffered further. I even skipped some classes, if I felt especially unprepared.

One afternoon, avoiding the medieval history class for two reasons—being unprepared, and knowing Tegan would be there —I felt compelled to escape. I took a cab up to Fifty-Third Street, thinking to walk through the Museum of Modern Art, worlds away from anything ancient or overtly religious. But after half an hour I had to admit I wasn't looking at the art. Or, rather, I was looking but not seeing. My mind would not settle on anything.

I left the museum and walked east to Fifth Avenue, where I turned north for no particular reason, staying on the west side of the street. It wasn't until I was facing the corner of Central Park from across Fifty-Ninth Street that I realized how close I was to where Mother had sacrificed herself.

I stood at the corner, across the street from the park, through maybe three light cycles. People jostled me from behind when a walk signal appeared, and irritated people moved around me as they crossed from the other side. Finally I let myself move forward with the crowd, but I didn't stay on the street sidewalk. Instead I headed into the park.

Central Park is not a bad place to wander vaguely. The farther north you go, the easier it would be to get turned around, to lose sense of where you had come from and where you were going. I didn't go that far; I was already confused enough.

It was one of those days in the interstice between winter and spring, not quite one or the other. A few white clouds wandered lazily around a blue sky. The air was chilly but not cold and seemed almost to embrace me in its stillness. I moved slowly, looking mostly down at my feet, ignoring people around me, even (despite my dream) ignoring the dogs some of them were walking.

At one point, not far from the zoo, as I approached a series of benches, I came to a complete stop. Sitting on one of the benches, apparently studying something that might have been the script from a play, was Donald Rainey.

I was convinced he had not seen me. *Should I turn around? Go another way? Sit down and say hello?*

Choosing a cowardly option, I left the pavement and moved behind Donald. For no reason that I could have justified I wanted to see what he was reading. There was a tree close to him I might duck behind if necessary.

When I was about five feet away, I saw a red-haired boy, maybe five years old or so. He wore a bright green parka, and a vivid yellow scarf streamed behind as he danced along the sidewalk in front of two women. The boy saw Donald and made a dash for the bench, plunked himself down, and stared at Donald.

I held my breath as Donald turned to the boy, then looked in the opposite direction along the sidewalk as if watching for something, then back at the boy. He lowered his head a little, and in hushed tones, said, "Can you see me?"

The child laughed delightedly and nodded his head.

"Rats." Donald sat back against the bench. "Guess I didn't take enough potion."

The two women stopped and smiled at Donald, and one of them held her hand out to the boy, who hopped off the bench and resumed his walk. Donald followed them with his eyes, a gentle smile on his face. As he glanced back down at his reading, something took control of me. I walked around the bench and sat where the boy had been.

Donald looked both surprised and not at all taken aback to see me.

"Hello, Spencer."

Now that I was here, beside him, seeing that expression between sweetness and mischievousness that came so naturally to him, I was at a loss for what to say. I went with, "Studying for a part?"

"An audition. Yes. If I could just make out this griffonage in the margins...."

"The... what?"

He shrugged. "It's my own writing. You'd think I'd be able to read it." He watched my face for a moment. "You're a long way from home. Uptown here, I mean, from Krom Moerasje."

"Pardon?"

"The original Dutch for the area now known as Gramercy. Something about a swamp, I think." I stared at him, having no words to respond to that. "So, Spencer. How's the world treating you these days?"

My mind flitted around, seeking something coherent to say, or even something to land on. It failed.

"Spencer? What's wrong?"

I told him the truth. "I don't know."

He folded his script and put it into a backpack at his feet. "Tell me."

I sat back and gazed sightlessly ahead. "My mother died."

"I'm sorry to hear that."

"She was hit by a bus." Donald said nothing. I added something I hadn't told Tegan. "I was with her. I should have stopped her."

"*Could* you have stopped her?"

I chewed my lower lip. "No."

He was watching the side of my face, waiting for me to say something else. But I had no words. Finally, he said, "What else?"

"What?"

"I think there's also something else bothering you. Of course, you don't have to tell me anything, but—"

"Why are you being nice to me?"

"Is there a reason I shouldn't?"

"I—I wrote you off. Kind of literally."

"You wrote, 'I can't do this.' You weren't mean or rude. You were truthful. At least as far as you knew."

"What does that mean?"

"I'll tell you if you tell me what else is troubling you."

I rubbed my face. My tone somewhat harsh, I said, "I've been seeing a really great girl, and I don't know how to tell her it needs to end. For her sake, as much as mine. I'm having nightmares and not sleeping well, and my grades are falling. I've realized that chastity is my only option in the priesthood. Is that enough?"

Donald gave a kind of snort in an effort to control laughter. It was a fruitless effort, and he gave up and laughed. Then, "Oh,

Spencer. Oh my god." I waited while his chuckles slowed and then stopped. "You, dear boy, are not destined for chastity. Maybe you don't want to fuck *me,* but you need to fuck."

I stared at him, dumbfounded.

He hadn't finished. "If you go into the priesthood with a stick up your proverbial ass, what kind of a prig will you be? Oh, darling, yes, there are men who can do that. Chastity, I mean. But you? No. You're already so uptight it shocked me when you followed me home that day. If you don't get some good sex, and get it soon, and then keep getting it, I'm going to pray—and I don't pray—that you never make it out of seminary. I would pity any congregation that got stuck with you."

My voice dripped sarcasm. "Thanks very much." Had I asked for his take on my personality? I had not. Did I agree with anything he said? I did not. I was beginning to be sorry I'd sat here with him. "Your turn."

"My turn?"

"You said you'd tell me what you meant if I told you what was wrong. That bit about my being truthful as far as I knew."

He nodded. "I think I just told you."

"You told me I'm a prig."

"I said you could turn into one. I said chastity is not for you."

I wanted to push back. I needed to push back. I tried to be angry, but in fact I was terrified he was right. "Who do you think you are to say that to me?"

"Oh, no one in particular. Just someone who was the recipient of a raw passion I don't think you knew you were capable of."

He had to be wrong about me. "You aren't giving God enough credit. If I'm sincere in my prayers and my intentions—"

"Here we go. Deja poo all over again."

I blinked stupidly.

His voice took on an edge. Maybe a few edges. "Spencer, please. I've heard it all. 'If I pray hard enough, I won't be gay anymore.' 'If I pray hard enough, I'll feel attracted to women instead of men.' Or, 'If I pray hard enough, I won't need sex at all.' Yeah, right. Bullshit."

"But—"

"And if I don't do all that, if I remain obstinately who I am and actually, you know, *live* it, I'll go to Hell. Well, like I told my dad, I can't go to Hell. Satan has a restraining order out on me."

He was angry. Maybe even furious. But not with me.

"Is that what your father told you? That you'd go to Hell?"

Donald gave a short, barking laugh. "What did your father tell you?"

I shook my head. "He never knew."

"He's dead, too?"

"Two years ago."

"And your mother."

It was difficult to breathe. I just shook my head.

"And now you're alone." He gazed intently at me. His voice low, even concerned, he said, "Am I the only one who knows?"

I managed a gasping breath. "You are."

"Are you planning to tell anyone at the seminary?"

"I don't know."

He shook his head in apparent disbelief. "So your plan to remain chaste is as much to avoid admitting the truth about yourself as anything else. Have I got that right?"

Was he right?

Quietly he asked, "They haven't guessed?"

I didn't know for sure, but I shook my head.

"Man. And I thought *I* was a good actor."

"Do you—do you think it's obvious?"

"Oh, honey."

"Tegan doesn't think so!"

"Tegan? Is that the woman chasing you around?"

"She's not…. She's…."

"You need to disabuse her."

I raised my voice. "Don't you think I know that?"

Donald stood and slung his backpack over one shoulder. "You have some thinking to do. If you change your mind about being able to—you know, 'do this,' you've got my number."

I wasn't ready for him to leave me here, alone. I was sick of being alone. And as annoying as our conversation had been, it was the only real one I'd had in weeks. "Donald!" I stood and watched him continue to walk away. He didn't turn around.

The next real conversation I had, just over a week later, was not annoying. It was devastating.

Dr. Dunfey called me into his office late in the afternoon. "I have to say, Spencer, this is not something I thought I would ever need to talk to you about."

That was his opening volley. I held my breath.

"You're aware, I know, that your performance this session has been less than satisfactory. I have here," and he touched a pile of papers on his desk, "everything you've written for your classes since you started here. The first few months, your creative thinking made your essays fairly sparkle. But since your mother died, it's as though you're channeling someone else, someone with no spark, no originality, and very little insight. You're missing classes. And when you attend, you sleep."

I started to speak, but he held a hand up briefly.

"I understand that your mother's death, and the manner of it, would be enough to take someone off track. But if things continue like this, your candidacy will be at risk. I know what you're capable of. So I'm going to offer you a possible reprieve. Unless you can convince me that things will change for the better very soon, I'd like you to consider taking some time off. A few months, at least. Maybe take a couple of tutored courses to keep up and start back in earnest in the fall."

He paused and looked at me, no doubt expecting me to respond.

I stammered, "I don't know what to say."

He let out a long breath through his nose. "Is there reason to believe you'll soon get back to where you were in December, in terms of commitment?"

"I—" My eyes focused on a few dust motes where a ray of sunshine from the window highlighted them. I shook my head. "I don't know."

Dr. Dunfey sat back in his chair and tilted his head. "Is there something troubling you besides your mother's death?"

I looked from one of his eyes to the other. I examined the creases on his forehead, imagining him as an old man, perhaps in his nineties. And then, as though it came from somewhere outside of me, my voice said, "I'm gay."

Dr. Dunfey sat forward, his forearms resting on the edge of his desk.

"Spencer, I'm going to ask you a question, and I want the truth. Have you searched your soul? Have you prayed? Have you asked God for guidance in this matter?"

I clamped my hands together so tightly my fingers hurt. I didn't want to admit that I hadn't been able to talk to God since Christmas. "I've known since I was sixteen."

"You're aware that the Episcopal priesthood is still open to you, despite what you've told me, yes?"

"Yes."

"There is a condition, however. That is that this aspect of who you are cannot be troublesome to you in a way that interferes with your ability to fulfill your vocational obligations to parishioners, to God, or to yourself." He paused, but again I didn't speak. "And I'm getting the sense that this is not a condition you are able to meet. At least, not currently."

Still, I was silent.

"Spencer, I need to hear from you. Is your homosexuality troubling you?"

"I was considering a vow of chastity."

Dr. Dunfey sat back again. "That is an extreme choice. Many make it, of course, but also many fail. It should not be made lightly, and it should not be made under a cloud of uncertainty. And because you did not answer my question, I must assume you are troubled and looking to chastity as a way out."

He sighed and shook his head. "Spencer, you need to take some time. And I strongly advise you to see a professional counselor. This is not something I believe you'll be able to work through on your own. I can provide you with a referral."

He fished in a drawer and handed me three cards. "I particularly recommend Kathleen Connolly."

"Why?"

"She's a lesbian who felt forced to leave Catholicism."

I stared at her card.

"Shall I make plans to set up your temporary leave?"

I was near tears. Although being here, going to classes, and feeling disconnected had been difficult, this was the only place I was in touch with other people. What would I do without an imposed schedule? How would I get through the days? And the nights? Oh, the nights!

I stood, nodded, and, in a strangled voice, said, "Thank you." I left as quickly as possible.

There was no place for me to go. I just walked, without a sense of where I would walk or why. I walked until I reached the Hudson River at Pier 63, where I bumped against the railing at the water's edge.

The hiatus of almost-warm weather was gone, and day was

very cold, the kind of winter day when you feel almost desperate for warmth to return. This time of year the sun shines brighter than it has for weeks, and it stays longer in the sky, but it's like a false promise; the cold continues long past when that promise is made.

The water, choppy from a brisk breeze that sent icy fingers through my thick wool coat, seemed almost to call to me. A coughing sound escaped me. Another calling?

How had I ended up right here, nearly dangling over a part of God's world that would kill me and not care? Was this my true calling? To follow my parents into whatever plane of existence was next? And would it be the same plane, or was there really a Hell awaiting those who throw their lives back in God's face?

I hadn't noticed the couple, a young man and woman, looking like college students, who'd taken a position a few feet to my right. I noticed them only when I laughed aloud, and they looked at me in some alarm.

I didn't care. Because what had made me laugh, what had occurred to me as I contemplated suicide and death and Hell, was that I was already there. I was already in Hell. There was no landscape of actual fire. No brimstone had been set alight beneath my feet to send columns of sulfuric pain up to burn my sinuses, my lungs, my heart.

Never before had it been so clear to me that Hell is nothing more and nothing less than separation from God.

An image of Lucifer, the fallen angel and proprietor of Hell, came to mind. According to the story, he was beautiful and intelligent and favored. His very name means light. But he became jealous of Jesus, whom he saw as favored by God above himself. And, like me, Lucifer had followed the crowd when the other angels bowed down to Jesus, though his heart was not pure. He went through the motions until, after a major confrontation in Heaven about his rebellion, he was cast out and into Hell.

Well, I was there. I was Lucifer. But my sin, what caused me to separate from God, was not jealousy. It was another of those seven deadly temptations: lust.

In Timothy, 5:28, it says "Everyone who gazes at a woman to lust after her has committed adultery with her already in his heart." All I had to do was change "woman" and "her" to "man" and "him" and there I was.

Then there's James, 1:15: "Lust, when it has conceived, bears sin; and the sin, when it is full grown, brings forth death."

John's first letter, 2:15, says lust condemns us. "Don't love the world, neither the things that are in the world. If anyone loves the world, the Father's love isn't in him."

Sin, in the most fundamental understanding, is separation from God. Separation from God is Hell. Therefore, in a statement as true for religion as it is for algebra, Sin is Hell.

Yup. I was in Hell. No question. And it felt like a Hell of my own making, and Father's love—I mean, of course, *the* Father's love—was not in me. If I lived past today, I would know myself as Lucifer.

CHAPTER NINE

Returning home after my epiphany, after realizing that I had already descended into the netherworld, I felt an odd sense of release. It was not a good feeling, but it created a physical impetus I'd never experienced.

There was no one—not parents, not school, not Dr. Dunfey, not even God—who cared what I did now. The shackles that had held me in place all my life had burst apart, and they lay where I had tossed them, at the bottom of the Hudson River.

I dropped my backpack where I stood and threw my overcoat across a chair in the foyer; who cared whether I hung it up or not? I placed a call to my favorite Chinese restaurant and ordered everything I wanted on the menu, not caring whether there would be what Mother had called "a complete meal" in the combination, not caring how many hungry children in China would go without dinner while I gorged on several dishes I would not be able to finish.

While waiting for the delivery I went to a package store and picked up a six-pack of Chinese beer. I was about to take it to the register when I realized there was no reason to stop with beer. So I fetched a hand cart and added to it an expensive bottle of scotch whisky, a bottle of costly vodka, and a few bottles of fine wine.

~

By the time I had eaten more than I thought I could hold, and three of the bottles of beer were empty, I felt sated in a way I never had before. I left the kitchen without taking any action about the mess on the table, on the counter, or in the sink.

It was only a little past seven o'clock. I set an album of Ravel to play on the stereo and lay on the drawing room couch, shoes still on my feet, and dozed.

The stereo needle, having completed its journey through the musical spiral of the record, hissed as it bumped into the revolving record label, and that roused me. I opened my eyes to the dim room, lit only by a small light behind me.

I should feel bad, I told myself. *But I don't.* Maybe I was a little ill from too much food, but nothing more important than that felt wrong. It surprised me.

What I would have expected was to feel guilty, sick in body and in spirit, remorseful at having taunted death at the water's edge, sorry that I had mistreated Mother's house, and regret that I had allowed myself to indulge in food and alcohol as I had. But—no.

I sat on the edge of the couch to assess who I was and what I wanted next.

"Piano!" I said to no one.

I went into the music room and turned on all the lights. But at the keyboard, I found that I couldn't play very well. I told myself it was the alcohol, and maybe it was. I left the piano in disgust and went back to where the stereo needle was still patiently repeating its drudging chore, grating eternally against the record's label.

I replaced Ravel with the most bombastic symphony

Tchaikovsky had written, and sat in Father's favorite easy chair. I wanted to read, but schoolwork was out. The Bible was out. I was not in the mood for the classics or for any of the few contemporary novels Mother had bought in the last couple of years. I made a mental note to go to the public library and find some books that qualified for the label "risqué," maybe even something bordering on pornographic. But then I realized that descriptions of heterosexual attraction and activity wouldn't interest me. Maybe there would be something more up my alley? I would ask the librarian. I wouldn't care might know I was gay.

Despite the bombast coming from the speakers, I nodded off again and didn't wake up until the music gave way to the near-silence of the needle, once again hissing against the label. I lay there for a moment, pondering the idea that quiet is what woke me up. I glanced at my watch: Nine-thirty, give or take.

Standing up made me realize I was still a little woozy, but only a little.

What the fuck am I going to do with myself?

Who am I without an imposed schedule of schoolwork and religious study?

Without external expectations, as things had turned out, did I really have only myself to please?

What do I want?

What does the wanting want?

One hand clenching my hair, I turned around in the room, eyes seeking almost frantically for inspiration. Nothing I saw called to me.

I wandered through the entire house, room by room, venturing even into Mother's room and then Father's room, and in my current state the reason for the separation of the two bedrooms hit me hard. Mother had suffered three miscarriages before she had me, and she was told not to try for any more pregnancies or risk serious damage to her own health. I'm fairly sure my parents were intimate after my birth, but no doubt separate bedrooms kept accidents to a minimum.

Then something else struck me. Telling either of my parents that their only child, the only child they would ever have, was gay would have been devastating. So I'd hidden who I was not just for myself, but also for them.

The kitchen was as I had left it: a disgusting mess, from table to sink to counter. I turned my back on it.

Whatever I wanted, it wasn't here. Aloud, I spoke the voice from my dream:

"What you seek is not here."

A barking laugh escaped me. The voice in the dream had not come from someone standing in this house. It had come from someone standing in the grounds at General.

Very quietly, I repeated: "What you seek is not here."

The voice was telling me I didn't belong at General. I didn't belong at a seminary. I didn't belong in the priesthood.

My knees went out from under me, and when I hit the floor I was weeping. Sobbing, I fell forward, elbows on the blue-tiled floor, head hanging. My chest heaved and clenched, gasping for air and screaming it out again.

Everything I was, everything I had ever known about myself, was tied up in the church. But not just in the church. I was swathed in endless lengths of cloth in all the colors of the liturgical year: royal blue and immaculate rose for the virgin, Mary; emerald green for the stunning realization of the perfection of the Christ; deep purple for the mourning of Lent; pure, angelic, gleaming white and iridescent gold, for Christmas and for that most holy and mysterious of liturgical events, the Easter resurrection. It was a veritable religious rainbow.

I couldn't say whether a sudden, mind-blowing hit of something ironic can be equated with an epiphany, but a stunning connection between the rainbow of the religious calendar and the rainbow of the flag that had come to represent who I was underneath all the swaddling made me gasp one final time and sit back on my heels, silent and breathless.

Had I been hiding the rainbow of homosexuality beneath the rainbow of religions trappings?

Coughing, I struggled to my feet.

"You're just drunk," I said aloud to the empty house. "Don't be so melodramatic."

When I awoke, morning sun shone through my bedroom windows. I lay on top of the quilted bedspread, an old and slightly tattered thing my maternal grandmother had completed just before dying, when I was three. I was still clothed. I had no memory of having left the kitchen.

How drunk was I last night? There was no answer, except that when I rolled over and came to my feet I did not feel the effects of an alcoholic hangover: no headache; no nausea; no lack of visual clarity. I felt like myself, physically. My stupor last night must have had some other source.

Reality crept upon me slowly as I reconstructed the events of the previous day. I had been taken to task by Dr. Dunfey. He had put me on temporary leave due to poor performance. When I told him I was gay, he had obliquely tried to dissuade me from the choice of chastity without really offering an alternative.

No alternative. That meant no choice. At least, not in that context. Not in that world. As for choice, my empty life was now all too full of it. I could choose anything. I could sell this old townhouse and move into a SoHo loft, full of light and contemporary furniture. I could leave New York and travel the world. I could study piano seriously; I might have enough talent to make something of myself in the music world. I could enter an advance degree program in almost anything.

But it seemed I could not be a priest. And that overshadowed everything else.

The first thing I did was take a long, hot shower, during which time I had some difficulty remembering that today was Saturday. Then I went out to breakfast, a little place Mother and I had frequented in the last year or so. I sat at the table, a plate now empty of eggs Benedict and hash brown potatoes before me. Beside that was a bowl with just bits of honeydew melon beside it. I liked fruit, but it seems to me there is just no point to honeydew melon, so although once upon a time I wouldn't have left it there, wasted, now—in my current mood—I ate only what I wanted. Staring into the murky, opaque liquid in my third cup of coffee, I contemplated my options.

There was a big difference, I mused, between deciding what to do right now and considering (let alone deciding) what to do for the next month, or the next year, or for my lifetime. With no commitments on my schedule—hell, with no schedule at all— the options for what to do right now seemed far too numerous.

Too many choices. Too many options. So I chose one my mind had skittered away from whenever that option had tried to surface. I was afraid of it, and I was sorely tempted by it. I finally decided it was a personal challenge, one that might help me figure out what direction to go in next.

I went home, and I called Donald.

"You don't sound like yourself." It was not what I had expected him to say, but I knew he was right.

"I'm not surprised. My whole life has—" I stopped myself from saying "turned upside down" and instead finished with, "changed."

"How so?"

I heard my own lengthy exhale. "Can we meet? I don't really want to talk about this over the phone."

After a pause that seemed much longer than it probably was, he asked, "Why me?"

It was a good question. I had other friends. Well, a few, anyway, but they all saw me as a priest-in-training. They all knew I had been destined for the priesthood. They would probably all be horrified—especially those I knew from General—to hear what had happened, what had changed. How *I* had changed. For I truly did feel different.

I told Donald, "You won't make a fuss."

"That sounds umbrageous."

"What?" *Honestly,* I thought; *Donald and his weird vocabulary*.

"Shadowy. Dark."

"Yes. You could call it that."

"Fine. Let's have coffee or something after my show tonight."

"You're in a show?"

"Nothing you want to see. Trust me. Meet me at the stage door. You know the place. Around, say, ten-fifteen." And he hung up.

The table wasn't actually greasy, or so I kept telling myself. Donald had led us to a place close to the theater. I'd had dinner already. Leftover Chinese, of course. But Donald had not.

"I don't eat before a show," he told me just before he ordered a plate of mac-and-cheese with a side salad.

He guzzled one of the two glasses of water he had asked for, set that glass aside, and wrapped his hands around the other. "So. Changed, confused, jargogled. Go."

I ignored "jargogled," tried to ignore the draft I felt on my legs, and contemplated how to begin. I decided to dive in.

"I'm not going into the priesthood after all."

Donald tilted his head, but his face showed no particular expression. "Because…?"

"I got kicked out of school."

"You did not." He didn't sound facetious. It was an actual denial.

"I might as well have."

His food appeared, and he dug into it immediately. Stabbing with a fork at his mac-and-cheese, he made small circles with his left hand to indicate I was to continue.

I felt myself scowl. I was not being taken seriously. "There's not much room in the priesthood for people like me."

Donald, bent over his plate, swallowed a mouthful of food, and raised only his eyes up to mine. "Gay?"

I fought the urge to look around to see if anyone had heard him. There were only two other occupied tables, they weren't close to us, and after all, why would it matter?

"Yes. I can choose to hide as effectively as I can and live in fear that someday someone will see something and report me, or I can choose to remain chaste. I don't need to hear your opinion about that again, by the way."

He sat back as he chewed a mouthful of lettuce, and frowned. Then he said, "Wait. I thought it was mostly okay to be gay and Episcopal."

"Oh, the church wouldn't kick me out for that alone. But, to paraphrase my advisor, I couldn't do anything that compromised my priestly life."

"Or what?"

I blinked. Dr. Dunfey hadn't outlined the consequences. "I'm sure I'd be defrocked. Shamed. Mortified."

"So they didn't actually kick you out. You left."

I shrugged and nodded. "It wasn't official, but I don't see how I could continue with my chosen career."

He wiped his mouth with the paper napkin. "And what now? What's next?"

"I don't know."

He took a few swallows from his second glass of water. "Did you ever finish reading *Equus?*"

"Yes. Why?"

"Sounds to me like you're blinding the horses."

"What on earth are you talking about?" His cavalier attitude toward my existential crisis was making me sorry I'd called him.

"What I'm saying is that leaving the priesthood behind has the effect of blinding the…. what school was it, again?"

"General. Theological. Seminary."

"It blinds the people there to what you did in the loft."

I felt my head shake, just once. "What did I do?"

He leaned forward, his voice low. "We fucked."

My back hit the back of the flimsy chair.

"See?" he said, his voice normal now. "See? You know exactly what's going on."

"Oh, wise one, please enlighten me."

"You think God can't love you. So you doubt your ability to love other people, or to love yourself, and maybe not even God, and if you can't do that, you can't be an effective priest." He closed his eyes, and his voice took on a chanting tone. "If I have all faith, so as to remove mountains, but don't have love, I am nothing." He opened his eyes on me.

I said, "First Corinthians, chapter thirteen."

"If you say so. I lose track of the verses and stuff. But truer words were never spoken. And you don't see any love in your life."

A waiter appeared, removed Donald's empty dishes, and offered me a coffee refill. I shook my head. Donald mumbled, "I shouldn't do this." He looked at the waiter. "Could I have some coffee and a slice of your apple pie?"

The waiter left, and Donald and I stared at each other for a few seconds. Finally, he asked, "Did your parents love you?"

"What's that got to do with anything?"

"Because mine didn't. Or, maybe my mom did, but she was too cowed by my dad to go against him in anything. I waited until I was ready to go to college on my own dime, between saving summer job earnings and working in a campus dining hall and being saddled with a certain amount of debt which I'm still paying off." He waved a hand dismissively. "As I was saying, I waited until I was ready to leave home to come out to my family. I expected Dad would kick me out. I was not disappointed. He was, of course. Disappointed. I'd done everything I could to hide my truth from him up to that point. I'd even followed behind him, the wise, Wenceslas-style sage." Now his tone changed to artificially ponderous to quote the Christmas carol. "'Mark my footsteps, my good page. Tread thou in them boldly.' So I stepped with feigned boldness in his proverbial footprints to get safely through the piles of snow that represented my burden. I wanted him thinking I'd follow him into the ministry."

He shrugged dramatically and added, "No wonder he was disappointed. It must have seemed like a betrayal to him. To me, it was survival."

"So…. Are you in touch with anyone in your family?"

He gave a quick nod. "My sister, Ruth. Good biblical name, that; I was named after some dead family member."

"Where is she?"

"Still living at home. Cedar Rapids. Mom died five years ago, and after Ruth graduated college, she moved back to take care of Dad. His health isn't great. We think he has Alzheimer's, but he won't admit it or get a medical exam."

"Iowa." It seemed like the last place someone like Donald would have sprung from.

"With any luck, he'll die soon, and Ruth will be free."

"How old is he?"

"Ninety. I think. Could happen any day, gods willing."

Donald's pie arrived, and I gave him a minute or two to enjoy it while I contemplated how very similar our early years had been: a lovable mother, cowed by a dominant, religion-oriented husband; a reasonable fear of owning up to our true natures to our fathers; both mothers now deceased, and his father possibly near death. The only difference seemed to be that he'd aimed at a career in the theater, while I had aimed at a career in the priesthood. But for me, the priesthood would also have involved a good deal of acting. I'd have to act straight. I'd have to act like someone I wasn't.

Well, well. Maybe we had even that in common.

We stood on the sidewalk in front of the restaurant, hands in our coat pockets against the cold, as someone on the inside of the glass door turned a hanging sign so that instead of OPEN it now showed CLOSED.

"Are you sorry you called me?" Donald's usual impish look was gone. He looked like he wanted a genuine answer.

Was I sorry? No, though it was true that seeing him again, here, like this, hadn't helped me decide on a direction.

I shook my head. "No. It was good to see you. Good to talk with someone who, you know, understands."

We stared at each other, and I was about to say good night when he asked, "And is that all you want? To talk?"

"What do you mean?"

He sighed. "Never mind. It's fine. Give me a call if you want another chat." He turned and walked quickly in the opposite direction from the one I'd been about to take. Not for the first time, I watched his slender frame diminish as the distance between us increased. This time, there was no crowd for him to disappear into, no softly-falling flakes of snow. Just hard, cold pavement, closed, dark buildings, and a damp cold that made me hunch my shoulders.

〜

At home, I hung up my coat and was about to tackle the piled-up detritus of plates and flatware in the kitchen when I noticed the answering machine blinking. I pressed the Play button and leaned against the wall to listen.

"Spencer? Um, hi. It's Tegan. I, uh, I heard something today, and I wanted to check with you. Are you—um, are you on some kind of sabbatical?" I heard a nervous laugh. "I mean, will you not be in school—at General, that is—for a while?" She paused, almost as though waiting for me to speak. "It just seemed so unlikely. So, are you okay? Is everything all right? Can you call me? Please?"

The call ended without the typical *Okay, then, bye, see you,* or any other traditional closing phrases.

I didn't move right away. I leaned there, holding up the wall (as Father used to say), as a swirl of emotions fought for primacy.

At first, hearing her voice, I had cringed. That was guilt. I really had just disappeared without a word to anyone, and if anyone at General deserved an explanation, it was Tegan. When had we last spoken? Over a month ago. Mid-February, if you didn't count the occasional superficial exchange in class. That's when we'd had dinner at her place. That's when I'd left without any acknowledgement on my part that there might be something between us. And, roughly, that's when I'd decided there could be nothing.

Next came irritation. Who did she think she was, demanding explanations from me? For all she knew, the reasons were personal enough that no one should pry. No one should ask anything.

After that, I felt some odd mixture of regret and melancholy. Tegan cared enough to call, but she sounded tentative, as though afraid she might be intruding. Then, as she ended the call, her voice was wistful, pleading.

And then irritation resurfaced. It was after midnight now, obviously too late to return the call. That meant the burden, the obligation of calling her back would hang over me until it was fulfilled.

Did I really need to call her back?

"Of course you do." The voice came from the silent house. Whether it was Mother's voice or Father's, I couldn't be sure.

CHAPTER TEN

As bad as Friday had been, Sunday was worse. I lay in bed as sluggish time ticked by. Since starting at General, I'd been attending church there instead of my family's church. Right now I couldn't imagine going to either of them.

Life had been so simple when I'd been on the cusp of realizing the dreams everyone had had for me, dreams I'd had for myself. What the fuck had happened?

Eyes closed, I pictured myself on some expanse of ground. To my right, several feet away, was a set of ecclesiastical robes —mine, if I would but go and put them on. On my left was something I couldn't quite identify: an amorphous shape, almost a human form, swaying and humming in a way that was almost sultry.

The robes pulled at me, and I felt myself move toward them. Even as I did, though, a force from the humming figure pulled harder, and I moved in that direction. But this made the pull toward the robes stronger. Back and forth I went, wanting the robes goal to win, but drawn to the mystery and the sensual, suggestive quality in the other direction. Faster and faster they pulled me, my figurative head snapping one way and then another.

"Ahhh!" I screamed as I sat upright in bed.

Upright. The only way out of this yanking competition was up, away from the compelling power of both sources. And where did "up" go?

I threw the bedcovers aside and padded around the house until I found those cards Dr. Dunfey had given me. Kathleen Connolly was the one he had especially recommended. I knew, or at least expected, that even though it was now close to ten o'clock, she wouldn't be in her office on a Sunday, so I thought it would be a safe time to place the call and hear her recorded voice. Maybe that would tell me something about whether I'd move forward in therapy with her. So I called.

"Kathleen Connolly."

Fuck. She answered. Now what?

"Um, hello. I, uh…. Dr. Dunfey at General Seminary suggested I call you."

"And you are…?"

"Spencer Hill. I'm sorry; I didn't expect you'd be at the office today. I'm not exactly prepared—"

"Ah, yes. Did Dr. Dunfey say something in particular that caused you to call me?"

"He—that is, um…." *He said you're a lesbian. Nope; can't say that.* "I'm having doubts about my vocation." That wasn't really an answer.

"And he thought I'd be able to help you work through that?"

"Yes. Something about you leaving Catholicism."

"I see. Have you been in therapy before?"

The conversation went on for at least ten minutes. She asked what my goals were for therapy, my expectations for the process, lots of questions I didn't know how to answer. I began to get the sense that she didn't need answers as much as she needed to assess whatever it was I did say.

At one point, unable to come up with specific issues I wanted to work on, I blurted out, "I'm gay."

She didn't miss a beat. "Did Dr. Dunfey mention that I'm a lesbian?"

"He did, yes."

This time she paused, but only briefly. "Do the doubts you're having about your vocation relate to your sexual orientation?"

"Yes."

"I suggest we meet to talk further so each of us can see if we might work well together. What is your schedule like?"

My turn to pause. Did I want to go through with this? "I, um, it's pretty open right now, as I'm taking a break from classes. But as I started to say, I don't know that I'm prepared to make a decision."

"And you shouldn't make a decision until we assess how well we'd work together." She waited, but I said nothing. "Let me ask you this, Spencer. How will you decide whether to work with a therapist? What is it you're waiting for?"

She had me. Was that a good thing or not? "I guess I don't know."

Silence.

"I've never done this before," I said, hearing in my own ears how lame that sounded.

"I understand. Keep in mind, this meeting would be an assessment, not a decision in and of itself. It commits you to nothing." When I didn't speak, she asked, "Would you be able to meet Tuesday at four o'clock?"

I felt my pulse and my breath quicken, and not in a good way. The truth was that I had nothing but time. And I was scared as hell. I inhaled and held my breath long enough for my brain to tell me, *This is just an introductory meeting.*

"Fine. Yes." It wasn't exactly a heartfelt affirmation, but it was enough.

~

I showered, dressed, ate a little breakfast, and then wandered vaguely around the house. I told myself I was thinking through my conversation with Dr. Connolly, but in reality I knew I was avoiding calling Tegan.

I picked up the phone and gazed at the keypad. I replaced the phone. I thought about whether I wanted any lunch, whether there was any food in the kitchen, or whether I'd prefer to go out in any case. I wandered around some more. When I felt myself wonder how much scotch I had left, I knew what I had to do. I picked up the phone and dialed Tegan's number before I had time to stop myself.

"Oh, Spencer, I'm so glad you called back. Please tell me I heard wrong, and you haven't left General."

I took a sliver of time to consider why Tegan thought she had any right to quiz me, and another to wonder why she cared.

"A little time off. That's all."

"But—why? You aren't giving up on the priesthood, are you?"

Suddenly I was back to why she thought I had to account for myself to her. "I'm not prepared to go that far. In fact, I'm not prepared to go into details right now. So...."

There was a pause, and then, "It's just that I'm worried about you."

She might have heard my irritated exhale. "Tegan, I think you'd be better off if you just forgot about me. Don't waste your time—"

"Look, Spencer, I'm not dense. I've figured out that you don't want a romantic relationship with me, though I must say I wish you could have talked with me about it. But that aside, I always liked you very much."

"Tegan."

"Yes?"

What have you got to lose, Spencer? "I'm gay."

"Oh."

"Yeah. 'Oh.'"

"Well, I guess that makes a certain amount of sense."

"What?"

"Can we meet someplace? Why don't you come to evensong here tonight, and afterward we could grab a quick bite."

A short, humorless laugh escaped me. "Evensong? Yeah, I don't think so."

Another pause. "You seem different."

"I am different. Of course I'm different."

"Okay, well, can we just get coffee or something? I don't have to go to evensong."

Exasperation was obvious in my voice. "Why?"

Her tone was less friendly now. "You owe me that much."

She was right. And, thinking quickly, it occurred to me that if I repaid this emotional debt, I might feel less guilty about having led her on.

We decided on a café halfway between her place and mine.

I walked very quickly to be sure I arrived first. There was only one table open, and I practically dived for it. By the time Tegan arrived, I had a café au lait and a plate of almond biscotti on the small table in front of me.

She pulled off her mittens—knitted in the style of Scottish Fair Isle, evoking an almost child-like innocence—and draped her coat onto an empty chair beside me. As she sat across from me, I caught the eye of the waiter. Tegan asked for the same coffee and biscotti I had and settled herself in her chair.

"So." She opened.

"So."

"Spencer, why all the Sturm und Drang?

"Pardon?"

"Why all the fuss, the drama, the—whatever you want to call it?"

I shook my head. "Not what I was going for."

"Why did you ask me out?"

"I… well, I guess I was hoping someone like you could, you know…."

"Someone like me?"

"Attractive. Intelligent. Keen sense of humor. Interesting. Playful. Articulate. Well-read. Shall I go on?"

"You left out God-centered."

I nodded. "At the time, that would have gone without saying, given where we met."

"And now? How much does that matter now?"

"Well, I mean, a relationship is out of the question."

"Am I still all those things you listed?"

"Of course."

"And God-centered. Are *you* still God-centered, Spencer?"

I looked at her face, a face that would age well, I decided. She would go from being attractive to being a handsome woman as the years went by. She would probably be a very good priest; she'd certainly landed easily on one of my soft spots.

"I don't know."

Her order arrived, the waiter left, and we were silent for maybe twenty or thirty seconds while Tegan toyed with a biscotti, the crisp confection making clinking sounds on the plate. Then, "Are you leaving because you've lost your connection to God, or because you're gay?"

I'd never said I was leaving. She'd made a logical leap, and it annoyed me that she was right. "I don't see much of a difference."

Tegan dunked one end of a biscotti into her coffee and munched on it. As she drowned the other end, she said, "Maybe you don't have a choice about being gay. But you have a choice about connecting with God."

"Do I? Do I, really?"

"Of course you do."

"Not according to scripture."

She waved a hand. "Don't go all fundamentalist on me. We're Episcopalians, for heaven's sake."

"Oh, right." Sarcasm lent an edge to my voice. "I can be a gay Episcopal priest, just as long as I deny part of my humanity. I can be a gay priest, as long as anyone who knows that, also sees me as chaste. I can be a gay priest, but I can't have a help-mate, a partner to support my work. Oh, yes, the church tolerates homosexual priests."

Without meaning to, I brought my hand down rather hard on the table. "Well, I don't want to be *tolerated*."

I leaned my elbows on the table and rubbed my forehead. Then I sat back, limp. "Tegan, I'm sorry. I'm sorry I misled you. I'm sorry I disappointed you. I'm sorry I wasted your time."

"Why do you think I agreed to that first dinner with you?"

I shrugged and shook my head.

"I like you, Spencer. I like your intensity. I like your dedication. I like your intelligence." She half-grinned. "And you're kind of easy on the eyes, too."

She leaned forward. "Look, we enjoy each other's company. Okay, so it didn't go anywhere in the romance department. I'm glad you've told me why. But I still like you."

"You said I was different. From before."

"Mmmm. And I think I'm going to like the new Spencer even better."

I shook my head again, in puzzlement this time. "How can you? I can't even talk to God anymore."

"That wouldn't stop Him talking to you. And it doesn't have to stop me talking to you, either."

Dr. Connolly's office-slash-home was on the western end of West Seventy-Fifth Street in an apartment building. The only things between the building and the Hudson River were Riverside Drive, a narrow strip of grass and trees, the Henry Hudson Parkway, and another strip of what would be greenery except in winter.

I entered the building, waited for the man at the front desk to verify that I was expected, and rode a walnut-paneled elevator to the sixth floor. The pale blue hallway carpet was thick and made my footsteps silent. Beside the door to apartment 5D was a chair, and on the wall was a buzzer under a sign that read, "Please ring and be seated."

I allowed myself several deep breaths before pressing the button.

The woman who opened the door was just over five feet, by my estimation. I guessed her age at around forty. Her long, light brown hair was pulled back and secured into a smooth knot. She wore brown slacks, a cream blouse, and a flowing, silken, kimono-like wrap of gold, brown, and olive green swirls.

"Spencer. Please. Come in."

She ushered me past the living room, which had views of the river, into what might reasonably have been called a study or a spare bedroom. Everything I saw looked neat but still lived-in, and the decor was eclectic while still being tasteful. The study, like the living room, was pleasing to the eye and seemed balanced in some way I couldn't have articulated.

Dr. Connolly had me sit in an upholstered chair, at a slight angle to the one she took.

"Please tell me a little more about the doubt you're having regarding your vocation."

Of course this is what she would ask. It's what I had tried to answer in the cab ride from my house. I had at least a semblance of an answer ready.

"I'm on temporary leave from General. It's unclear to me whether I should return in the fall or choose a different path in life."

"And how much does your sexual orientation enter into the question?"

Okay. Pulling no punches. "I'm not sure I want to live a life in which I'll be constantly on guard against offending the authorities or the parishioners. I'm also not sure a life of chastity is viable for me."

"How does the idea of leaving your calling behind make you feel?"

I exhaled audibly, a stalling tactic. "Empty."

"Can you say why?"

I told her about Father, and how he left the Catholic priesthood to marry Mother, who left her calling as a nun behind as well. I told her about growing up in the Episcopal church as a result of my parent's decisions. I told her how long ago I'd felt called to the priesthood. I told her how long ago I'd realized I was gay. At some point, I stopped talking.

"You've said almost nothing about your sexual orientation. How active have you been?"

I blushed. I'm sure of it. I felt the heat rise even as I adjusted my posture in an attempt to appear casual. "Not at all, really."

"No encounters?"

I shrugged, my muscles tense. "One. That's all."

She nodded. "How strongly did your parents support your vocational intentions?"

"Completely. But they never pressured me."

"How do they feel about this temporary leave?"

"My father died two years ago."

"And your mother?"

I'd known mentioning only Father was not going to allow me to escape this question. I had tried it anyway.

"She… um… she died in December."

There was a brief pause, and I wondered if she'd offer the usual *I'm sorry*. She didn't. "Did either of your parents know you're gay?"

"No."

"But you confided in Dr. Dunfey?"

"Yes."

Dr. Connolly gazed for almost a minute at her clasped hands before speaking again. I would have expected her voice to take on a soft, soothing tone, but it didn't.

"Here's what I'm thinking at this point, Spencer. You've known you were gay almost as long as you've felt a calling to the priesthood. You told your parents about only one of those things. I'm sensing some shame around your homosexuality. I think that in order to help you determine your best path forward, we'll need to explore the triangle formed by your calling, your parents, and your orientation. These three areas are swirling with things like love, sex, expectations, approval, escape, shame, hope, and confusion."

She paused to see if I had a comment. I did not.

"If we go forward, I will ask you to dig deep into emotional areas you've probably barely examined. I will not mince words, and I'll expect you to be as honest as you can be—with me and with yourself. If I sense you're covering something, whatever the reason, I'll be as gentle as possible, but I will go after it. The more honest we are with each other, the more progress we'll see. This is a team effort. You are not alone, and I am not always right."

I liked her. Even so, I wasn't at all sure I wanted to go through what she described. At the same time, the only other path I saw was a choice between a life of deception and a lifestyle that would be best described as self-destructive. And, I reasoned, I could always end this.

I expected her to ask if I was willing to commit to this journey she had described. She didn't. She waited.

Finally, I said, "When would our appointments be?"

She nodded once and got up to fetch a small, black-covered notebook. "Do you have your calendar with you?"

I shook my head. "I have no regular commitments at the moment."

Consulting her notebook, she asked, "I would suggest Tuesdays at four o'clock as a regular time. For the first month or so, perhaps longer, I suggest an additional meeting on Fridays at one. What do you think?"

"Twice a week?"

"We can discuss a different arrangement at any time, but twice a week at first would give us a bit of a jump start on things."

She gave me a card with appointment information on it, told me her fee, and said there was no charge for today. She stood. So did I.

"I'll see you Friday at one, Spencer." She walked me to the door of the hallway. "And Spencer?" She waited until I looked at her. "I'm very much looking forward to working with you." She closed the door without waiting for a response.

CHAPTER ELEVEN

When I got home, my answering machine was blinking with a message from Donald.

"Hey, Spencer, um, odd question here." His voice didn't have his usual note of veiled glee. "I'm hoping you wouldn't mind coming to see the play I'm in, this Friday or Saturday. You'd be doing me a big favor, because my sister Ruth is visiting. She wants to see me perform, but she's anxious about being alone in the theater. So you'd be a sort of paper date. You know, like a paper tiger. I mean—shit, I'm not saying this right."

I laughed and shook my head as though he could see me. The message went on.

"You can't tell I'm nervous or anything, can you? Listen, forget it. This is embarrassing. I'll think of something else. Sorry to bother you."

He hadn't said anything about the play itself, so I was curious about that. But I was even more curious about Ruth. What had he said about her? That she was taking care of their aging father, I think. She'd graduated college, but beyond that I didn't know how old she was.

I called Donald back. "Hey. What's this play you want me to squire your sister to?"

"Are you—are you saying you'll do it?" He sounded tentative, almost pleading.

"Depends. What's the play?"

"Oh. Well. Something contemporary about two friends who get lost in the woods. It's okay, I guess. Probably not something you would want to see unless you were doing a huge favor for someone."

Someone. That made me wonder, for the eleventy-eleventh time, just what he and I were to each other. Friends seemed like it missed the mark. Lovers was way too much.

I hoped he could hear the tease in my voice. "Well, I guess I could do it. But just this once. Um… does she know anything about me?"

"She knows enough not to imagine a romantic entanglement between the two of you."

"I see. Well, would Friday or Saturday be better? My calendar is almost completely open at this point."

"Right. Okay, then, Saturday. Would you be willing to pick her up?"

"Where is she staying?" I pictured Donald's cramped studio apartment.

"Here. I'm on the floor. Air mattress."

"I, uh, I didn't notice the actual address."

He laughed. "I'm not surprised."

He gave me the address, and we agreed on a pick-up time.

I was glad Donald had suggested Saturday; I wasn't sure what shape I'd be in after my first real session with Dr. Connolly. Turned out to be a good thing, too; I was in rough shape Friday night.

~

"What would you say is most important to you in your life right now?"

At the start of the Friday session, Dr. Connolly had asked me to take her on a whirlwind tour of my childhood, assuring me that we would come back to various aspects of it in future sessions. I'd been fairly straightforward with my narrative, though I'd had a bit of a struggle when describing how Mother had died. Dr. Connolly had interrupted me only once, to ask whether I had referred to my parents as Mother and Father in their presence. She didn't seem to react when I said I had, just asked me to continue.

But when I had finished, she asked a question with no easy answer. What *was* most important to me in my life right now? Did I have a clue? Not really. So I gave her what was *missing* that was most important.

"I wanted to be a priest. Now I can't. Not without, you know, hiding my proverbial light under a bushel."

Surely, she got the scriptural reference, but I saw no reaction.

"Why did you want to be a priest?"

Once, my answer to that question would have been the pat, packaged bullshit I'd said during the Discernment process. Then, recently, I'd had that epiphany inspired by *Equus*. I said, "I see Hell as a state of separation from God. Heaven, therefore, is a state of unity with God. I wanted to help others find that unity."

"Others?"

"Parishioners. Anyone, really."

"And you? Are you united with God?"

"I—well, that's the problem. Lately I don't feel any connection with God."

"But you did." Not a question. "What happened? What changed?"

It was a topic I'd gone over in my head, round and round, until I was dizzy, confused, and disheartened. I repeated the only conclusion I had come to. "I don't believe I have a choice about being gay. This tells me God made me this way. But His words tell me that what I am is abomination."

I waited. Dr. Connolly waited, as well. So I went on.

"Why would a God worth worshipping create abomination? How could He create me in His image unless He's gay? How would that God expect me to give my whole self to His people when I can't let them *see* my whole self? Why would He make me gay and then tell me I'm something He can't love?"

My voice had been growing louder. I nearly shouted, "How can I love that God? How can I believe that God loves me? And how the hell can I go around telling other people how to get close to a God like that?"

Dr. Connolly waited for me to calm myself a little. Then, "Anything else?"

"Yes, actually. What kind of God would make me gay, and then thumb His nose at me and tell me to fix it?"

She nodded once and repositioned herself in her chair. "What do you think your earthly father would have said if you had told him you were gay?"

That one stopped me cold. Time ceased. The earth halted in its spinning. There was only silence in all the world for about five seconds. When time began again, I think I opened my mouth to speak, but nothing came out.

What *would* he have said?

I closed my eyes and pictured Father. "He would have quoted Bible verses. He would have told me I need to pick myself up by my bootstraps and come to my senses."

"Did you love your father?"

Another full stop. Even my breathing stopped until I managed to say, "I wanted to."

Dr. Connolly let a few beats go by and asked, "Do you believe he loved you?"

I'd thought I'd been prepared for this. She had warned me, during our introductory meeting, that she would "dig deep." I thought I knew what that would mean. I thought I knew how it would feel. I thought I knew how I would handle it. I was wrong.

She hadn't asked if Father loved me. I would have answered, "Of course." No; she asked if I *believed* he did.

I was determined not to cry. Not in the very first session. Not in front of this person I barely knew. But the truth—which, she was right again, was not something I'd considered before—was that I did not believe he'd loved me. I did not believe it because I'd never felt it. Not really. Not in any way that survived an off-hand compliment, or his chuckle at a witticism, or his approval of my vocational choice.

I closed my eyes and tears leaked out from beneath my eyelids. I knew I couldn't speak, so I shook my head, No. I pictured in my mind the box of facial tissues I'd seen on a small table to my right. I'd told myself I wouldn't be needing them. Again, I was wrong.

Dr. Connolly was silent as I grabbed a tissue, dabbed at my eyes, and blew my nose. After I recovered myself, in a voice that was gentle but not sympathetic she prompted me with questions about what my relationship with Father had been like. By the time I left her building, I wasn't entirely sure where I was.

Half-way home, in the cab, it occurred to me that Dr. Connolly hadn't asked the same questions about Mother. She hadn't asked anything about Mother, really. I would have to gird my prover-bial loins for Tuesday's appointment in anticipation of questions about her.

I went to a neighborhood bistro for dinner, not wanting to sit alone in the kitchen or the dining room. Somehow, though, I felt at least as alone, at least as lonely as if I had.

At home again, I sat with a glass of scotch and listened to a record of Chopin nocturnes. Or, I played the record; I didn't so much listen as let the music wash over me as I reflected on my therapy session.

It felt odd that I'd been so sure, so immediately sure that I didn't believe Father had loved me. When Dr. Connolly had asked, the answer had been right there on the surface. Now, sitting alone, trying to focus on that question and its answer, my brain slipped around inside my head.

We don't see a lot of stars in the sky here in the city, but Father had taken us on a few vacations—a Long Island beach town, a country inn in Vermont—where I'd learned that if you want to see where a star is, you must look to the side of it. Looking directly at it made it disappear. That's the approach I had to take, feeling like my own father hadn't loved me.

I wanted to face it head-on. I was sure there was a world of information buried inside the realization, if I could just accept it.

But I wasn't there yet. It was too much to feel.

Saturday evening, I had the cab wait at Donald's address on St. Mark's Place, and I rang the buzzer beside the name "Rainey." A distorted voice came through the intercom.

"I'll be right down."

And she was. Ruth Rainey looked remarkably like her brother, which was disconcerting for me.

We said little on the cab ride to the tiny theater. I asked her inane things like whether she was enjoying New York, if she'd been here before, how long she was staying. She seemed shy and answered politely but briefly.

Donald had left comp tickets for us. The theater wasn't crowded, and no one sat on either side of us, but Ruth was reluctant to set her coat on an empty seat, so I helped arrange it behind her as she wrapped it around her shoulders.

Before I could come up with another superficial question, she said, "It's very kind of you to sit with me."

"Not at all. I'm looking forward to the play. I've seen Donald in only one before."

"Puck."

"Yes."

"Type casting."

This nearly facetious response took me by surprise, and I laughed. "I know what you mean."

"Do you see a lot of my brother?"

"Well, no, I wouldn't say a lot."

"He'd probably kill me for saying this, but he talks about you all the time."

That information gave me an odd jolt. I needed to get the focus off of me. "Do the two of you speak frequently?"

"We've always been close. Did he tell you we're twins?"

"Twins?" Fraternal, of course. Still, it was surprising. "He didn't mention that, no. He did say your father was not well. Is someone with him while you're traveling?"

She shook her head. "I had to move him into a home."

I nodded. "Donald mentioned he might have Alzheimer's."

"He was too much for me to handle."

The lights flashed, and just as someone came on stage to introduce the play, Ruth whispered, "He likes you very much."

The play itself was at least creative if a trifle predictable. There were just two characters and only one act, though the stage lights would dim and brighten as the plot moved between night and day. Donald's co-star was a dark, attractive man, and as the two grew more dependent on each other through the trials of being lost in the woods for a few days, I felt an odd sense of jealousy. Ridiculous, of course, but there it was. And it didn't help that I wasn't entirely sure whether the play intended to point toward an attraction that went beyond friendship. The feeling was slightly assuaged by what Ruth had told me.

So Donald talks about me "all the time." So Donald likes me "very much." These thoughts made me feel like a schoolboy— every bit as ridiculous, I told myself, as the feeling of jealousy.

We went backstage after the final curtain. Donald was in a small dressing room, removing makeup with something that looked like facial cold cream. He wiped his face hurriedly with a small towel when he saw us.

Ruth went to him and as they hugged, he said, "You frothy, elf-skinned dewberry."

"You reeky, knotty-pated pignut! You were wonderful, Donnie. So much better than the other guy."

"Shhh! He's just on the other side of these thin walls." He looked at me. "I hope you weren't too bored."

"Not at all. I had a delightful companion." Ruth looked at me and blushed. "Interesting names you have for each other, I must say."

Donald grinned at me. "Yeah. Shakespearian insults. Great fun. So, I'll finish up here and we'll go grab dessert or something. Sound good?"

I watched as "Donnie" removed the last of his makeup and changed into his own clothes, evidently unfazed to have Ruth see him in his underwear. They chatted comfortably with each other about the play as I listened, feeling a different kind of jealousy. Or maybe it was more a kind of longing. If I'd had a sister, I would love to have been as close to her as Donnie was to Ruth.

We walked about five blocks, Donald and Ruth ahead of me on the sidewalk, to a different place from the one where I'd met Donald recently. Over pastries and coffee for Ruth and me, and a sandwich and pastry for Donald, they engaged in lightning-fast conversation I could barely follow. I learned a few new words: quanked, which I took to mean overcome by fatigue; zowerswopped, or bad-tempered; pisstified: being pissed off and mystified at the same time; mumpsimus, an incorrect view on something that a person refuses to let go of; and that's all I can remember.

Listening to their banter was like watching a ping-pong game in which no one slams the ball; the goal seemed to be to keep it in play as long as possible.

"Oh, before I forget," Ruth said, "I must visit an apothecary tomorrow to buy potions."

I couldn't help myself. "You what?"

Donald laughed. "Don't mind us. We get a kick out of expressing things oddly. She needs to find a drug store." He took a forkful of his pastry, an eclair, into his mouth. "My, how very butyraceous this custard is."

"Really?" Ruth asked. "Mine seems a little thin."

I grinned and shook my head; they were like bookends. We moved on to talk about what Ruth wanted to do tomorrow.

To Donald, she said, "I don't suppose I can talk you into coming to church with me."

"Ha! No, but maybe Spencer would take you to an Episcopal high mass someplace."

I felt myself cringe involuntarily. I hadn't attended mass last week, and I hadn't intended to this week either, not at General, and not at St. Ignatius. The surreptitious glances, the questioning looks, and the spoken questions from some would be more than I felt able to face. I didn't know how to explain my feelings to myself; how could I answer anyone else's questions?

Ruth turned to me. "I've never done that. Lutheran services are probably drab in comparison. Would you?"

Before my silence grew conspicuous, Donald spoke up again. "Say, if you go to St. John the Divine, I'd go with you. It'd be worth it for the drama. Then, we wouldn't be too far from The Cloisters." He looked at Ruth. "That would take up pretty much the whole afternoon, but I think we'd really enjoy it. I've never been there. There are stone cloisters brought from overseas, and lots of medieval art. Right, Spencer?"

"Wonderful!" Ruth looked at me, clearly assuming I would have no objection. "What time is mass?"

I could do that, I decided. No one there would know me, and the cathedral is quite large anyway. And I hadn't been to The Cloisters in too long. "I'm pretty sure holy eucharist starts at ten-thirty. Dress warmly. The Cloisters is in the middle of Fort Tryon Park, and there are some great river views you'll need to walk around outside to see."

I told them to be ready by nine forty-five, and I'd pick them up.

Donald eyed me sideways. "That's going just a wee bit out of your way, isn't it? Down to the lower east side, and then w-a-a-a-y up to the cathedral?"

"Let me worry about that."

I didn't worry about that, of course. I had a plan for transportation. What I didn't have a plan for was the way I still felt, based on what Ruth had told me. I wondered if Donald thought about me as often as I thought about him.

CHAPTER TWELVE

Sunday morning I had the car I'd hired through Mother's service wait outside Donald's building while I got out to ring the bell to his apartment. But he and Ruth were waiting inside the foyer, all ready to go.

"Oh, Spencer!" Ruth's eyes were wide with excitement. "A car, all for us! I'm positively whelmed."

I decided to accept "whelmed" as a less extreme version of "overwhelmed."

Manhattan's streets are significantly less crowded on Sunday mornings than at any other time during the week, and our ride north was smooth and uneventful. The spring equinox meant that the morning sun was brilliant, showing off the city at its best.

I told the driver what time to return as gentleman Donald helped Ruth out of the car. She had clearly decided to get into the spirit of luxury, walking in a stately manner, head high, as we entered the cathedral.

We were fairly early. Making our way across the large entry, the narthex, I saw we would have our choice of seating, and I ushered our group to about mid-way into the nave. We left our coats on chairs, on the aisle so we could leave as easily as possible when we were ready.

Ruth lifted her head and sniffed. "What's that smell?"

"Incense. You'll see how they use it during the service."

Although I'd been here before, I wasn't especially familiar with this cathedral. The basic characteristics don't vary very much, although the larger the cathedral, the more specific features any of them might have. Here, I pointed out the fourteen small bays on either side of the nave, dedicated to the contributions of different groups and lay individuals—categories such as education, sports, the military, art, and so on.

Ruth said, "We call it the nave in our church, too. Where everyone sits."

"Everyone in the congregation, yes. Cathedrals are cruciform in design."

"Shaped like a cross," she said.

"Right. This section we're in now, the crossing, is where the long arm of the nave intersects with the short arms of the transepts. The altar here is the low altar, used for smaller services and the like."

I felt comfortable in my role as tour guide; maybe my knowledge was limited, but it exceeded Ruth's and Donald's. I pointed overhead. "This tiled dome is said to be the largest free-standing dome in the world."

When we had finished craning our necks, I pointed ahead. "We can't go very far today. They give tours if you're interested in seeing all the separate chapels around and behind the high altar."

Donald took Ruth's arm and stepped slightly ahead of me to see the chapels better, directing her gaze by pointing. He turned to me. "Those chapels look like small churches."

"They kind of are. Specific small services can take place in any of them."

Ruth turned slowly as she gazed around. "I just can't get over the windows! I've seen stained glass windows before, of course. But that...." Looking up high, she nodded toward the entrance, over my shoulder.

I turned around. My breath caught in my throat as the brilliant sunlight filtered through the vivid colors and intricate patterns of the massive rose window, soaring high over the entrance. It wasn't a surprise. Rose windows are common in a lot of churches, particularly Roman Catholic and Anglican, or Episcopalian. But seeing it suddenly, the glory of it sent a shaft of pain through my heart.

This should be mine! Not mine, personally. But mine, by dint of my commitment to God through the Episcopal priesthood. Mine, through the community I so wanted to belong to. Mine, but for what God Himself had caused me to be. The profound injustice of it brought tears to my eyes.

I should not have come. I nearly said it aloud. The words screamed inside my head. I muttered, "Why don't you take your seats. I'll be right back."

Without waiting for a reply I nearly stumbled back outside into the bright daylight, away from the sights and sounds and scents of the inside of that house of God. Weaving among the incoming worshippers, I moved unsteadily over to the side and sat down on one of the steps that led up from the sidewalk. I lifted my head toward the sky, to where—as I was taught in Sunday school—God lives.

Stained glass windows, which came into their own in the Gothic European cathedrals, were made possible when architecture had advanced enough to allow for the soaring arches we take for granted now. The brilliant colors and elaborate tracery were meant to bring heavenly light into what once had been smaller, low-ceilinged chapels. God's people were to be awed by their immensity and beauty, and the images depicted sacred scenes. They were meant to be both uplifting and remonstrating, to make people understand their own lowly starting point and still remain aware of the heights to which they could ascend if their devotion was sincere.

There had been nothing wrong with my devotion. It was sincere. It was deep. It was real. Or, at least it had been, before I'd been cast out of heaven, Lucifer once more.

I rubbed my face, and Father's voice spoke to me. "So melodramatic, Spencer. Must you?"

Angry for a new reason now, I stood suddenly. I strode purposefully to where Donald and Ruth waited. Damn it, if I wanted to attend mass, I would fucking well attend it.

Before taking my seat, which was directly on the aisle, I stopped to genuflect; I dropped to one knee, made the sign of the cross, and sat down. It was routine, automatic. And it wasn't until after I'd done it that I chided myself for treating a sacred ritual as a thoughtless gesture.

Donald had been right about the drama. It was the Lenten season, closing in on Easter, and there was purple everywhere, from the clergy's voluminous damask chasubles and silk stoles (all with gold embellishments), to the flowers, to the clothing on many people in the congregation. Ruth was fascinated by the procession of the clergy up the aisle through the nave, accompanied as it was by one of them swinging a metal sensor on a long chain, leaving a trail of scented smoke wafting behind. She poked me gently in the ribs and whispered that she understood the smell now. The professional choir sang chants and tropes and anthems, and the priest intoned the prayers. It really was like theater.

One thing surprised me. As I sang through the hymns, following the bass lines rather than the melodies, I heard Ruth beside me sing the melodies in a light, sweet soprano, and Donald's confident voice on the tenor line was clearly audible. I knew some of these hymns by heart, but there was one that wasn't familiar to me. As a good sight-reader, I had no trouble with the bass line. I listened to Ruth and Donald, expecting them to falter, but they sang as confidently as I did. I was fairly sure today's hymns would not have been standard fare in a Lutheran service, which told me I was not the only one of us who could read music.

I found the sermon disquieting. Often, that should be the goal of a sermon, for without some discomfort most people easily resist change for the better. But I was not moved to betterment that day.

The congregation hushed as the priest took the pulpit.

"Today's sermon is about suffering, blindness, and light.

"When we encounter affliction, we want to know why we are suffering. We are tempted to believe that when something bad happens, it comes as a punishment from God. Our vision is distorted by the belief that suffering is caused by sin. We believe that when we suffer, in some way we get what we deserve."

He paused here and looked around. "It's especially tempting to think this way when someone else appears to be punished." He was rewarded by respectful chuckles.

"When we're suffering, we want a reason. We want someone to blame. But even as we blame ourselves and each other for sin, we blame God. God is the punisher. God is the deliverer of suffering. We become nearsighted, seeing only what fits into this false belief. And it is a false believe, because He does not dole out disease, or blindness, or pain. The works of God are healing.

"As we see in the beginning of John, Chapter Nine, Jesus encounters a man who has been blind from birth. The disciples ask what sin this man committed that he should be punished in this way. Jesus responds that there was no sin, that this blindness is in fact a path to see the works of God. Jesus spreads mud on the blind man's eyes and tells him where to go and wash the mud away. When the man does this, he washes his blindness away as well."

The priest paused again, and again he looked around, this time with intensity rather than humor. "Where is the mud of darkness in your life? How are you blind? Name it. Acknowledge it. And when you've done that, go and wash it away. Because when we wash the darkness away, we make way for the Light of Christ."

One more pause, as though to let that sink in. Then, into the silence he said, quietly, "May the Light of Christ be in your lives and help you to see His truth. Amen."

During the collective rustling that followed, I realized that my back had stiffened—not just because I was paying close attention, although I was. I felt accused.

It wasn't that I felt I was being punished. But that didn't mean I wasn't suffering. I was suffering the disappearance of Light. Of Jesus. Of God. Of purpose. And it wasn't because of anything I had done. It was because of something God had done. He had made me gay, and His church denied me the life a straight priest was allowed.

If I wanted to blame God for my suffering, that's what I would do.

When it was time for communion, the massive organ released deep, contemplative chords progressing in a slow counterpoint. The lowest notes reverberated throughout the building, seeming to pull my very bones with them. The power of this sound was evocative of every mass I had ever attended, and its effect on me today, in my current state, made my eyes burn with unshed tears.

As the front rows began filing up to the altar, my companions gazed at me with something like concern. I gathered they didn't know what they should do. I leaned forward.

Whispering, I told them, "If you want to participate in communion, when the people in our row stand, you can go up with them. But you don't have to."

Ruth asked, "We don't have to be Episcopalians?"

I shook my head. "It's between you and God. No one else will know why you partake unless you tell them."

"Will you go?"

Would I, indeed. I was torn. "I haven't decided. But if you do, just follow the lead of the people in front of you."

Would I go? Was this, as Tegan had suggested, one way for God to talk to me? I would find out.

There were so many people in the nave, it took a very long time for everyone in front of us to file up and be forgiven for their sins through the body and blood of Christ. When it came time for our row, I moved forward, Ruth and Donald behind me.

The line in front of me moved very slowly, as the parishioners kneeling at the altar were served and blessed, and then moved back to their seats. Anyone who spoke did so in hushed tones.

When it was my turn, I forced myself to avoid any feeling of familiarity, as though this were my first communion all over again. I knelt on the long, purple cushion I shared with several other people, made the sign of the cross, set my elbows on the railing, my head bowed, prayerful hands open to receive the sacred wafer.

Would God speak to me?

All I heard were the words of the two priests, one after the other, offering in the usual way:

"The body of Christ, the bread of heaven."

"The blood of Christ, the cup of salvation."

❧

Leaving a church service had always left me feeling subdued yet hopeful. Not today. Today I felt almost angry. I recognized the anger for what it was—an effort to avoid feeling betrayed and hurt—but it lingered as I led the way, walking a couple of long blocks to a café I had located ahead of time. Both Donald and Ruth remained quiet as though in deference to my mood, which I struggled to set aside. I had mostly succeeded by the time we were seated around a small table overlooking the street but shaded from the bright sun thanks to buildings close by.

Ruth looked at me, a gentle expression on her pretty face. "Does going to church usually make you quiet?"

I did my best to smile. "Yes. It does. I hope you enjoyed the experience."

"It was a far cry from anything that goes on in our church." She looked at Donald. "What did you think?"

Donald shrugged. "I didn't know all the responses, of course, but it's still the same old, same old. Just dressed up purtier. Lipstick on a pig. Nice building, though."

Over soup and sandwiches, we talked about the cathedral, the people we'd noticed, the "gorgeous outfits" (Ruth's phrase) of the clergy, and the very impressive choir.

I told Ruth, "You have a lovely voice."

She gave me a demure look.

"What about me? Do I have a lovely voice, too?" Donald's teasing tone lifted my mood, just a little.

Tongue in cheek, I said, "Oh, the voice is fine. Now if only you could train it to sing the right notes."

Our car drove north and onto the meandering road through Fort Tryon Park to the entrance of The Cloisters. I paid the entrance fee for the three of us, and we entered what felt like a collection of hallowed spaces. There were several other people around us, but no one spoke much, and when they did it was in near-whispers that echoed slightly. Everything around me felt holy, despite the relocation from overseas, and despite the knowledge that all of it was a museum project, not associated with a house of God any longer.

I led the way through the Romanesque Hall, starting with the small Sainte-Guilhem cloister and its intimate chapel, all stone, starkly overpowering. The reverberation in here was more intimate than in the hall.

In hushed tones, I said, "Sometimes performances take place in here."

Donald raised his voice just barely above a whisper. "Wow. What a space! Listen to that resonance. I'd *love* to perform in here."

Ruth added, "I'd love to sing in here." She pointed toward the apse, the semi-circular space where performers would stand, where a large crucifix on which Jesus of Nazareth hung throughout eternity, suspended some distance away from the windows of the apse. Unlike many other pieces of its kind, where the head would be bowed in humble death, here His face is visible, eyes fully open, a kingly crown in place of tangled thorns, triumphant over death.

We moved slowly on from there, surrounded by an impressive collection of sacred art and artifacts. Here was stained glass, natural light shining through it, that pre-dated anything at St. John. Everything here harked back to medieval Europe, transporting us back palpably to another time and place. Books of ancient parchment, opened in their protective cases, revealed hand-calligraphed text—almost unintelligible to us—surrounding brightly colored images of figures rendered in primitive yet glorious intricacy.

The items were not limited to the sacred, despite the atmosphere. There were chess pieces, playing cards, and other items that had been used by people who had died hundreds of years ago.

Soon we came to an opening into the main cloister area, the large Cuxa Cloister. Around the medieval garden, open to the sky, were covered walkways. Paved paths from four directions met in the center forming a cross at the stone fountain that would bubble with water in warmer seasons.

Ruth stopped. "Can we go out here?"

I nodded and lifted an arm to indicate I would follow. Slowing my pace to allow Donald and Ruth to move ahead of me, I took some time to imagine what it must have been like for the monks who padded alongside these columns centuries ago, the open sky above them implying access to God. I kept my hands firmly in my coat pockets, self-consciousness preventing me from positioning them in an attitude implying prayer. Even so, I allowed myself a bit of the melodrama Father had disdained, imagining the hem of heavy, coarse, woolen robes dragging at my feet and ankles. As I paced, my feet in imaginary leather sandals, I admired the slants of sunlight falling through the marble structures. The gardens were beginning to promise new life where crocuses and snowdrops poked through grass that showed just a hint of green. Brown coneflower heads, leftover from last year's crop, looked almost punk with their bitter-chocolate spikes. Monkshood stalks had collapsed near the ground, taken down by the rot caused by successive freezing and thawing.

My eyes, resting on the stilled fountain in the center, sought the contrast of shadows bent by sunlight on matte marble. *What must it have been like,* I wondered, *to have trod these stones, the very ones now beneath my feet, in medieval Europe? To have been awakened throughout the night by bells for worship rituals that left little time for selfish pursuits? To have put God always above all else?*

And did the monks really do that? Deny themselves earthly pleasures? One reads stories….

Back inside, the stone rooms led inexorably to the famed unicorn tapestries. They lived, I knew, in a room darkened to protect them from harsh light that could dim their colors, all of which had been made with fragile plant materials.

Ruth and Donald both came to a full stop inside the entrance to this dusky space. I walked around them to where I could get a better look at one of the tapestries in particular.

Several of the tapestries led up to this one. They depict hunters, on horses or on foot, accompanied by dogs, chasing the unicorn through scene after scene. The one I wanted to examine was the one that touched me the deepest.

Between other museum visitors, I moved in closer to get a better look at the face of a woman in the scene, something I had missed during my first visit and had seen only the next time I'd been here. Initially I had accepted the purity of the supposed maiden, a purity that was the only effective bait for the unicorn. I had been fooled as surely as the mythical creature. For the woman's expression was not that of a demure maiden, but that of a cunning conspirator. And, in fact, as I followed the line of her gaze, she was actually looking not at the trusting creature before her but at its hunter.

Betrayal!

Bad enough that mankind chased the beautiful animal to kill it. Worse, still, that someone it trusted had lured it into a deadly trap. Obviously, purity had its limits. Virgin, she may have been; trustworthy, she was not.

My eyes moved from the battle-bloodied unicorn to the dog whose teeth sank into its flank to the hunter nearly concealed behind a wooden railing upon which roses rambled. The hunter, spear in right hand, was blowing on the horn in his left to call the other hunters. Horn of the unicorn, horn of the hunter. The woman betrayed one horn for another. Despite my attachment—emotional and cerebral—to the art before me, I chuckled.

A voice close to my ear startled me. "What's so funny?" Donald had moved quite close to me. Now my eyes caught on something else: his.

Ruth, gazing around the room, approached and broke the spell, if that's what it was.

"Amazing, aren't they?" She made a small gesture with her arm to indicate the tapestries on the walls all around where we stood. I watched as she turned toward another tapestry. "This one," she said, "this is the one that I—that seems… I don't know. It calls to me, somehow."

The Unicorn in Captivity. No dogs, here. No hunters. No maidens. Just the unicorn, lying under a pomegranate tree, within a small enclosure. I smiled, admiring the workmanship in the millefleurs detail, the whimsical positioning of the strands of hair in the animal's tail, the delicate stitching to indicate the twisting of the horn—

"It's so sad." Her voice was soft. I barely heard her words.

Donald said, "Do you think so? It's safe there, at least. No hunters, or dogs."

Ruth appeared transfixed. "She's wounded, and she's trapped."

"It might look like that," I told her. Common misconceptions, I knew. Also, the unicorn was widely viewed as male. I nearly voiced these corrections, but something about Ruth made me want to tread lightly. "The red on his coat is not blood, actually; it's juice from the ripe pomegranate fruit in the tree."

"Oh. I—oh…. But she's stained." Her tone imparted a sense of being warped, or shamed. Something to be hidden.

Stained. I'd never looked at it like that before. I knew that the fruit symbolized fertility and marriage to the medieval artist, and so I'd always perceived it in that light.

"Well, then, the fence," I pointed out. "Look how low it is. The unicorn could easily jump over it and escape."

With a jerk, her face turned to me. "So she could leave? Whenever she wanted to? But that's worse!"

I was at a loss. Donald was not. He moved to his twin, took her hand, and led her to a bench against the wall. His arm behind her, he spoke to her in apparent tenderness, and she rested her head on his shoulder. She didn't seem to be in distress, exactly, just perhaps a little overcome by some feeling. I admired the unicorn a few minutes more before moving to join them. Ruth was now sitting upright, holding one of Donald's hands.

"Is everything all right?" I asked, wondering what had happened.

She waved a hand before her face as if to dismiss concern. "Oh, yes. Um, could we maybe go out onto the terrace? I'm dying to see that marvelous view."

And it was marvelous. I'd seen it before, but I was no less stunned today. In silent admiration, we leaned on the top of the wall overlooking the river, forested land sweeping away in both directions, and on both banks.

I spoke first. "I won't give you the whole history of this place except to say a heartfelt word of thanks to the man who got it started. George Grey Barnard. And then to John D. Rockefeller, who relocated the buildings to this rise and then bought all that land across the river to preserve this view."

After another couple of minutes Ruth said, "You'd never know we were in Manhattan." Then she shivered and excused herself to find a restroom. Donald and I stayed where we were, a foot or two apart, still leaning on the wall, still looking across the river.

"I have a bone to pick with you," I told him.

"Do tell."

I wasn't convinced he was taking this seriously, but I charged ahead. I'd been stewing about something since the previous evening.

"I know you're aware of how I've been struggling with my vocation. Did it not occur to you that attending mass in an Episcopal cathedral would be problematic for me?"

"It did occur to me, as a matter of fact." I waited, but he said nothing more.

I turned to face him. "Then why the hell did you put me on the spot last night? Why did you encourage Ruth to ask me to take her?"

He shrugged. "Seemed to me you needed a push."

"What are you talking about?"

He turned to face me, but his attitude was still casual. "You avoid things."

I shook my head, scowling, nonplussed.

"Oh, come on," he said, his face losing the cavalier expression. "You hit a bump at school, and rather than face it head-on you try one avoidance tactic and then another. First you're going to be chaste. Then you claim they kicked you out." We glared at each other. He added, "Am I wrong? And if you need another example, what about us?"

That got me. "What *about* us?"

He turned away from the view and leaned his back against the wall, face toward me, arms crossed over his chest. "You want me. You want to be with me. You want sex with me. But you avoid that, too. You avoid anything that points in that direction. And yet you call me when you're struggling, as you describe it."

I began to protest, but he held a hand up. "I take the blame for asking you to squire my sister around. But as I was leaving that message, I thought better of it. You, however, rose to the challenge, and then you followed us like some kind of puppy dog for the rest of the evening."

"Puppy dog?"

"So I dangled church in front of you. And you went for it.

You aren't ready to leave God behind, Spencer. You're just sulking because you think you've been handed this bum deal. I wanted you to face the Father. Your father."

More glaring. Then I said, "Like you faced yours?"

His voice grew harsh and almost loud enough for the people several feet away to hear him. "At least I told my father who I am. I *did* face him. And he really *did* kick me out."

"That's not fair! My father died!"

"And if he hadn't?" Donald snorted. He actually snorted. "If he hadn't you still wouldn't have said anything. You probably wouldn't even have told—whoever that guy is at school."

"Dr. Dunfey."

He waved a hand much as Ruth had done, only in anger. "It doesn't matter. Look, what I'm saying is I wanted you to face what it is you'd be giving up for the luxury of being who you are. I also wanted to you to realize that being who you are involves people like me. You're convinced you can't have both, and you might be right. But you've turned your back on all of it. You're avoiding all of it."

He pushed away from the wall and headed back inside just as Ruth appeared in the doorway. He draped an arm across her shoulders, and I barely heard the words, "You ready to leave, sis?"

I lay awake a long time that night. Was Donald right? Was I avoiding things?

I shook myself mentally and retraced the day in my mind. The church had been painful. I had felt betrayed by God, who seemed to be not only denying me my vocation but also thumbing His nose at me.

The museum had been lovely, up until that scene on the terrace, and as I turned in bed to lie in another position my mind skittered away from that and landed in the tapestry room with the unicorns.

The unicorn. A metaphor for the Christ. Pure, true. Able to be captured by someone who professed love. *Judas, do you betray me with a kiss?*

Unlike the unicorn, Jesus *allowed* himself to be captured and sacrificed. He is said to have done it for love. I could almost hear Donald's voice: *Yeah, Jesus didn't avoid that one, did he?*

But they have much in common, Jesus and the unicorn. The unicorn represents our striving for good. Our need, our compulsion to come to know God. And we, flawed and limited creatures that we are, can be our own worst enemies. We're always getting distracted by things that matter very little, in comparison, but that are immediately available, obviously attainable. Or, at least more obviously reachable than God.

I gave up sleeping and propped myself against the headboard. I switched the bedside lamp on and rubbed my face.

In the tapestries, mankind kills the unicorn. Two thousand years ago, mankind killed the Christ. And as I'd heard in sermon after sermon, all around us are Christ-figures in the form of people who help us, people who care for us, people who do their best to live up to the example Jesus set for how to treat each other. If we ignore those people, are we—yet again—killing the unicorn?

Why doesn't God give up on us? God's faith doesn't falter, so the unicorn keeps appearing in various guises, each time trying to show us the way to God. But, so often, we manage to ruin things.

Suddenly I was back on the terrace again.

Was Donald right? His case was compelling.

My next therapy appointment was Tuesday. Would I have the courage to raise this with Dr. Connolly before she raised it for me?

I almost fell asleep. I was in that half-dozing state when it hit me what had come over Ruth as she'd gazed at the unicorn in captivity, and why she'd referred to it as "she." Ruth was that unicorn. She'd been trapped for years, taking care of an irascible old man rather than going off to live her own life. And when I'd pointed out that the unicorn could have jumped over the fence, it challenged Ruth's dedication, her belief that she couldn't leave her father. To think that she might have escaped at any time, that she might in fact do it right now, must have felt like a shock.

For once, I didn't remember any dreams when I got up the next morning.

CHAPTER THIRTEEN

"Why do you think your parents chose St. Ignatius for their church?"

Dr. Connolly was in fine fettle at my Tuesday appointment, asking questions that made me think, whether I wanted to or not. I had told her about how miserable the service on Sunday had made me feel, and she clearly wanted to pursue that thread.

"I truly don't know."

"It's a far cry from St. John the Divine. From what you've said about your father, don't you think he'd be more likely to go for something grand rather than otherwise? And if St. John seemed too large, he could have chosen The Church of St. Mary the Virgin."

I chuckled. "Smokey Mary's."

"I beg your pardon?"

"They use a prodigious amount of incense."

"Why St. Ignatius?" She wasn't going to let it go. She must have been convinced there was something meaty there.

"I haven't a clue. Honestly."

"Is it possible it was an attempt at humility? Did he feel guilt over having left the Catholic priesthood?"

I stared blankly at her. It was the first time I had ever thought of Father in that way.

I said, "Saint Paul was like that. He frequently demeans himself, humbles himself, apparently to subdue something in his nature that could lead to arrogance. Self-importance."

"And that sounds like your father?"

I held her gaze. "It sounds very much like him. But also I think Mother preferred the smaller church. She always shied away from anything ostentatious, anything grand."

"Did she deny herself?"

I closed my eyes, picturing Mother as she waited in anticipation for after-Christmas sales, delaying the purchase of that lambskin coat despite the fact that someone else might have walked away with it before she got there.

"She did. And whether Father chose St. Ignatius because he felt he had fallen from grace or because Mother would be more comfortable there, I can't say."

"Was he often protective of her?"

I shook my head. "No. But he cared deeply for her. He loved her very much. And you never know with people, do you?"

She switched the subject so quickly I felt dizzy. "There is some speculation that Saint Paul was homosexual."

Two things happened at once, but so fast they could have been in the same gunshot. One was that my head jerked toward her, and the other was that my voice spoke unencumbered by any thinking my brain might have done: "That's blasphemy."

In the several seconds of silence that followed, I saw her reveal something she probably wouldn't have wanted me to see. Because so far, she had revealed little or no emotion that didn't seem deliberate.

One corner of her mouth lifted ever so slightly. She had scored a hit, and she knew it.

She recovered quickly. "Why is it blasphemous?"

The breath I exhaled was laden both with annoyance at

myself for having responded without thinking and with irritation at her for acting, for the second time since we'd met, as if she didn't recognize a scriptural reference.

"I think you know what scripture has to say about homosexuality." I wanted to add, *This affects both of us*. But I didn't.

She gave me a look that implied confusion. "As a divinity student, you must realize that the word 'homosexual' didn't appear in any language, in any book of the Bible, until the middle of the twentieth century."

I'm sure she heard the exasperation in my voice. "We both know what behavior it referred to."

The look on Dr. Connolly's face was as revealing as that hint of a smile had been, and I expected her to say more about this topic. But she closed her eyes for a second and gave her head a slight shake as if to refrain from the temptation to enter into a longer discussion.

"We might have time for more on that later. Right now I have another question. Did you go alone to mass at St. John?"

I felt my chin rise involuntarily, just a tiny bit. "Why do you ask?"

"Why do you answer a question with a question?"

I forced myself to feign nonchalance. "I just don't think it's relevant."

"To what?"

I waved a hand. "Anything."

Without hesitation, she said, "That's our time for today. Before we meet on Friday, I'd like you to ask yourself how you would have answered my question if it were truly irrelevant."

It wasn't until I stepped out of the elevator on the ground floor of Dr. Connolly's building that it hit me what she had done. She knew what time it was. And yet, with mere seconds to go in the session, she'd asked me a question that—damn it!—she must have known I wouldn't want to answer.

~

As though I were trying to prove Donald right, I avoided Dr. Connolly's question quite effectively. Instead, my thoughts turned to the unicorn.

The summer after Father's death, Mother had confided in me that she had always wanted to see Paris. I'd tried to hide my surprise, but her shy smile had told me I hadn't been especially successful.

"But," she had added, "I couldn't go alone." She'd watched my face carefully.

I'd felt a smile work its slow way across my face. "Of course I'll go with you."

And I did. And one day, at Mother's suggestion, we visited the Musée de Cluny, also known as Musée national du Moyen Âge. She particularly wanted to see the display of unicorn tapestries there.

I asked, "Are they so different from the ones in New York?"

She smiled, almost to herself. "You'll see."

And she'd been right. She knew as well as I did that the New York tapestries depicted betrayal. And agonized suffering. And sacrifice. And death. In contrast to the bloodied, savaged creature at The Cloisters, the Cluny versions showed the polar opposite.

I sat transported in that dark, semi-circular space for over an hour, surrounded by gently-lit depictions of medieval scenes. At first I sat under a recessed light and read the small book I'd bought on the tapestries, but it yielded only facts. I put aside the printed information about the neglect and even abuse they'd received, about ill-advised repair attempts, about the techniques of weaving, about the various owners—some callous and some caring. I recalled how it was often said that the artist must suffer. In this case, it could be said the art itself had suffered. But now these glorious creations belonged to the Cluny. No one owned them; no one should.

Their images called to the eternal. Beauty. Truth. Divine love.

What I saw was that the Paris and New York tapestries were like two sides of the same coin: equally universal, yet demonstrating the opposing realities of life.

By Friday, when I met next with Dr. Connolly, I had given precious little thought to the question she had asked. So as I sat in my chair and she in hers, and she asked whether I had given the question any thought, I knew what I wanted to say.

"I thought about something else. That is, about another question you had asked, and about what my answer had been."

I waited to see if she would protest, but she said nothing. Even her face told me nothing. So I described the differences I had seen between the unicorn collections, divided both by geography and by what they represented.

"You asked what was most important to me," I reminded her. "I said what was important was what was missing. I said that as a priest, I would have wanted to help others find unity with God."

Again, I gave her space to interrupt. She was attentive but silent.

"Combining the concepts represented by the two versions of the unicorn's depiction—that is, spiritual and physical—into a unified whole is at the heart of what I wanted my role as a priest to be."

Dr. Connolly blinked a few times, as though trying to make sense out of what I was saying. I decided to wait until she spoke.

It took several seconds, but finally she said, "What part of glory is agony, and vice versa? How can you unify these ideas when you avoid half of the whole?"

My turn to blink. "How… how can you say that?"

She released a sigh that reeked of calculated exasperation. "By avoiding the question I asked last time, and instead spending what must have been quite a bit of time contemplating these philosophical issues, you avoided something you didn't want to see."

I couldn't keep the sarcasm out of my tone. "And what would that be?"

"Saint Paul."

Confused, I felt my head make two or three small shakes.

"Spencer, do you remember how you reacted when I mentioned him Tuesday? Let me tell you how it looked from where I sit. I saw horror. I saw condemnation. I saw agony. *Your* agony." She leaned forward slightly. "It doesn't matter about Saint Paul. People will argue his nature to no avail. He's dead. His mission was pretty well accomplished, on the whole, regardless of who he was or wasn't as a person. What matters now is you."

My brain cast about wildly for an angle, any angle, that would let me push aside what she was saying. "When you said that about Saint Paul Tuesday, I thought you were suggesting that my father was gay."

Her eyes widened briefly. I'd surprised her. But she said, "Nice try."

I was angry now. "I don't know what you mean."

"Who went with you to St. John?"

I stood suddenly, turned my back on her, and grabbed at my hair with one hand. Maybe thirty seconds went by. Maybe it was thirty minutes.

"Spencer, I could tell you who I think was with you, and I'd probably be right, though I don't have a name. But it does no good for me to say it. You must say it. You must say it here. You must face not only that person, but also yourself. I can't do that for you."

I wheeled around. "No. All you can do is goad me until I respond the way you want."

"Please sit." She waited until I did. "Part of my job is to help you look directly at things you would prefer to avoid. It's understandable that you'd want to avoid facing your agony, but I ask you not to do that. Because the end result, Spencer...." She let out a long breath. "The end result is glory."

I don't know where they came from, or why, but suddenly there were tears on my face. I wasn't sobbing, I was just looking at the face of someone I was paying to goad me, and my eyes were like open faucets.

Dr. Connolly's gentle smile contained something I never expected to see in her: tenderness. Her voice was softer than I'd ever heard it. "I dislike the expression, 'No pain, no gain.' It implies, almost, that pain is to be sought. We don't need to seek pain, Spencer. It will be there whether we look for it or not. What matters is how we respond to it. What we learn from it. And what we learn about ourselves if we won't face it."

I leaned forward, hands gripping my hair. Avoidance wasn't working. I had to admit that. Almost silently, I said, "His name is Donald."

She gave me a minute or so to collect myself. Then, "How does he make you feel?"

I reached for a few tissues. Hands limp in my lap, eyes closed, I said, "Excited. Terrified. Furious."

"Furious?"

"He won't go away."

"Do you want him to?"

I opened my eyes. "No. Yes. I don't know." Then, "No."

Dr. Connolly resettled herself in the chair and folded her hands in her lap. "I know you understand the concept of limbo, even if you were never Catholic. Is it fair to say that's where you are?"

I nodded.

"Can you describe what it's like? Can you articulate why you're there?"

I took a long, shaky breath. "It's an imperfect comparison, but…. I thought I was in heaven. I was accepted at General. I was doing very well. I was taken seriously as a candidate for my vocation, the only career I ever wanted. And then…."

"And then?"

"And then I met Donald." I closed my eyes again; that made it easier to avoid avoidance. "He approached me first. He teased me. After a time, he kissed me. After more time, I kissed him. And then we had sex." Another shaky breath. "And then I told him I couldn't do this." I stopped talking.

"Do what?"

I opened my eyes and scowled. "Be together." In a detached voice, devoid of emotion, I described that unbearable morning after I'd been with Donald, the ghastly way I'd felt, how repulsive I'd found the incident, how hideous I'd felt myself to be because of it.

Dr. Connolly sounded equally unemotional as she said, "It sounds like what you couldn't do was face yourself."

I think I moaned.

"Spencer, what was it about being with Donald that made you feel hideous?"

Eyes closed again, I frowned in an effort to recall those excruciating hours. The words I'd flung at myself were still alive: Unnatural. Sick. Twisted. Perverted. But they were far from the worst.

"It separated me from God."

"Why?"

I looked directly at her. "Isn't our time up?"

"We have a few minutes. Why do you ask?"

"Because you seem to like asking questions just as it's time to end the session."

She actually chuckled. "If you're astute enough to realize that, you're astute enough to know why. Can you answer the question?"

"With another question. Why do you pretend not to know your Bible?"

"These sessions aren't about me, Spencer. They're about you, and the meaning scripture has for you is what's important. Are you saying scripture is the source of what's causing this separation?"

"Of course it is."

"You know, Spencer, I could tell you all kinds of things about scripture that would countermand anyone using it to condemn gay people. I could tell you that ancient, mistaken ideas of where life comes from affected the attitudes of the people in Biblical times. I could describe the reality of those times that meant having children was the only safety net one had as one aged, and how high rates of infant and maternal mortality meant having many children was the only way to be sure two or three survived. But none of that would make you feel any better. What you're feeling isn't something anyone else can dispel. You'll have to do that yourself, with God's help."

"God got me into this mess!"

"And He offers two ways out. One is using the brains He gave you. The other is love."

I opened my mouth to protest, though I didn't know what I would say. Dr. Connolly spoke first.

"And that *is* our time for today." She stood. "Your homework for Tuesday is to do a little exegesis. Matthew, chapter twenty-two, verses thirty-seven through forty."

~

All the way home, I grumbled under my breath. *Matthew twenty-two, thirty-seven through forty*. I knew exactly what those verses say. I could quote them from more than one edition of the Bible. *Who does she think she is,* I grumbled silently, *to assign me the task of interpreting those verses? Of explaining them? They're some of the best-known verses in the New Testament!*

Inside my silent house I was still grumbling as I went through the mail delivery, until I noticed a square, light blue envelope with the return address of Cedar Rapids.

"Dear Spencer," Ruth had written on blue stationery that matched the envelope, a delicate, lacy cut-out pattern along the top of the page. "It was such a pleasure to meet you at last. I so appreciated your company at Donnie's play. And the blissful morning at St. John the Baptist Cathedral will stay with me always. That spiritual experience could not have been followed by anything better than our visit to The Cloisters. I hope to visit Donnie again soon, and it would be wonderful if I have the chance to see you again. Bless you. Yours in Christ, Ruth Rainey."

I had liked Ruth. I had enjoyed her company. She had seemed fresh, perhaps even innocent, guileless. And her brief note was perfectly worded. Nonetheless, as I read it for the third time, the tone of her voice and the expression on her face at one point in particular during her visit came to mind. It was when we were waiting for the play to begin. I had said I'd seen Donald play Puck. She had looked at me almost coquettishly, head slightly tilted. Fondly, yet in a voice laden with shrewdness, she had said, "Type casting."

So on that third reading of her note, between the carefully-worded lines, I knew she was hoping to encourage me to see more of Donald, to let whatever might happen between us take its course. There was so much meaning in "… a pleasure to meet you *at last*."

~

Before retiring that night, I read through the Gospel According to Matthew, paying special attention to several verses before and after those in my assignment. I had always enjoyed these passages, which depict Jesus outwitting the Pharisees and Sadducees even as they attempt to trap Him with God's Word.

Sleep came easily. But then there was the dream.

I was perhaps seven or eight years old. Before me was a pond, its water an intense blue and so clear I could see to the bottom from where I knelt on a ledge. Two feet or so below me, on the white sand under the water, were jewels of rich colors.

Behind me, bending down closely, was Father. There were no words, but I knew he wanted me to reach into the water for the jewels, not for their monetary value, but for a more ephemeral reason. They were imbued with a kind of spiritual significance.

Father held onto my hips as I leaned forward. I held my breath as my head entered the water, and I reached for the jewels. My hand hadn't touched even one before I realized that instead of preventing me from falling in, Father was holding me under. I would drown.

I awoke, gasping for air, in absolute shock that Father would do that.

Bathrobe held tightly around me, I paced through the house and ended up in the doorway of Father's room.

"Why?" I asked of the empty space. "Why would you do that?"

Of course I knew he would not have drowned me in water. Was he trying to get me to see that the jewels were more important than life? And what were they?

Knowing Father, the jewels were probably scripture.

But... wasn't scripture, wasn't God's Word, supposed to help us *live?* There's a line from somewhere that speaks of the Bible as something that will "help you to live and prepare you to die."

Was Father confused about which was which? Or was I the confused one? After all, it was *my* dream.

"You shall love the Lord your God with all your heart, with all your soul, and with all your mind. This is the first and greatest commandment. A second likewise is this: You shall love your neighbor as yourself. The whole law and the prophets depend on these two commandments."

I quoted the verses aloud. And for the first time, the full meaning of the phrase "law and the prophets" came to me. Jesus was a Jew. Torah (meaning instruction, sometimes referred to as law), together with the books of the prophets, comprised the entirety of sacred texts as He knew it. So what He's saying in Matthew is that loving God and loving each other take precedence over any other commandment—over anything else in the sacred texts. Love trumps Law.

I felt my butt hit the floor, right there in the doorway to Father's room. Was this what Dr. Connolly wanted me to understand? And if it was true, why the hell hadn't I already heard it expressed in this way from any number of sources?

Had I heard it and ignored it? Had I heard it and just not let it sink in or take root?

My knees were not altogether steady as I got to my feet. I moved to the bed, Father's bed, and sat on the side, staring out a window at the city lights. New York at night was brighter than this room. And that was the only thought in my head for several minutes.

Eventually my mind wandered over to another topic. Donald. "Love over Law" did not mean "Sex over Law." And Donald and I had had sex without love. At least, without romantic love.

But Jesus wasn't referring to romantic love. He meant divine love, a love that is not necessarily personal in nature.

"Christ!"

What was I to do with this conundrum? Did what I had done

with Donald really separate me from God, or had something else done that?

Limbo. Dr. Connolly had certainly been right about that. And I had to find my own way out of it.

I went back to my room and read through every verse I could find that mentioned same-sex activity of any kind. There were precious few of them.

Saturday afternoon I called Donald.

"I received a lovely note from your sister," I told him.

"Yeah, she's like that. Verily, a steward of etiquette." I thought he'd say more, but he didn't.

"Are you all right? You don't sound like your usual self."

"Got turned down for a part I really wanted. So I'm deep into the mulligrubs. I'll survive. What's up?"

I tried to fill my lungs with air, but I still felt a little short of oxygen. "So if you don't have a show tonight, would you like to get dinner someplace?"

There was silence for so long I nearly asked if he were still on the line.

"Tell you what," he said finally. "How about if we pick up some groceries and make dinner at your place?"

Now I was incapable even of trying to breathe. His suggestion was in the direction of where I had wanted to go, but it went further. There would be no escape, here. We would almost certainly have sex, here.

"Forget it," he said.

"No. Wait. I just—Yes. Let's do that."

"Are you sure? 'Cause it's kind of a big step for you. I know that. It's why I suggested it. But here's the thing, Spence. I'm kind of over this dancing around. If I come to your place, it's like you're saying you want to know what this is. What it might be.

And if I don't, then—and this isn't a threat, or an ultimatum, it's self-preservation—if I don't, then I don't want to hear from you again."

"I don't want that." It was true. It had been true all along.

Another pause, a short one. "What's your address? And what time should I show up? And, by the way, can you cook?"

Grocery shopping with Donald was fun. Perhaps I would have enjoyed it even more if I hadn't been so nervous. He was his usual self again, somehow not seeming any different for knowing what the evening might hold.

We'd met at the store, rather than at my house. Donald seemed to know what he wanted to buy, which was fine with me. At one point, as I waited at the meat counter, Donald headed off to locate a few other items. When my order had been filled, I looked around and couldn't see Donald right away, so I headed in the direction of the aisle for pasta, one of the items on his list. Before I got to that aisle, I heard whistling. Someone was whistling along with the recorded music the store was playing. Only the whistler wasn't following the melody. The whistling was in harmony to the melody.

As I turned into the pasta aisle, there was Donald, crouched down to examine something on a low shelf, whistling away. I stood still and watched him, and a warm feeling crept through me. How could I not find this man adorable? How could I not be attracted to him?

I recalled the condemnation of those few, paltry Bible verses. Those verses weren't about me. They had nothing to do with a relationship based on mutual regard or genuine attraction, let alone the love that might develop between any two people. Maybe I'd feel differently tomorrow, as I had after being with Donald in his apartment. In his bed. But right now, that amusing, intelligent, musical man whistling harmony to crappy music, that man who talked to his sister about me, was making me feel—God, was I feeling horny?

I laughed out loud.

Donald stopped whistling, looked at me, and smiled, almost sheepishly. "Can't help myself. The best way not to be annoyed by the stuff is to join in with it."

CHAPTER FOURTEEN

After a tour of the house, during which Donald remained interested but made few comments, we worked in the kitchen, preparing dinner. I had felt decidedly uneasy, walking through Father's house with a man I was very likely to have sex with at some point. If Donald noticed, it wasn't evident. He was his usual playful self, and perhaps thanks to his ability to keep it light and not stray into areas that implied attraction, my anxiety largely subsided. I'd been afraid he might ask about my parents having separate bedrooms. If he was curious, he didn't let me know it.

Even without anything overtly sexual, being here with him felt very different from how I had felt in Tegan's kitchen. There I had nervously avoided her in the tiny space. Here, in my large kitchen, I found myself standing close to Donald. At one point, as my arm extended across his body to grasp something on the counter, he turned his face to mine and we kissed, lightly, almost teasingly, and he smiled. I smiled. I actually smiled.

It was a simple meal: ground beef flavored with garlic ("It's okay if we both have it," Donald assured me) and cheese over pasta and parsley, a green salad on the side, and a bottle of

Chianti classico I had bought the night of the Chinese take-out gluttony.

"Cheers," Donald said, lifting his glass to mine.

The pasta dish was excellent, and I told Donald so. "Do you have this recipe at home?"

He gave me a sardonic look. "What's a recipe? I enjoy throwing things together to see if they like each other."

I laughed. "Typical."

"Is it?"

"Not surprising, then."

He grinned. "I'll take that."

Setting my glass down after another sip of wine, I said, "I really enjoyed meeting Ruth. You two seem very close."

He nodded. "Partly it's that we're twins, and we have no other siblings. Partly, I guess you could say we were thrust into it."

He went on to describe what sounded like a peculiar childhood, with a mother who was sometimes loving and tender and sometimes distant and unreachable, and a father whose presence was either stern or outright Draconian.

"Ruth and I kind of clung to each other like we'd been cast into a lifeboat on a turbulent sea. We followed the same interests. Like music, and art, literature. We developed a way of communicating that isn't our own language, or anything, but—well, you commented on it. The Shakespearean insults. The odd vocabulary." He shrugged, but I saw pain behind the casual motion. "It allowed us to escape into our own world."

I found myself genuinely moved, not just by his description but also by his honesty, by the trust he gave me in revealing these intimate personal experiences. And then he asked me to reciprocate.

He said, "We didn't have a lot of money, but we never wanted for anything important. Even so, I can't imagine growing up in a place like this. Especially in New York. Does it make you feel different, or did most of your friends exist in the same financial stratosphere?"

Odd way to put it. But I tried to answer. "I've often had cause to realize how sheltered I've been. Financially, and in other ways, too. My father was stern, and unemotional, and critical. But I gave him few reasons to be anything worse. Mother and I seemed to have a kind of silent conspiracy, never openly acknowledged. But after Father died, we could allow ourselves some emotional leeway. It was silent, perhaps, but we did acknowledge our bond. But I had no one like Ruth as a cohort."

"Did you have many friends?"

"Not many. No. I was afraid friends would expect to visit me here. And I didn't want that."

"Because of your father?"

"I don't think I refined my reasons. Mostly, I think it was because of the atmosphere Father's dominance created. You know. Humorless. Dry. Quiet by silent decree."

"Devoid of fun?"

I gave him a half smile. "Completely devoid of fun."

He eyed me carefully. "But you're not."

"Not what?"

"Devoid of fun. I get the sense you try to be, but it's an act."

I set down my fork and sat back in the chair. "And you know this how?"

He winked. "Give me a chance, and I'll show you."

I felt my breathing halt, just for a moment.

Kitchen clean-up in my house had always been a sober affair. With Donald, it was anything but that. He snapped the drying towel at my butt until I lifted my hands from the dishwater and threw bubbles at him. He stole items out of the dish drainer, items he was supposed to be drying, and dropped them back into the soapy water, laughing at the consternation on my face. He was Puck incarnate, but with none of the disdain that fictional character heaped upon his victims.

With everything finally washed, dried, and put away, I leaned a hip against the counter, and Donald did the same, and we regarded each other.

"Tell me," he opened. "What *do* you do for fun?"

"Tonight?"

"Or anytime in the past."

"Follow me."

I'd had just enough wine to soften my nervousness about what might happen after dinner, but I grasped at this opportunity to delay whatever that would be, and maybe show off just a little. I led the way into the music room. I had Donald sit in an easy chair, and I left the room. I brought back two scotch snifters with a few splashes of a very nice single malt in each. I handed him one and made my way to the piano.

I propped up the lid of the black baby grand to release as much sound as possible. I sat on the leather-covered bench and lifted the keyboard cover to expose those clear, definitive black and white surfaces—reliable keys to the sublime, despite their predictability.

I sat for just a moment, quietly contemplating what I was about to do. Then I suspended my hands over those keys. And I allowed the music to happen.

That's what it felt like. The barcarolle that had so moved my mother had been my favorite piece since I'd learned it, and I played it now. For her. For Donald.

For myself.

He was in the room. I knew that. He was watching, listening. I knew that, too. And all that had its place. But it wasn't the place where I was. I was in the music in a way I had seldom felt before. I *was* the music.

As the final chord hung in the air, slowly fading to silence, I breathed for what felt like the first time since I'd begun. Hands now in my lap, I sat for several seconds, silent and yet still reverberating with the sounds I had brought forth from the piano's strings. I looked up only when I heard a sound from Donald's direction.

He was watching me, rapt, tears running down his face, his breath catching just slightly every so often. Neither of us spoke.

Then he stood, not wiping his tears away, and walked over to me. He held a hand out, and I stood and took it. We held each other for a long time, two men damaged in very similar ways, each of us retreating from pain in very different ways: I into a self-contained, emotionally-restricted carapace, and he into a life where emotional release was safest when it was through the emotions of fictional characters.

Donald pulled away first, just enough to reach my mouth with his. We kissed, softly but deeply, acknowledging the connection between us that was not just physical. When the kiss ended, I took his hand, we retrieved our glasses, and I led him to my bedroom.

The first time we had been together could reasonably have been described as fucking. What we did that night was to make love. We covered each other's bodies with kisses. We left trails of evaporating, golden liquor on sensitive skin. His penis in my hand came to life in a way that made me feel both powerful and loving. I found Donald's anus with my fingers, loving the gasp I heard.

We didn't speak until Donald pushed me gently away. He said, "If you're not ready for this, please say so. But would you come inside me? Could you do that tonight?"

I knew he was not referring to his mouth. "I don't really know what to do."

He smiled. "I do." He got off the bed and reached into a pocket of his jeans. A condom packet in his hand, he glanced at my erection. "Would you like me to put it on for you?"

I nodded.

I couldn't have said what it was about the back of Donald's neck, of the side of his face with closed eyes and panting mouth partially open, that I found so wonderfully inflammatory. He spoke little, just enough to guide me, just enough to help me find my way deep inside him before the spasms began.

I had thought about this act. Lord knows I had imagined it, both as it was happening now and as it might have happened if our roles were reversed. Nothing had prepared me for the intensity, the muscular, masculine sense of dominance tempered by longing and surrender. Never had I felt so completely inside myself and yet not limited to myself at all.

It was as though Donald and I were one.

We lay dozing, sides touching, until I heard him chuckle. "I do think we just cracked your halo."

I tried not to laugh. I failed. I wasn't even sure why it was funny. A few minutes of quiet later, I said, "I'm sorry you didn't get that part."

He sighed, but it sounded more like contentment than regret. "Yeah. I've indulged in a few intense episodes of jouska because of that. The guy they hired is all wrong for the part."

I laughed again. "You and your odd words. What's jouska?"

"Oh, you know. That exercise where someone says something mean or hurtful or wrong, and you want to come up with a great comeback, but you don't. Until later, that is, when you play an imaginary scene endlessly in your head with you throwing one pithy, unassailable comment after another at the other person. In this case, the director."

"And what was your favorite imaginary comeback?"

"Hmmm. Not sure. Maybe, 'So he's the son of which of your sisters, again?'"

I was laughing a lot tonight. Despite our lazy afterglow, I was nearly giddy.

"Hate to go all prosaic on you," Donald said as he stroked my chest with the back of a hand, "but am I leaving tonight or not?"

I turned toward him, head propped on an elbow. "Stay as long as you like."

"Then I'd like to stay the night." He lifted his chin without raising his head off the pillow. I obliged the implied request and kissed him.

Lying back again, I asked, "What was the real reason you approached me in acting class? The day you told me you could help me?"

"I didn't lie. When you mentioned your intended vocation I was fascinated if also repulsed."

"Repulsed?"

"Are you forgetting about my father?"

"Was he that bad?"

Donald let out a long breath. "He didn't abuse us, or anything. Not physically, anyway. But he often said he had a personal relationship with God deep enough that he knew what God wanted. And it was seldom what I wanted. He was always right. Always *in* the right. Always righteous. There was no space for me in that." He turned his face toward me. "But that's only part of the reason I spoke to you."

"And the other part?"

"Your voice."

"My voice?"

His turn to prop himself up on an elbow. "I can almost see your body reverberate when you speak. The sound is deep, and rich, and profoundly masculine. It turned me on like I can't even tell you. Like you read about."

Controlling my urge to smile, I spoke in the deepest tones available to me. "And now? Does it still turn you on?"

"Ha! See? You *are* playful!"

The wrestling match that ensued ended with each of us coming again, in each other's hands this time, so close to simultaneously that I was once again struck by how connected with Donald I felt.

We burrowed under the covers, and Donald curled into a ball against my side. After a few minutes I heard his breathing go quiet and slow. I opened my eyes to the grey ceiling, and deliberately thought about Father. How horrified he would be! His son, a faggot. But I was a child no longer. I was under his stern looks, his unquestioned jurisdiction, no longer. I whispered, to that ceiling, to that controlling parent.

"I am a man."

When I awoke it was mid-morning, and I could hear the shower running. I relished being alone in the bed. I felt reborn—new, as though I had morphed into a magnificent butterfly. My wings at the moment were quiescent, but they were there, waiting to unfurl and be warmed by the sunshine of self-actualization.

The house felt occupied for the first time since Mother had died. I dozed until I realized the shower was no longer running. My turn, I decided. I didn't see Donald until I emerged, my wings still damp. He was in the music room, sitting cross-legged on the floor in front of the cabinet that held our family's—or, I guess now, my—record collection. I couldn't tell which album he held as he examined the back cover.

He smiled when he saw me. "Good morning."

"It is a good morning."

"It's pouring rain, you know."

I grinned at him. "I hadn't noticed."

"How do you turn this thing on?"

I powered up the turntable and amplifier, components of a

very expensive audio system Father had indulged in the year before he'd died. He'd declared music "worth it."

The album began to play. I reached for the cover, not recognizing the music.

Donald said, "I absolutely love Russian male choirs. The same reason, probably, that I like your voice so much."

He turned the volume up until the room nearly shook. I swear I heard vibrations from some of my piano's strings. I sank to the floor and closed my eyes, letting the sound fill me. The deep resonance permeated my every cell, making me nearly quiver. Again, as had happened last night, I was infused with a sense of masculine power. It was both unfamiliar and completely intrinsic to my core identity.

The first song ended, and I opened my eyes to see Donald watching me.

He said, "Enthralling, isn't it?" I let my expression speak for me. Donald moved so that his knees and mine were touching. "You are a man who wants a man. I pray you can become comfortable with that."

I grinned. "You once told me you didn't pray."

He threw back his head and laughed. "I lied. Come and make me some breakfast."

I wasn't an especially practiced cook, but I could throw together a decent breakfast. We sat across from each other at what I still thought of as Mother's kitchen table, grinning foolishly at each other.

A half-eaten piece of toast in my hand, I asked, "So, *do* you pray?"

He sipped some coffee and waved a hand. "Oh, all the time! For all the good it does. I prayed to get that part, and look where that got me."

I shook my head gently. "Will you be serious for just a moment? I'm trying to find out where you stand regarding God."

"Over breakfast? Are you kidding me with this?"

"Well, it is Sunday morning."

He chewed thoughtfully and sat back in his chair, eyeing me but not really seeing me. "The irony is that if Dad hadn't been quite so… well, so much like himself, I might have considered the life of a preacher. Of course, my sex life would have precluded success, but I had the leaning. Though, in any case, I would never have stayed in the Missouri Synod."

This information came to me as a slight shock. "When you said 'Lutheran,' I didn't realize…. So your church holds that everything is about obedience to law? And that because we're sinners and can't obey law, only the gospel saves us from God's wrath and judgement? From damnation?"

Donald's chuckle was without mirth. "You understand my father so well."

"It seems a very dark philosophy. So you left that behind. I'm glad. And now?"

His smile was wry. "Now it's hard to tell whether religion in general rejected me or I rejected it. But I will tell you this: I miss it."

"And do you pray?"

"I think of it more as communication. But don't get excited. It doesn't go very deep."

"Why not?"

He regarded me again, this time apparently as though trying to decide whether to give me one of his droll responses or his genuine feelings. He chose the latter.

"It hurts too much." He tilted his head and shook a finger at me. "And that's all I'm going to say on the subject. So. What shall we do today? Are you chasing me off home? Shall we wander through MOMA and giggle at some of the art pieces and weep over others? Shall we listen to music all afternoon and consume all the scotch in the house?"

"Do you *want* to go home?"

"Not especially. Though I realize I'm still in yesterday's clothes. I can tolerate that if you can."

"MOMA then. I have a fondness for modern art. Though I can't promise to giggle."

It had stopped raining by the time we left the house, though the overcast was thick. We took a cab uptown, one that I hailed with that voice Donald so admired.

Wandering around the museum, my feelings bounced around so much the art was secondary. I was still on a kind of high from the way I'd felt the night before, and this morning's conversation with Donald had given me much to ponder. Then there was the odd, unnamable set of emotions I felt looking around and wondering how many of the other people in the museum would look at Donald and me and know that we were together. And, how many of them would be able to tell we'd had sex last night.

As much as I had felt new born earlier, it took me by surprise —and not in a good way—when, standing with Donald before an especially large and inscrutable piece of metal sculpture, he took my hand. My arm jerked automatically, and he let go.

Sotto voce he asked, "Too much too soon?"

"We're in public."

"Oh? Do you know anyone here?"

I craned my neck to examine the upper reaches of the sculpture. "My parents and I dined a number of times with the current director."

"Okay then." And Donald took a sideways step away from me. "I didn't realize I was in the presence of one of New York's elite."

That got me. My neck complained at the suddenness with which I turned my head to look at Donald. "What are you trying to say?"

He glanced around to be sure no one was close enough to overhear. "Look, Spencer, this is new to you. I get that. I'm sorry if I took a step you weren't ready for, just now. Let's leave it at that, okay?" He gave me a smile I didn't believe and moved away toward another exhibit. I stood where I was.

Dr. Connolly's words echoed in my head: *What part of glory is agony, and vice versa? How can you unify these ideas when you avoid half of the whole?*

Was Donald showing me that with the joy, the rapture of allowing my true self to have loving expression, came the sting of society's condemnation? Could I not have the pleasure without the pain?

On the sidewalk beneath the overhang at the museum's doorway, we huddled against the rain, which had returned with a vengeance.

Donald said, "Off home now, I think." He looked at me almost like he wanted to kiss me. Almost. "Thanks for last night."

He threw what looked like a perfunctory smile at me and turned west, away from the direction he knew I would be taking, hands in his jacket pockets, shoulders hunched against the pelting rain. I almost called out to him, to remind him that if he was taking the subway, the other direction—my direction— would be the better choice. Just in time, I realized what he wanted was to get away from me.

So much for all the warmth I'd felt. So much for feeling as though that warmth, and the connection I'd felt with Donald, might mean I could speak to God again. So much for beginning to hope that the creature God had made me did not preclude Him loving me, and allowing me to love.

How could all this change in the course a few minutes?

A voice in my head reminded me that last night's changes had happened pretty quickly, and maybe *they* were what wasn't real.

I was still standing where Donald had left me, paying no attention to anything around me, when he reappeared.

"I'm sorry." He stood before me, bedraggled and dripping. "I tried to push you. I shouldn't have done that. And when you reacted, I didn't handle that well, either. I'm supposed to be the one with some experience, and I acted like a sulky child."

I was still staring at him in surprise when he stopped talking. I said nothing, so he continued.

"Please don't let this afternoon spoil what you felt—what we both felt last night."

"You're shivering."

"It's cold. I'm wet."

I took his arm. "Let's find a cab. I'll take you home."

We didn't speak on the ride south to St. Mark's Place. But about half-way there, I reached for Donald's hand and held it for the rest of the ride. And I thought about what he had said over breakfast: that, but for his father, he might have considered becoming a minister. And it occurred to me for the first time that, but for my own father, I might not.

Instead of having the cab drive me home, I directed the driver back uptown, all the way to West End Ave and Eighty-Seventh. Saint Ignatius of Antioch Episcopal.

Mass was long over. The worshippers were gone. I asked the cab to sit for a few minutes, meter running, while I considered my next steps. The front was just as I remembered it, on the corner, looking a little squashed between some building on one side and the street on the other. No grand plaza here, as there was at St. John. But the massive, severely vertical stained glass windows left no doubt as to what was inside.

I paid and dismissed the cab and dashed through the rain to the front doors, only a little surprised that one side of the double entry wasn't locked. I paused for just a second in the tiny vestibule, so much more intimate and welcoming than the cavernous narthex at St. John. I stood for a moment, testing myself to be sure I wanted to take the chance I'd come here to take. Something about the fragrance of the incense they had used during mass pulled me forward, and I walked slowly up the center aisle of the nave.

So familiar. Everything here was so familiar. The old, dark wood of the pews. The tall, narrow stained glass windows, respectable but not showy. The high altar, draped in purple for the last time this liturgical year; next Sunday was Easter, when all would be gold and white.

Lent. The season when we acknowledge that without God, we are dust and nothing more. In recognition of the forty days Jesus spent fasting in the wilderness, we forebear to indulge in something we love—a token for the suffering borne by Jesus on our behalf. It reminds us to place our trust in the spiritual resurrection to come—not just that of Jesus, but also of ourselves, if we will but accept the sacrifice God has made to save us from what we would be without His love.

I had vivid memories of Father asking my young self, "What will you give up for Lent this year, Spencer?" I had chosen things like dessert, or maybe an hour of television each evening. Later, as a teen, I might give up playing the piano or red meat. And I had always done my best, during the times of these paltry sacrifices, to relate to the suffering of Jesus. I never got close. How could I?

Now, Lent felt significant. There were two things I might

give up, and not just for Lent. Whatever I gave up would be gone forever. One was my vocation, the one I had felt God had called me to. The other was… well, the other was my self. And I was here today, in the church of my childhood, the House where I came into my faith, to see if Tegan was right. To see, if I asked Him penitently and sincerely, whether God had a message for me.

There were two other people in the pews, not together, widely separated. I chose a pew that preserved respectful distance, genuflected, and kneeled. At first I leaned my arms on the back of the pew in front of me, head bowed, my mind as clear as I could make it. If it's possible to will oneself to be calm, that's what I did. I was a supplicant. I was humble. I was open.

Nothing came.

I sat back in the pew and regarded the lighted altar, glorious in its purple mourning, but empty of information or guidance. I closed my eyes and spoke to God silently.

God, Father, I know You can hear me. I know You know I'm struggling. I come to You as a beggar, ignorant and without the means to find my way without You. You are perfect. I am anything but perfect.

You do not make mistakes. I am not who I am by choice, but by Your Will. How much of my self would You have me set aside in order to serve You, in order to minister to Your people? I understand the concept of a pebble in my shoe. But, dear Father, this is not a pebble. It's a thorn in my side.

My eyes opened in surprise. No; in shock. Saint Paul had spoken of a thorn in his side. Could it have been the same one? Dr. Connolly's remarks came to life in my mind.

It didn't matter.

"Spencer?"

I turned sharply to see who was in the aisle. It was Father Fleming, a priest here for the past several years. He had been one of my most ardent supporters during my Discernment, the process through which I had to pass to be accepted as a candidate for the priesthood.

"I apologize if I'm interrupting your prayers, my son."

I shook my head. "Nothing to interrupt, it seems."

He moved into the pew in front of me. "Is there anything I can do to help move things along?"

This wasn't a confession, and yet it felt as though one was called for. "I'm not at General any longer." I waved a hand. "Well, that is, I'm officially on leave. And I don't know whether to return."

If this surprised Father Fleming, he didn't let on. "What prompted the leave, may I ask?"

I looked into this kind man's eyes, so full of genuine concern, and I felt my shoulders slump in surrender. "I'm gay."

"I see." There was no hint of judgement, just acceptance. He looked around, then back at me. "I don't like to think we're disturbing others, but I would like to talk about this. Will you come into my office?"

I nodded, not entirely sure I wanted to talk at all, but—I was here.

He sat in one of the two chairs in front of his desk, and I took the other. He said, "So you fear being gay will interfere with your ability to minister?"

"I don't see…" Deep breath. "I don't see how I can feel fully alive in my role as a priest if I must be on guard not to reveal something important about myself. I don't see how I can work alongside priests who are allowed full lives when I am denied that very same freedom. I don't see—" Whatever I was about to say was lost in the catch of my breath as I attempted to stifle a sob. Tears filled my eyes. I dropped my head down and clenched my jaw hard.

"I hear you, Spencer. I understand. I can't say whether you would be able to go forward in full commitment. Many do, but there is always a price to pay. Most of us in the clergy are very much hoping things are changing for the better. Just look how far we've come with the ordination of women. But we are not there yet for you, and there's no telling whether we'll see those changes in our lifetimes. The Church moves slowly. It takes the long view."

I lifted my tear-stained face. "And in the meantime it leaves shattered lives in its wake."

"Oh, Spencer." His voice was gentle, but I heard no hope in it. "And how is your faith otherwise?"

"I came here to see if God had anything to say to me. I've been listening for weeks to no avail. I thought, perhaps here…."

"Have you asked for guidance?"

"It's why I'm here. And I've heard nothing. I've felt nothing but emptiness."

"You know, sometimes God doesn't speak to us directly. Sometimes His messages come through His servants."

"If that's you, what message is He sending through you?"

"Far be it from me to send promising young people away from the Episcopal priesthood. But consider that there are ministries other than the Episcopal Church. God is non-denominational."

I blinked stupidly. "What are you saying?"

"If ministering to God's people is truly your vocation, you might find fulfillment in another denomination."

I couldn't take in that idea. I sat back, stunned, a kind of shivering traveling through my body.

"Spencer, you need to weigh the vocation you feel called to against your attachment to the Episcopal Church. If you feel you cannot leave the church and you cannot live honestly as a priest within it, you can still remain quite involved with the parish of your choice. If, however, God is calling you to the ministry, perhaps His message is 'Not this one.'"

What you seek is not here. It was that dream, come to life in the words of Father Fleming.

I couldn't breathe. The idea of leaving the Episcopal Church had never occurred to me. It felt like anathema. It also felt like a door had just opened.

Father Fleming folded his hands in his lap. "Do you want a suggestion?"

I nodded; speech was not an option.

"I suggest you return to General and finish your Masters of Divinity. During this time, you can get a sense of whether you could live the kind of life you would need to, in order to live as a priest. If the answer is no, you still have the degree, and it could open the door into a different ministry. Or it could provide you with the beginnings of a career in teaching. There are so many ways to serve God, Spencer. The Episcopal Church is only one path. The priesthood is only one path."

"So… feeling this way, being who I am, might just be God sending me down another path?"

"It might very well be just that."

If that was true, then that voice from my dream might be referring more to the Episcopal priesthood than to the seminary itself.

"You've given me much to think about." I gave a short, humorless laugh. "Maybe too much."

"Keep asking God for guidance, Spencer. Keep the line of communication open. He will find ways to speak to you."

I sat up for a long time that night, my mind bouncing around at random. I recalled how it had felt, looking up at the rose window in St. John, furious that all the glory, the beauty, the ceremony there should have been mine. Is that what the church was to me? Flowing robes of rich colors, somber words heavy with meaning spoken to crowds of subdued worshippers? How important to me was the theatrical aspect of high mass, of the liturgical year, of the majesty of the priestly role itself? Because none of that was a calling. It wasn't a vocation. It was spectacle. It wasn't ministry.

I had told Dr. Connolly that I felt called to help people find unity with God. What props did I need in order to do that?

I fell asleep in the chair, no answers to show for all my mental ramblings.

CHAPTER FIFTEEN

Monday as I was finishing breakfast, the phone rang. It was Donald.

"Hey, I'm thinking that on a gorgeous day like today, even though it's a little cool, it's arguably insalubrious to hang around indoors. How would you like to give me a tour of Gramercy Park? I figure you're my only way in to see that statue of Edwin Thomas Booth."

I paused a little too long as my brain scrambled to define "insalubrious." So Donald spoke again.

"You do have a key to the park, right? I mean, I'm assuming, here…."

"I do. I do have a key." I stood and moved to where I could see out of the living room window to verify his assessment of the weather. "You've never been in there?"

"Be real, guy. How would I get in? You're the most well-heeled person I've ever met, let alone knowing anyone else who lives anywhere near that park. What do you say? And we could grab lunch someplace after."

So far, nothing he'd said smacked of the possibility of sex. "Sure. Let's do that. Do you want to meet there?"

"Only if you get there first. If I hang around loitering, I'm likely to get arrested. I could just come to your place. Ring the bell. Wait for you outside. Just so you're clear about my intentions."

So, no sex today. A sense of disappointment hung over the time I waited for the sound of my doorbell. After yesterday, this surprised me.

Turning the key in the Gramercy Park gate, I couldn't remember another time when I'd opened this for anyone but myself, with or without Mother. Visitors aren't forbidden, by any means, but I'd never brought anyone here—not even Tegan, who had specifically requested a visit.

Donald and I didn't talk much, except for when I described something, some tree that was special to me, or some planting that had significance for the park itself. Donald had referred to the Booth statue, so I walked him all around the park first before heading for the bench in front of it, glad to see that although there were other people in the park today, that bench was free. It's where I had sat after seeing Donald play Puck, and I had gazed at this same statue, determining to be no one's fool.

"Feel that marvelous apricity. Verily, spring has sprung."

"And what, pray tell—"

"The feel of warm sun coming through cooler air."

Donald's hands were in his jacket pockets, his eyes on the statue. I lay my hand between us on the bench, palm up, and watched the side of his face as a smile slowly lifted the corner of his mouth. Without looking at me, he pulled his hand out of the pocket and took mine with it.

We sat, silent, happy just to be together, for several minutes. Finally I said, "Did your father have a deep voice?"

"He thought he did."

"Do you resent him for being the reason you left the church?"

"Hmmm.... Resent...."

"Hate?"

He shook his head. "Oh, I try not hate anyone. That's where evil lives. Why throw yourself into that hell? I mean," and he turned to look at me, "you know as well as I do that what we give out to the world is what we get back."

"So love—?"

He nodded and turned to face the statue again. "Yeah, being loved is great. But the real joy comes from loving."

"That doesn't sound like what I know of the Lutheran Missouri Synod."

"And that was probably the single biggest reason I rejected it."

I felt my head shake slowly. "For someone who left the church behind, I think you're one of the most Christian people I know."

He laughed, pulled his hand away and leaned forward, elbows on knees, and rubbed his forehead. "Gah! My head hurts. Must be my horns coming in."

I chuckled. "Like a spring stag feeling his oats?"

Still leaning forward, he turned a roguish face toward me. "Sure. Those are the horns I meant." The sarcasm in his voice led me to understand the devilish reference he had intended.

He leaned back in the bench, hands back in his pockets, eyes still forward. "So. Spencer. Have you decided what to do with your life?"

"I'll tell you what I did yesterday. After I dropped you off."

I described my return to the church of my youth, my struggles to hear a message from God, and how it had come through Father Fleming.

After a few seconds of silence, Donald shifted on the bench, the leg near me bent so that his body faced me. "Let me get this straight. You went to an Episcopal church to find out what God wanted you to do. An Episcopal priest—your staunch advocate —told you to go preach someplace else. That's the message from God you've been waiting for?"

I shrugged. "Maybe."

"So, what are you going to do? Will you take his advice and go back to General?"

I rubbed my face with both hands. "I don't know. I don't know what the hell I'm going to do. I don't know what I *want* to do."

"Sounds like you're all in a zwodder." I felt Donald's hand on my shoulder. "Take me."

"What?"

"Take me to your church. To the one that drew you to God. I've seen what St. John has to offer. Let me meet St. Ignatius. I think I'll like him a lot better."

I smiled and shook my head gently. "How many times have you been inside a church since you arrived in New York?"

He was silent for long enough to confuse me. Then, "More often than you might have guessed."

I blinked stupidly, unsure what to say next. I stepped around his last comment. "Next Sunday is Easter. There will be lots of parishioners there. Lots of joyful hymns, lots of celebration of the risen Christ."

"I know all about the risen Christ. At least, from my Lutheran roots. I think it's the same Christ, yes?"

I tilted my head at him. "All right then. It's a date."

He stood. "Speaking of dates, is it time for lunch? I'm famished, and my stomach is wambling fit to beat the orchestra."

"Band."

"What?"

I laughed. "Never mind. Let's go."

⌖

I insisted on treating Donald to a restaurant where they had actual cloth on the tables, and cloth napkins, and small bud vases with a few fresh stems of colorful blossoms, and menus that weren't laminated, and stemware already set and waiting.

As we followed behind the host to our table, Donald whispered, "I'm not dressed for this, you know."

"It's only lunch. And it's Monday." I gave him a significant glance, delighted at my own clever reference to the theatre as I added, "A lot of these houses are dark on Mondays, you know."

"Oh, ha, ha."

Playful. I was playful. Who knew?

Donald had known.

He kept me entertained with his own brand of playfulness through our meal.

"Oh, take a gander at that debutante over there. To your left. Don't look! Her face is a lovely oval, kind of like a circle compressed by a Thigh Master."

Of course I looked, and Donald kicked my shin under the table. "Just take my word for it. And that matron behind me has a throaty laugh. You know, kind of like the sound a dog makes right before it throws up."

Later: "There's a young fellow behind you committing an act of Verschlimmbessern."

"Okay, now you're just showing off."

"Seriously! You should see the prodigious amount of salt he's pouring into his soup. He's making it worse by trying to improve it."

Later: "This antediluvian guy just came in with the most corvine hair I've ever seen. It's jet black and so thin upon his lily-white scalp that he can't possibly think he's pulling that look off."

And over dessert: "Give me a moment." He held a mouth full of food without chewing, his eyes closed. He swallowed and said, "Excellent. I needed to degust."

I tried not to smile and failed. "You can stop trying to impress me now."

"Hell, Spencer, this isn't about you. Look around you! This place is rife with cockalorums and snollygosters."

I threw him an artificially shocked look. "That includes us, you know!" I wasn't sure about snollygoster, but I knew a cockalorum is someone with a mistakenly favorable opinion of himself.

He dropped a hand at the wrist, a decidedly gay gesture. "Oh, honey, we're the worst of the bunch." In spite of myself, I laughed again, and then looked around for our waiter. I had to get Donald out of here before his enjoyment of our bottle of Chablis became any more obvious.

Out on the sidewalk, we stood before the restaurant's window, and Donald said, "That was heavenly. And now I'll take myself off home."

It felt as though my jaw wanted to drop. I'd had no specific plan for the rest of the day, or for the night, but I'd hoped that whatever happened next would involve Donald.

"You—but, well, how about if we go back to my place and listen to some music?"

He smiled and patted my cheek as if I were a child. "Not today, sweet man." He retracted his arm, hand back in a pocket as he turned toward the nearest subway station. Over his shoulder he said, "Always leave 'em wanting more."

How many times had I watched him walk away from me? And how many of those times had I felt so very powerfully as though I wanted to chase him down, heft him over my shoulder, and carry him off to my lair to do unmentionable things to him?

Once.

So far.

～

At home, I threw my coat aside and shed clothing as I made for my bedroom, where I masturbated like I'd never done before. This act had always felt like almost enough. Today it was nowhere near enough.

～

I didn't know what to expect in my Tuesday appointment with Dr. Connolly. My assignment had been those verses from the Gospel of Matthew. Certainly, I had given them a good deal of thought since Friday. And I believed they had finally revealed to me what she wanted me to see.

"You seem in good spirits today, Spencer."

I smiled and nodded. "I had a very interesting weekend." I took several minutes to describe everything that had happened, while she sat still and seemed to listen intently.

When I came to the end of my tale, she asked, "How do you feel about yourself today?"

I couldn't help smiling. "I think I understand what you wanted me to see in those verses from Matthew." She nodded, so I continued. "If I am to love God with all of my body, mind, and spirit—that is, with everything I am—then I can't leave any part of me out. The color of my eyes. Whichever hand is dominant. Whether I'm gay or straight or something in between. I have to love Him with all of me."

I waited to see if Dr. Connolly would comment, but she didn't. So I went on.

"The message of Jesus is a message of Love. Capital L. So loving God is first. Second, loving others as I love myself, makes no sense unless I love myself. So I'm commanded to do that."

I waited again, and this time she said, "And are you following both of those commandments fully?"

"Not yet. But I think I'm getting there. At least I know what I'm supposed to do."

"What about all those verses calling you an abomination?"

"'The whole law and the prophets depend on these two commandments,'" I quoted. "If there's a conflict between a law and what Jesus tells us is most important, He wins. Love wins."

I thought Dr. Connolly might be about to cry. Certainly her eyes watered. She took a deep breath and let it out slowly. "Have you made a decision about what you'll do next? Will you take Father Fleming's advice?"

"I'm giving it serious consideration. I think I need a little more time learning to love God with all of myself first. Loving myself might take a little longer. But I'm not saying I'll wait for perfection before making that decision."

"How does the idea of leaving your Episcopal roots make you feel?"

"A little lost. Well, at sea, anyway. It's been my world for so long. I just don't know whether I could love myself and live in that world as a priest without feeling as though there's an empty place inside me."

"You strike me as someone who will settle for nothing less than total commitment. I mean, you're an all-or-nothing kind of person. Do you see yourself that way?"

"I need a minute to think."

Was I like that? Was I so intense that I wasn't comfortable with—with what? With flexibility? With adaptability? Was I rigid? Intractable?

Finally I said, "I don't know. I don't want to be unyielding. Or stubborn. Is that what you see?"

"Not exactly, no. But I do wonder whether you're uncompromising when it comes to yourself. Whether you expect too much. The expectations you have of yourself seem to be set extremely high."

Something about her comment hit me hard. Almost without

thinking, I said, "That makes my head ache. Maybe my horns are growing in."

I was not prepared for what happened next. Dr. Connolly laughed. She laughed until tears rolled down her face. She was barely able to say, "Forgive me, Spencer. This is quite unprofessional. But you—Oh, my God!" And she laughed some more.

I joined in, although not quite with the same abandon.

It was a good session.

I wish I could say that the positive way I felt leaving my Tuesday appointment with Dr. Connolly had lasted longer than it did. I made it through the night, still on a kind of high. But Wednesday afternoon, when I was back at that coffee shop with Tegan, feeling good took at least a few steps back. It was as though in a game of "Mother, may I?" I'd forgotten to ask for permission when told I could move forward.

Tegan's invitation when she'd called that morning had been innocent enough.

"Hey, Spencer. Just thought you might like to catch up on some seminary gossip. How about meeting me at our place around four?"

"Our place?"

"Almond biscotti?"

"Ah. All right. See you there."

So I went, and I think we sat at the same table, and we ordered the same things. There wasn't really a lot of gossip to talk about, but I hadn't been fooled; I knew she wanted to know what was going on with me. After a few minutes of superficial pleasantries (how her father was doing, what she was working on in classes, and me doing my best not to say "No, I'm really doing nothing at all with my days"), she got down to business.

"Have you given any more thought to returning? It's still an option, isn't it?"

"It is. As far as I know, anyway."

"And?"

I could have told her about my visit to St. Ignatius, but for some reason I felt guarded. "Of course I've thought about it. No decision, though."

She tilted her head as though to see me from a different angle. "What are you doing with yourself? Couldn't you be doing some work privately, just to keep up?"

"I suppose I could. It was offered."

"And?"

"There's no 'and,' Tegan."

We regarded each other silently for several seconds. Then, "Are you and God talking again yet?"

I was tempted to ask whether she was deliberately ministering to me. Instead, I said, "In a manner of speaking." God and I had communicated, if Father Fleming had been correct, through him. Maybe even through Dr. Connolly.

Tegan's face, and her tone, indicated impatience. "Spencer, I understand what's holding you back. I really do. You were very clear about that the last time we met. But I have to ask: Are you throwing away your vocation based on a feeling you haven't really tested yet?"

"I have no idea what that means."

She touched a finger to her forehead, a gesture of frustration, and perhaps a stalling tactic. "On one hand, you have a promising future in the Church. On the other, you have vague feelings you haven't tested, feelings you believe will hold you back—"

"Vague feelings? What do you mean, not tested?"

"Well, last time we met here, I took you to mean that you hadn't actually… you know."

It took me a few seconds to get her meaning. "Wait. You

think I'm—shall we say, inexperienced? You think I haven't ever had sex with a man?" I stretched my mind back to our last conversation, struggling to remember anything that might have led her to think I was a virgin. If I'm honest, I also didn't want to admit how close to correct that assumption would have been at the time.

Her head pulled back, suddenly, just a little. "I thought you had implied as much, talking to me across this very table."

I shook my head. "Sorry if I misled you. I'm not inexperienced. And my feelings are not, as you put it, 'vague' or 'untested.' On the contrary."

"I see." Tegan's face was unreadable. The silence between us felt stony. She toyed with her biscotti for a few seconds. "Are you in a relationship now?"

None of your business, I wanted to say. But if I considered her a friend, why would I hide that aspect of my life?

"In a manner of speaking." It was the second time I'd spoken that phrase. Perhaps I was being vague after all?

"And it seems you aren't willing to give it up."

"What did you say?" My tone was pure ice.

"I mean, otherwise, why wouldn't you do what you could to get back into the seminary?"

"Tegan, you're the one who said not to go 'all fundamentalist.' Did that advice apply only to gay candidates and priests who remain chaste?"

Her tone changed suddenly to something close to dismissive. "Oh, now, don't get all huffy. In fact, maybe a solid relationship would be a good thing. If you can get through seminary without an indiscretion that would get you into trouble, that would bode well for life as a priest."

Disbelief made me shake my head. "Were you not listening last time? That isn't a life I want to live. I shouldn't be denied the same kind of full life, as full a relationship, as any other priest."

"But it's not the same kind of life."

"What are you talking about?"

She leaned a little over the table toward me, her voice just above a whisper. "Spencer, you're gay. Relationships for you will be very different from what they'd be if you were straight."

Was I hearing her correctly? Was she telling me that as a gay man, I would be incapable of having a relationship that would last?

Was she right?

I sat back in my chair. Whether she was right or not, I was not going to yield the point to her. "If a straight married couple were to go through a rough patch, especially if one of them is a priest, the entire community—other priests, and parishioners who knew about it—everyone would rally around and do whatever they could to support that couple, to encourage them to work things out.

"But if that couple were gay?" I gave a snort. "Tegan, if that couple were gay, everyone around them would just throw their hands into the air. 'Oh, well, what can you expect?' they'd say. 'It was bound to happen,' they'd say. No one would try to help. No one would offer support." I leaned forward, my voice a hoarse whisper. "If gay relationships fail, maybe it's not just because we're gay. Maybe it's also because we're expected to fail. Maybe it's because no one *wants* to support us. Did you ever think of that?"

"Of course I have. Spencer, I've had several gay friends. I've seen what their lives are like. I know what I'm talking about."

I threw a handful of bills on the table and stood. "Really. Well, however many gay friends you've had, what you're saying tells me you're as ignorant as everyone else."

I heard Tegan call my name twice before I made it out to the sidewalk.

～

By the time I got home, my shins hurt because of how hard and how fast I had planted my feet on the pavement. Initially it was because of how angry I was. Then it was because of how hurt I was. But then it became about how confused I was.

It's true I'd given a lot of thought to the discrimination that would prevent me from living a full life as a priest. But in none of that thinking had I pictured myself in whatever semblance of marriage I could have with a man. I hadn't imagined a scenario where my partner would have the same role as my female spouse would have had. I hadn't pictured him visiting sick parishioners. Or hosting pancake suppers. Or organizing "bring and buy" events or bake sales. Or pressing my surplice or ordering replacement collars.

And I certainly hadn't given any thought at all to what it would be like to live with a man as my "married" partner, let alone what would happen if our relationship began to founder. Yet that's exactly what I'd thrown at Tegan. That is, she wouldn't support us. No one would support us. I didn't even know if that were true. But it certainly felt as though it would be true.

What *was* true was that if I were in that relationship with a man, I could not be a priest in the Episcopal Church. Not until such time as Father Fleming and a few others hoped for, when the Church would turn itself around, a long and awkward barge in a narrow canal, and accept me the way God made me.

Sitting alone at Mother's kitchen table, working my way excruciatingly slowly through my dinner because of thinking so hard between forkfuls, I began to feel resigned. It was a resignation that came from a place of anger and hurt, but no longer from confusion. I would probably resume my studies at General in the autumn. I would take whatever remedial courses I could over the summer. And if I went forward, I would earn my Masters of Divinity as an unashamed, unrepentant gay man. I would live life as though I loved myself, even as I was still learning how to do that—not only because it felt absolutely necessary, but also because I was commanded to do so by Jesus Himself.

And I would remind anyone who needed reminding what the two most important commandments were—and what they meant to me.

My self-absorbed ruminations were interrupted by the ringing of the telephone. In no mood to talk to anyone, I stood before the thing and waited for the sixth ring, when the answering machine would kick in, and I could hear any message being left.

"Spencer? Um, this is Tegan. Listen, I want to apologize. I'm so sorry I offended you. That isn't what I wanted to do at all. I just—oh, Spencer, I just don't want to see you throw away your gift. I know you'd make a wonderful priest. I really hope you don't give up. And please don't let my stupid comments affect your decision. Please. Again, I'm so sorry."

I think it was this message that gave me the push I needed. But I would have to be very brave. I would have to be very determined. If the Church managed to turn itself around in that canal before I finished at General, so much the better. But if it didn't, then so be it. I would do whatever I had to do.

I was not going to tell God, "Hey, God, great job, here. Beautiful world, and all that. There is just one tiny mistake, though. I mean, you made me gay. But don't worry. I'll fix that for you. And if I can't, I'll lie."

Lying about who I was began to feel like slapping God in the face. I would not do that. I would not live a lie.

CHAPTER SIXTEEN

Thursday morning I called Donald. I was ready, I'd decided, to start being brave, to admit to myself and anyone else who cared that I was who I was. I would make no apologies about it. And if I wanted to be with a man, if I wanted to hold a man's hand in public, then—damn it—that's what I would do.

He wasn't home, or he didn't answer. I left a message: "Spencer here. I'm hoping we can get together in the next day or so. There are a few things I'd like to talk with you about."

After I hung up, I began to worry. What if he was out walking through parks with another man? What if he was actually home, but was making love with another man? What if he'd decided I wasn't, after all, someone he could grow to love? What if he'd found another Jonathan who wasn't me?

I told myself I wasn't exactly ready to be his next Jonathan. Not quite, anyway. I wasn't ready for a step like that. And, after all, Donald was the first man I'd ever been with, so how did I know what I wanted in a partner?

And then I told myself that even if I wasn't Donald's next Jonathan, I wasn't about to go out and find someone else to start a relationship with. This was my first one; and, all right, it wasn't likely to lead to permanence, but it would be the first romantic relationship I'd ever had. Ever. In my entire, fucking life. I didn't want it to end prematurely.

The look on Donald's face when he'd realized I was a virgin plagued my mind's eye. He'd been not just astounded, but almost all the way to horrified. He'd said he didn't want to be the one to show me to myself. He didn't want to watch me figure out that I was now a kid in a candy shop. He didn't want to teach me how to love a man and then have to watch me go off and do just that, elsewhere.

Why would he want to be in a relationship with me? Why would he want to take that risk? He'd be crazy. So he probably was seeing someone else. Maybe more than one. All right, so he'd told me he wouldn't ever again sleep with someone he knew he couldn't love. But that still left a lot of men in the picture frame.

Who was I to him? Just one more possibility? And not a very promising one, at that, because of that candy shop beckoning to me even as he began to love me.

By the time Donald called me back, late in the afternoon, I'd spun myself into a tizzy. I'd gone back and forth between wanting to see where things with him could lead and feeling like just one more fish in the proverbial sea, and the bouncing had left me emotionally bruised, needy, and painfully vulnerable.

"Hey, Spencer. What's up?"

What's up? Is that how you respond to a lover? Or even to a potential lover?

When I didn't speak quickly enough, he asked, "Everything okay? You said you wanted to talk?"

I was feeling less like I wanted to talk with him than I'd felt since we'd met. But I had said that. "Yes. If that's okay with you."

"I have a show tonight. Can we meet after that? Or maybe tomorrow afternoon?" He sounded so casual, as though setting a time to get together for drinks with a friend.

An actor. He was probably seeing another actor.

I clenched my jaw. "Let's say tomorrow afternoon. I'll come to your place. Is three o'clock good?"

If I had tortured myself before Donald had called back, the shape I was in after that phone call was as though I'd spent a day on a medieval rack while little demons stabbed at my naked body with pointed sticks. Once or twice I remonstrated myself with the idea that I was enjoying the torture, that it was allowing me to feel wronged and righteous and virtuous, deserving of vengeance and retribution. Three or four times I managed to remind myself that I was the one performing this torture, that I could stop any time.

I spent a sleepless night, feeling alternately like a sulky teenager and a jilted lover.

My Friday one o'clock session with Dr. Connolly did something, metaphorically speaking, that Father used to threaten when I misbehaved: It jerked a knot in my tail. In her usual way, she goaded me until I confessed to the self-flagellation I'd indulged in because of what were unsubstantiated suspicions about Donald.

"So which is it?" Dr. Connolly asked. "Is he seeing other men and therefore unworthy despite not having said he wouldn't do that, or will you try every piece of candy in the store, now that you've acquired a taste for sugar, making you the unworthy one?"

I stared at her. "There's no way to answer that."

"Indeed." We sat in silence for maybe a minute. Then, "Spencer, the last time you were here, you said you knew what you needed to do. You said one of the things Jesus commanded was for you to love yourself."

"I also said I wasn't there yet."

"Agreed. Many people are not. What I want you to think about is the gulf between what you put yourself through yesterday and your intention to follow that commandment."

She was right. What I'd done to myself was not in line with loving myself. That didn't make me a bad person. It meant only that while I was tying myself into emotional knots, it never occurred to me that I was acting against my own spiritual interests. It would have been one thing to have those concerns trouble me. It was another to enable them to continue doing that for hours.

So on my way to meet Donald after my session with Dr. Connolly, I did my best to pare away the flotsam and jetsam of yesterday and arrive at what was important. And what was important was what I needed to tell Donald.

By the time I climbed the stairs to Donald's apartment I was no longer in a froth. I felt deflated, emotionally collapsed, and more like a man being led to the gallows than like someone about to meet his lover.

Donald leaned against the frame of the open doorway, arms crossed, an inscrutable expression on his face.

"Come in." He stepped aside and closed the door behind me, sliding the police bar into place. "Take your jacket?"

I plunged my hands deep into the jacket pockets. "I'm not sure how long I'll be here."

He let out a noisy breath and walked to one of the two chairs in the tiny space. "Then let's get right to it. What did you want to say?" His tone told me he had some idea already, and that served to confirm my suspicions.

"I had a conversation yesterday with a classmate from General. It helped convince me that I need to be who I am, no apologies, no excuses, and no nonsense from anyone." I paused, more because I didn't know what to say next than from any sense of instilling drama.

He scowled. "Do you feel like you're getting nonsense from me?"

I shook my head. "No. Not nonsense. But the thing is, I need to move forward. I need to begin living life as who I am. And I need to be with someone willing to do that with me, at least for a while, and not with anyone else. That person would be my only partner. And I'd need to be his."

He looked totally confused, so I added, "And I gather that isn't you." My voice nearly broke. I did not want to end things with Donald. But he was forcing me to.

"What—I—you—Spencer, what the fuck are you getting at?"

"I get the sense I'm only one of some number of... well, of people for you."

"You 'get the sense.' I don't know what that means. What gives you that sense?"

A jolt of something hit me from somewhere. It was the realization that I had no good answer for that question.

He said, "You think I'm seeing other men? Is that what you mean?" He threw back his head and laughed. "Oh, my God, Spencer. You silly man. Don't you know I'm head over heels in love with you?"

Tears stung my eyes. I could barely hear my own voice say, "You are?"

"Well, at least head over heels in lust. Maybe it's a little early to be exchanging the big L word with each other. But—seeing other men?" He smiled and shook his head. "That ain't me, honey. I'm a one-man's man. I thought I made that clear the last time you were here."

I had to clear my throat. "You said you wouldn't sleep with someone you knew you couldn't love."

He shrugged. "Okay, all right, I admit that's not quite the same thing. So let me be clear now. I want you, Spencer Hill. I want you, and right now for as long as we want each other, you're the only man I'll want." He chuckled. "Or at least the only man I'll be with. After all," and he waved a floppy hand, "there are a lot of men out there. But they'll have to wait."

A loud puff of air escaped me, a kind of sobbing sigh. But I was too happy to weep. I closed my eyes.

"So, are we okay? Is that what you wanted to talk about?"

I looked at him, feeling my shoulders slump in relief. "I guess I was having unreasonable doubts."

He shook his head, his expression fond. "And are they gone? Do you trust what I'm telling you?"

I nodded, and he stood and reached for my hands. We held each other for what felt like seconds but was probably closer to a minute and a half.

He pulled away enough to reach up and hold my face in his hands. "I want you, Spencer. I want to be with you. I want to sleep with you and fuck with you and share meals with you and laugh with you and cry with you. I want to memorize all the lines on your palms and bury my face in your crotch until all I can smell is your musk. I want to hear you play the piano for hours. I want to talk with you about philosophy and religion and literature and art. I want to gossip about silly people we meet and get as angry as you do when we aren't treated like real people because we're together."

He paused, as if waiting for me to speak. But I couldn't. I was too ecstatic.

"Do you want those things with me?"

"Yes." A strangled whisper was all I could manage.

One side of his mouth lifted in a sly grin. "And are you ready to show me? Over there?" He tilted his head toward his bed.

I shrugged out of my jacket and, wanting to do something—anything—surprising, I slid one arm behind his shoulder and another behind his knees. I lifted him up and carried him the few steps to the bed. And I made love to him. With him. I nuzzled his neck. I gripped his scalp with my hands, pulling his head back until his mouth opened wide enough to let me nearly caress his throat with my tongue. I sucked his nipples and squeezed his ass and massaged his balls and bit his thighs until he cried out.

"Fuck me! Oh, God, Spencer! Fuck me now!"

I barely got the condom on in time.

We dozed until around four-thirty, when Donald had to shower and get ready for his show.

When he emerged from the bathroom, I was lying on the bed, genitals exposed, an arm behind my head. "Can I come see your play?"

He grinned and tossed me something metallic. "Believe me. You don't want to."

I glanced at what I'd caught: a key ring, with three keys on it. "What's this?"

He gave me an arch look. "Sweetie, if you don't know, then we just wasted an afternoon. It's the keys to my place, silly. The thickest one is the outer door. The one with the yellow dot is for the police lock. Take your time showering, and lock up before you leave. And take those with you."

Giddy. I was positively giddy. He'd just given me the keys to his home. I was still staring foolishly at those metallic representatives of regard when he finished dressing and came over to the bed. He pulled me to my feet and gave me a deep, loving kiss.

"I'll be out by ten-thirty or so. Can I come to you after?"

I grinned idiotically. "I'll feed you. Bring a change of clothes this time. I can give you your own toothbrush."

"Throw in my own bathrobe and we'll call it a deal." He winked and was gone.

Joy. Joy like I'd never felt. Don't misunderstand me; I'd felt joy before, many times, mostly the kind associated with religious passion. This was different. So it was joy like I'd never felt before.

For the first time in my life, I was in a relationship. A real, honest-to-goodness-romantic-sexual-fabulous relationship. I knew that there would be ups and downs, that not all would be sunshine and roses. But—holy crap.

I bought groceries and flowers on my way home, for a post-theater dinner and breakfast and just to make the place look welcoming. As I waited for my lover (an old-fashioned term, perhaps, but I relished it) to arrive, I listened to piano music by Schubert. His lyric, melodious style—deceptively simple, I knew from experience—was romantic without being sugary.

As I listened, I pondered the difference between the joy I had felt in the past from my connection with God and the joy I felt now, because of a connection with another person. Did this latest joy seem more intense because it was more recent? God was perfect. Donald was not. I was not. Did imperfection make love easier? Was God's perfection perhaps even a little off-putting?

What I wanted to believe, based on those verses from Matthew, was that my feelings for Donald were like a window into the incomprehensibly massive Presence that is God. Isn't that why God came to us as Jesus? So that humans, with our limited capacities, could have a personal aspect of God to relate to?

I had nearly fallen asleep when I heard the bell that signaled someone at the front door. As soon as I opened it, everything about the quiet, empty house changed. Donald gave me a quick kiss as he breezed past me.

"What a weird play! I'm not even going to tell you about it. It made no sense to me, and I was the lead character. But I take the parts I can get. For now. Maybe someday…."

Donald devoured nearly half of the roast chicken I'd bought, pre-cooked. Between us we killed a bottle of sauvignon blanc. We made short work of the pastries I'd bought for dessert, and I had to protect the ones I'd bought for breakfast or he would have eaten those as well.

"You must be too full to move," I told him.

He sighed and nodded. "I don't eat like this often. Gotta keep my slim, girlish figure. But happiness makes my hungry." He grinned at me. "That said, it might be a little while before I'm up for ravishing you."

I laughed. "That's worth waiting for. You sit there while I do a little clean-up."

"Are you going to play piano for me again? Please?"

He made it so easy to tease him. "What, you think because you've been entertaining others all evening, you can come here and demand to be entertained? Is that all you want me for?"

"And there he is again, folks, the playful guy he didn't know was in him."

I did play for him. I played piece after piece while Donald sat, peaceful and contented, in an easy chair, listening. I played Chopin, of course. Beethoven. Schubert. Debussy. There was no

particular order to the pieces I chose; they weren't even chrono-
logical. But they were all contemplative, gentle.

By the time I stopped and looked up, he was asleep. I sat still
and watched him, saw his chest smoothly rising and falling,
heard the soft sound of his breathing, noticed the slight slack-
ening of his face.

Quietly I left the room and went into Mother's room.
Although she had not indulged herself in most ways, she'd
relished well-made nightclothes. And she had at least four
bathrobes. I chose a plush, soft blue robe, standard style with a
belt, and laid it across the chair in my bedroom. I stood there for
a moment, assessing my feelings about what I was doing. Father
had been even taller than I was, so any robe of his would have
swallowed Donald. But was I really comfortable, I asked myself,
letting Donald use one of Mother's?

I nodded and whispered, "Yes." If I put aside the fact that I'd
never know how she would have reacted to my being gay, I felt
sure Mother would have approved of the happiness I felt. She
would have been delighted to see me like this. Letting Donald
use her robe would have been just fine with her.

We didn't have sex that night. We slept together in my bed,
always touching somewhere—legs, hands, sides, foreheads—and
although I didn't sleep very much, the sense of peace, the depth
of contentment I felt did more to refresh me than anything else
could have done.

Morning was a different story, sex-wise. I would never have
imagined what Donald showed me how to do. He grinned his
Puck-ish grin and said, "How about we take advantage of
morning wood?"

As I reclined on my side, and he on his, his head at my knees
and mine at his, we gave each other head, as the expression goes,

simultaneously. It was the first time I'd swallowed his cum. It felt like a very special kind of baptism.

Later, over breakfast at a nearby diner, he asked, "So who is this classmate who convinced you to fuck men with abandon?"

Something between a snort and a chuckle escaped me. My tone teasingly remonstrating, I said, "Now, wait. I thought we agreed not to go around fucking other men."

Donald's eyes opened wide. "I'm not sure why, but I'm shocked to hear you use that word. Not in a bad way, mind you."

I laughed and shook my head. "I can't remember the last I said 'fuck' aloud within anyone else's hearing." I pointed my fork at him. "You're a bad influence."

"Thank you. Now, who was that person?"

"Her name is Tegan. She and I were in a production of *Everyman* last December. I think she very much wants me to return to seminary."

"Does she have a crush on you?"

"Oh, I don't think so. She knows I'm gay."

"And does she have a crush on you?"

"What are you suggesting?"

He waved his fork. "Never mind. Doesn't matter. What did she say?"

"She's convinced I have a lot of promise as a priest."

"She doesn't think having to hide who you are would be a problem?"

"It was a little confusing to me. I think she said that of course my life would be different, but—" What the hell *had* she said, anyway? "Something about how my life would be different regardless, because I'd never have a partner the way I would if I were straight."

"You mean, whether you're a priest or not?"

He was right. That was the point she was trying to make. "Yes. I think it was somewhere between not having just one sexual partner and not being able to maintain a committed relationship. And if that implied undesirable way of life was going to be mine anyway, why not live it chaste, as a priest." I scrunched my face up, perplexed. "I think that's what she meant."

Donald took a mouthful of scrambled eggs, chewed and swallowed, and, looking down at his plate as he loaded his fork again, said, "Don't ever let me anywhere near her."

"Why not?"

"I suspect I would not fare well in prison." He burped loudly, looked astonished, and added, "Oh, my. Pardon my unpardonable eructation!"

~

Walking back to my house, Donald said, "Are we on for Easter services at St. Iggy's tomorrow?"

"If you're sure you want to do that." I wouldn't have gone on my own, and I wasn't entirely sure I wanted to take Donald, but if that's what he wanted....

"I do. I have a show this afternoon and again tonight, so I'll just stop by your place now long enough to pick up my things. So, would you prefer not to spend tonight together before going to God's house tomorrow, where you'd have to confess your many sins?"

"You're joking, yes?"

"Only a little."

"St. Ignatius of Antioch Episcopal," I said, leaning on the full name of the church, "is way uptown. If you have a show tonight, would you rather be in your own place for the night, even though you're farther away from our destination, or would you rather show up at my place, fresh clothes in hand, after the show?"

He stopped walking. "I like the way you think. Very rational. Your place, I think. I'll take my Sunday clothes to the theater."

~

It felt decidedly, gloriously sinful to have sex with Donald the night before going to Easter services. Twice.

In the morning I woke first and was soaping myself in the shower when suddenly I was not alone. Wrapping his arms around me from behind, Donald pressed his genitals against my ass.

"Good morning, gorgeous." I stiffened, and he released me. "Too much?"

I closed my eyes and took a deep breath. "No. Just unexpected."

"Good." He resumed his embrace and slid his hands down to my crotch. "May I help you wash up?"

I gasped audibly as my penis throbbed into life. Donald chuckled. Neither of us spoke as he worked me into a lather that had nothing to do with soap. As I leaned against the shower wall, I said, "I am going to have so very much to confess today."

Donald laughed. "But wait. There's more." And he guided my hand to his erection and braced his back against the tiles as I returned the favor he'd given me.

I watched his face as his breathing calmed. He opened his eyes and smiled. "God, but I love being gay."

It was a sentiment I wanted to share but didn't. Not quite. Not yet.

"St. Ignatius is a far cry from St. John," I told Donald in the cab ride uptown.

"How so?"

"It's not a cathedral, for starters. I love the place, and I think it's truly beautiful. But it isn't nearly as impressive."

"Or as overwhelming?"

"Were you overwhelmed?"

"Absolutely."

I didn't know whether to take him seriously or not, but it didn't matter.

We joined the throng of people heading inside the church; as I'd predicted, many parishioners would attend Easter mass.

Sotto voce, Donald said, "Look at all the finery. This is a well-heeled group of people, eh?"

I just shrugged and found us a place about two-thirds of the way back, away from the aisle. Donald sat and then stood again immediately.

"What on earth," he pointed, "is that?"

"The baptismal font." It was truly eye-catching. The white marble stand, and the bowl to hold holy water, were surmounted with an ornate, gilded spire that came to a peak fully three times the height of the marble stand.

I added, "We can go closer after the service, if you like. It depicts St. John the Baptist, as well as symbols representing water. The candles there are lit today for the first time since Epiphany. They represent the risen Christ."

Donald shook his head slowly and whispered, "I have my doubts as to whether Jesus would have approved of all this expense."

"Maybe not, but He chastised Judas, who criticized Mary when she washed His feet with expensive oil, saying the money for it could be used to help the poor. Jesus told Judas, 'You always have the poor with you, but you won't always have me.' So, who knows?"

Donald was mostly quiet through the service. He followed along in the Prayer Book and did his best to respond to the liturgy. He sang harmony to the hymns. But he couldn't help himself when the organist took harmonic liberties with the hymns' final verses, which it seems all organists are wont to do, perhaps to relieve their boredom from everything else they have to play.

Donald whispered, "Why is it they always 'f' with the last

verse? That's when I want to sing the loudest, but the harmonies are all 'f-ed' up!"

I think the high point for Donald was the changing of the garb. He gasped as the clergy at the altar, with their backs to the nave, removed their deep purple chasubles and robes and donned raiment of white and gold.

Donald leaned toward me. "Christ is risen!" Then, "Do we clap now?"

I stifled a giggle and did my best to ignore him.

"How will we know when it's over? Will there be a stage curtain?"

"Will you stop?"

"I'll try. But, Spencer, maybe this isn't a cathedral, but it's still quite a show."

After the service, as Donald and I stood at the baptismal font so he could see it more closely, I heard a voice behind me.

"I'm so glad to see you here today, Spencer."

Father Fleming beamed first at me and then at Donald. Fumbling my words, I introduced them.

"Welcome, Donald. I hope you will both join us again." Father Fleming smiled broadly and walked away, no doubt to save me from my own ridiculous embarrassment. Doubtless, he knew enough about who Donald was to me to know that I would be at least disconcerted by the encounter.

"I hope you've seen enough," I said quietly. "Ready to leave?"

Donald turned toward me and, I'm sure, was prepared with some sardonic rejoinder. But he seemed to swallow his words when he saw my face, where my distress must have been clear. "Sure. Let's go."

We found our way to a nearby Jewish deli, where we both

ordered cheese blintzes. We sat back, waiting for our coffee to arrive, and he said, "You okay?"

I took a shaky breath. "There's no reason I shouldn't be. I mean, Father Fleming knows about me, so even though he must have known we were together it wouldn't have mattered. And he was friendly enough. I'm just not used to this."

"This? What this is that?"

I waved a hand as though that would help put me at ease. It didn't. "Oh, you know. Being seen in public as gay."

His face playful, he said, "I didn't hold your hand or anything."

I laughed. "No. And thank you. But, Donald, that was my childhood church. That's where I grew up. That's where I learned to love God, and where I made the decision to serve Him and His people. And now—"

The waitress set our coffees before us and left.

"And now?"

"I know. I know. I can still do that. Just not in the way I always pictured. And being there, in that church, draws a hard line between what I wanted, what I can't have, and the only options open to me."

"Spencer?" He waited until I looked at him. "I'm sorry. I shouldn't have asked you to do this. I should have known it would be difficult for you, even if I wasn't with you, and even more if I was. I'm not sure why…." His voice trailed off.

The blintzes arrived. Each of us stared down at them for several seconds. I didn't know what to say. Probably Donald didn't either.

Finally he sighed. "Can't have these getting cold."

We ate at least half our meal in silence. Then he said, "I think I wanted to see another church service, is all. I mean, sure, both this and St. John are Episcopal, but when I said I was over-whelmed earlier? In the cab? It wasn't just the grandeur and the glitz. It was the meaning."

"I don't follow."

"Do you remember once I told you I missed religion?"

I nodded. "You also said you didn't pray because it hurts too much."

"Oh, yeah. I did say that. Well, it does. But I don't want it to. Sometimes I think if my father hadn't ruined religion for me, I'd still belong to a church somewhere. Just not," and he looked at me from under his eyebrows, "the Missouri Synod."

I smiled. "You could join St. Ignatius."

He shook his head. "Don't think so. Nice place and all, but way too frou-frou. Though I did like how many families were there together."

At first I wasn't sure what to make of that. But then I remembered his exchange with the young boy in the park, the day I'd spied on him. He'd seemed like a natural. I didn't pursue it. "What do you think you would want in a church?"

He sat back and pushed his empty plate a little to one side. "A place where I feel not just okay. Not just tolerated. I want to feel welcome. Like I belong." He grinned. "I think maybe I'm looking for a tribe."

"I don't think I know what that means."

"Neither do I, really."

"Well… I think I felt like part of a tribe, so maybe I do know. I felt it especially at General, like it was mine alone, not anything to do with my parents." I looked out the window for a moment, seeing nothing. Then, on impulse and for reasons I couldn't have explained, I said, "Would you like to see it?"

"See what?"

"General. Just the grounds, though."

He chuckled. "Yeah, that's about as far as they'd allow a heathen like me. Or maybe I'd just peer through the wrought iron fence, if there is one, like the street urchin I am."

"So, you'd like to? This afternoon?"

He watched my face as he said, "It wouldn't be too much for

you? I mean, it's part of what you've given up. To be fully yourself."

I nodded slowly, thinking. Did I speak too impulsively? Was I up for this? Or would it be too much like how I'd felt today when Father Fleming had talked to us? Was I willing to test myself a little more? Would I handle myself any better at General, which in some ways would be a bigger challenge for having been my religious home more recently?

As though jumping directly into freezing cold water, I said, "If I do go back, it will be as a gay man who doesn't need to hide."

Donald looked at me from the corners of his eyes. "It might feel like ripping the bandage off. Are you sure?"

I laughed. "No. But I don't want that to stop me."

"It's like some remote hermitage," was Donald's take, as we stood in the close at General, trees around us just beginning to show pale green leaves, spring bulb flowers showing off their Easter colors. The brick buildings around us appeared less formidable than in winter but still diffident, almost unwelcoming, only slightly softened by the burgeoning nature around them.

"Hermitage?"

He shrugged. "You know. A place apart from the world. Protected. Sheltered. But not cushy. Not soft. Nothing that would coddle you."

We stood quietly while I considered his impressions and compared them to mine, both when I'd felt at home here and now that I felt more like an outsider. I regarded the place through the eyes of someone who would very likely come here again, to learn, to gain a certain authority, but not to further the specific mission the place pointed toward.

"Spencer?"

I turned, startled, to see Tegan. Her pure white coat and blond hair echoed the colors of the service I'd just attended. Only a touch of purple eye shadow hinted at the change from Lent to Easter.

Painfully conscious of the fact that Donald, beside me, had also turned to face Tegan, I nearly stammered. "Hello. Um, happy Easter. Christ is risen."

She tilted her head charmingly. "Christ is risen."

We stared at each other until Donald said, "Is that some kind of ritual greeting? Should I say it, too, or is it only for the initiated?"

"I'm sorry," I said, flustered, grabbing figuratively for the manners I'd been taught. "Tegan Langley, this is Donald Rainey. Donald, Tegan."

She shifted a basket from her right arm to her left so she could extend her freed hand. "Pleased to meet you, Donald Rainey." She eyed him closely as if to discern why I would be attracted to him. I held my breath; he had once implied he would murder her.

"And you, Miss Langley."

She reached into her basket, and from the tangle of green plastic strings she extracted a brilliantly wrapped foil egg shape and held it toward him. "Allow me to extend the offer of Pagan fertility, as delivered by a mythological rabbit."

"Ooh, I love Pagan rituals. And you in your rabbit-white fur! Thank you. Though I could do without the fertility. As long as it's just chocolate inside...."

She laughed. "It is. Spencer? One for you?"

I took the colorful object she held out to me. "Thanks."

Donald had unwrapped his already. "Fabulous. Dark chocolate."

"Of course!" Tegan chirped. "Nothing else is really chocolate, don't you agree?"

They regarded each other long enough for me to wonder what secret meaning was passing between them. Finally Tegan turned to me.

"What brings you here today, Spencer?"

I lifted a shoulder, going for nonchalance and fully aware of failing. "We attended mass uptown this morning. This is a kind of field trip, really."

To Donald, she said, "So you're not considering becoming a candidate? That's too bad." I heard something in her voice that was an odd mix of genuine regret and teasing sauciness.

"No, alas. I'm hopelessly reprobate."

"Oh, you shouldn't let that stop you. Most of us here are, too." Her laugh was musical, flirtatious. "Well, I must dash. Nice to see you, Spencer. Truly. And Donald, don't be a stranger." She smiled sweetly and turned away. We watched as the movement of her body brought the purity of the white coat into question.

"Tell me," Donald asked, "does she have a lot of gay friends?"

Surprised, I said, "According to what she's told me, yes. Either has or had. Why?"

He turned away from Tegan's retreating path and looked up at me. "She's a hag." He moved away from me, toward the street.

I caught up with him. "A hag? *Tegan?* But she's lovely! I know you said you didn't want to meet her. Is that why you called her that?"

He waited until we were on the sidewalk, outside the grounds, before he said, "Very lovely. She's charming. Great accent. And she's a fag hag."

I shook my head, confused. "What does that mean?"

"Walk with me."

"Where are we going?"

"East."

He said nothing else until we reached the river, almost the very spot where I had dubbed myself Lucifer not so very long ago. With about six inches between us, we leaned our arms on the railing and gazed across the water, which was calm today if looking slightly grey.

"A fag hag," Donald said finally, "is a straight woman who hangs out with gay men. She typically has a number of gay friends, though commonly she will latch onto one of them in particular, and his gay friends become hers. She enjoys flirting with them, dating them when the opportunity arises, and on rare occasions even having sex with them if they're into that."

"Why would she do that?"

He shrugged. "It could be that flirtation with a gay man is safe. Usually there's no sex, so the flirtation can be indefinitely maintained. He can use her as his 'beard,' as the saying goes, when he wants to appear straight, with her traveling on his arm to social events, while both of them act for all the world as if they're together romantically. It's also possible that a hag might want to avoid relationships with straight men, for her own reasons."

He turned away from the water and leaned with his bent arms on the railing. "If you recall, one of the plays I had in mind for you was *California Suite*. Neil Simon wrote it. Most people know it because of the film that came out a few years ago, in nineteen seventy-eight. Five different couples converge on Hollywood at the same time for different reasons. A lot of it is comedic. I was going to have you work on the parts that involve one of the couples, Diana Barrie and Sidney Cochran. She's an actress up for an Oscar. He's gay. Their marriage is pretty much in name only, but as the story unfolds we see that while Sidney admires and even loves Diana in his own fashion, she loves and desires him in a more traditional way."

He looked at me as if waiting to see if I had any comment. I didn't.

"Diana is not exactly a fag hag. But she exemplifies the corner a fag hag can paint herself into. Because very often the hag either fancies herself in love with her gay man, or she is genuinely in love with him. But here's the thing a lot of hags don't get."

Donald pushed away from the railing, turned to face me, and shoved his hands into his jacket pockets.

"He'll never want her. She'll never mean to him what he means to her."

"Even if they have sex?"

His smiled a patient smile at me. "For her, each time that happens it will deepen the relationship. For him, each time that happens, it happens. And it's over. It doesn't affect the relationship."

"I don't understand why—"

"Did you and Tegan ever fuck?"

"No! Of course not."

He chuckled. "Don't say 'of course not.' It wouldn't be out of the question. But think of it like this. Let's say the sex happens in the bedroom. You go in, you close the door, you fuck, you have a good time. For her, on the other side of the room is another door. It leads to the rest of her life. But you never go through it. For you, there is no other door. There's no way out except the door you came in."

He turned again to face the water. "Now, let's say you go into that room with a man. You fuck. You have a *great* time. Now, for you, on the other side of that room there's another door. It leads to… maybe the rest of your life, maybe just to the next few months. And maybe, because of the guy you happen to be in the room with that time, that other door is shut, bolted, boarded up—that is, it ain't opening. But it's *there*."

He watched my face for a few seconds. "Is this making any sense to you, Spencer?"

I felt my jaw clench. I didn't want to think of Tegan being one of the women he described. "I'll need to think about this."

"Fine. Meanwhile, remind me to lend you my copy of *California Suite*."

I didn't really hear him. I was already thinking. "Okay, I hear what you're saying. But Tegan went out with me before she knew I was gay."

He gave me an arch look. "Are you sure?"

"What?"

"Are you sure she didn't know? Fag hags are really great at sniffing out gay men. And let me ask you this: When you told her, how did she react?"

I stretched my mind back to the phone conversation. She had not been surprised. Donald saw that on my face.

"Aha! You see I'm right."

"I do. But I don't want you to be."

CHAPTER SEVENTEEN

Donald and I spent a lot of time together that next week, walking all over the city. He knew areas I'd never ventured into: Tribeca, Turtle Bay, Alphabet City, and—of course—Greenwich Village. We had drinks one evening in Stonewall, the bar where the riots had started in nineteen sixty-nine, the riots that had planted the seeds for the movement that became known as Gay Rights. And Saturday, because Donald didn't have a play that night, he insisted on what he called a very special outing.

"I guess I shouldn't be surprised that you've never seen *Rocky Horror*. But now that you're determined to be yourself, it's a requirement."

So we stood in line that night, starting at around eleven o'clock, outside the 8th Street Playhouse, surrounded by people in the most outlandish costumes imaginable.

"I decided to cut you a bit of a break," Donald told me as he did his best to avoid being bumped by the man in front of him. "I didn't make you dress up. Maybe next time."

The guy who'd stumbled backward wore a black, silver-studded leather jacket and hair slicked back into some style from the nineteen-fifties, and he was laughing uproariously at something his wildly-dressed companion had said.

Donald wore jeans and a simulated leather jacket, dyed pink. He had told me to dress as casually as possible, but in jeans and a grey sweatshirt, I still felt out of place in this crowd—though whether I had underdressed or overdressed, I wasn't sure.

The doors opened around eleven thirty, and our motley crew (a wild understatement) streamed inside. Donald took my arm and steered me to seats on the center aisle. "You have to see the whole show," he said, "not just what's happening on the screen."

When our row was full and we no longer had to keep standing to let escaped circus denizens past us, Donald pulled something out of his pocket and handed it to me.

"Your rice." It was a small plastic bag containing a few spoonfuls of white rice. He grinned at my confused expression. "You'll see."

I sat still, not wanting to call attention to myself, even though I knew that no one was looking at me; there was far too much else to see, and all of it far more interesting. I felt uneasy, out of place, and very glad I was on the aisle in case I decided to leave.

There was a pre-show event billed as a meeting of the Rocky Horror Fan Club. In front of the stage were people dressed as oddly as some of the audience members. They shouted out questions, and when they liked an answer from the audience, two of them would hold up a large piece of what looked like poster board, painted red, with vertical lines drawn onto it in several places. This item turned out to be a kind of award, and when it was given out everyone in the audience but me shouted out, "The three-foot dick!"

By the time they'd handed out the third dick, I was giggling. Not chuckling; giggling. I couldn't help it. But I stopped quickly when one of the characters in front demanded that any virgins— anyone who'd never seen the film—identify themselves, and Donald elbowed me in the ribs.

"That's you!" he hissed. But I refused to comply.

When the movie itself began, the role of the people who'd stood in the front became clear. There were several of them, and each was dressed like a different character from the movie. As the show went on, these people acted out the same scenes, simultaneously. They didn't limit themselves to the front area; they ran up and down the aisles, sometimes right past my seat. I wasn't sure where to look.

There's no way I can describe the movie itself. Any sense of plot, any message, was obliterated by the deliberately ludicrous things that happened in scene after scene. If I had to sum up my impression, I'd say it was to be who you are—wild, unfettered, unorthodox, gay, straight, goth, wacky, whatever, because there's really no such thing as a misfit, and we're really all weird in our own ways.

The audience was clearly made up mostly of people who'd seen the film many times. They often chanted along with the script, and sometimes they called out responses in unison to what someone in the film said. It was uncannily similar to a worship service.

I got to throw my rice toward the beginning of the film, during a wedding scene.

I don't think I'm likely to see *Rocky Horror* again, though there was one scene I'll never forget. Tim Curry, as a character called Dr. Frank N Furter, bursts into a ballroom where insane-looking people have just collapsed after the "Time Warp" dance. He's dressed in torn black lingerie—the sort of sexy, undergarments I wouldn't have imagined a man would ever put on. His hair is dark, curly, and bushy, his black eye makeup is extreme, and he's wearing the brightest red lipstick ever made on his full, sensual lips. The way he sashays across the room, the sex-heavy looks he gives the camera, the masculine power clothed in ambiguous trappings all conspired to bounce me back and forth across that line that separates male from female. I could never have imagined that the overall androgynous effect would have caused me to… well, to nearly come in my pants. But that's what it felt like. It was outrageous. It was beyond reality. And it was profoundly compelling.

Afterward, outside, Donald wrapped his arms around one of mine, and we walked so close together our hips touched.

He laughed, a joyous release. "Wasn't that fun?"

I didn't exactly laugh—perhaps still too stunned for that. But I did chuckle. "Yes. I have to admit, it was."

His mouth almost touching my ear, he said, "My place is closer." So that's where we went. And we had what I think I might always look back upon as the best sex I've ever had.

I spent the next two weeks or so in a kind of lustful fog, learning more than I would have imagined about sex between men. I even experienced the deep intensity of feeling Donald inside me, and the rich fullness of penetration.

I didn't fulfill my intention to talk to Dr. Dunfee during that time. Blame it on sex, blame it on Tim Curry, blame it on that aching sweetness when spring coincides with a burgeoning romance, blame it on whatever you like. But I still very much wanted to return to seminary, and I wanted to do so as my new self, not hiding who I was.

When I did eventually talk to Dr. Dunfee, in his office at General, I sat in the same chair where I had told him I was gay. And now, I told him, "I had a conversation with Father Fleming, up at St. Ignatius."

He nodded. "That was your family church, as I recall."

"Yes. He convinced me that if I decide the Episcopal priesthood isn't going to be my destiny, there are other ways I can serve God. And the Masters of Divinity would be a solid foundation."

He nodded again. "He's correct. And, Spencer, I'm glad you'll be with us again. To be honest, I've missed you. And I truly believe it would be a shame to lose you. Who knows? Once you graduate, you might decide to join our community after all."

I confess, it felt good to hear him say that. And I liked having options open to me. We set up a couple of courses for me to take over the summer, along with some independent study beginning immediately. A review before autumn classes would ensure that I was ready to proceed as though there had been no break.

It seemed as though right after my conversation with Dr. Dunfee, I felt a change in my relationship with Donald. It disturbed me. I had felt as though my life was starting to come together in a good way, arguably for the first time. But something was shifting.

It seemed as if the Easter service at St. Ignatius had awakened something in Donald, something he had buried, no doubt because of his father's Draconian approach to religion. He asked me to go with him to Sunday services at different churches. One week it was Baptist. Another, Presbyterian. Then Congregational. He didn't request Lutheran; perhaps any flavor of that denomination was too close to his family's church.

At first I saw this as a good sign. I liked that his connection to God was coming to life again. Once or twice I asked him what had prompted it, but his response didn't really help me understand. "I told you. I miss it." Once he said, "I do like seeing all the families." And another time, "It's your fault, you know, being all focused on God and everything."

Then, one Monday afternoon in early June, he asked if we could go to Gramercy Park and pray together.

"In the park? You want to pray in the park?"

"Why not? It's a gorgeous day, warm but not hot, and nature

is a great place to be, no?"

I couldn't refuse just because it seemed unusual. So we went. We sat on "our" bench, close but not touching. I waited for Donald to take the lead; I wasn't entirely sure what he had in mind. He sat quietly for a couple of minutes, facing the statue of Edwin Booth, but with his eyes closed. Then I heard his quiet voice.

"Dear Lord, be with us here in Your beautiful world, the world we will one day leave behind for Your glorious heaven. Help us to understand that this physical beauty is all that we can appreciate until we're ready for Your Glory. We are grateful for this worldly beauty, Lord, even as we do our best to prepare for what lies ahead when we fully accept Your Son, Jesus, as our Savior. It is in His name we pray. Amen."

I was transfixed. Not in a good way. It was as though some other entity, some other persona had moved into Donald's body and was speaking for him. Though quite the opposite from the tortures suffered by the little girl Regan in that film, *The Exorcist,* the contrast between the person before and after the demonic possession was almost as startling.

Perhaps a minute went by, and then Donald asked, "Won't you pray?"

I did my best to prevent sarcasm from creeping into my tone. "Oh, I think you've said enough for both of us." What I wanted to say was more along the lines of asking what play that script was from.

Donald sighed, a soft sigh, with a satisfied note to it. He stood and faced me.

"Think I'll head home now."

"Home?"

"Yes. I'll walk. It will be lovely."

Lovely. This wasn't my Donald. I think it was at that moment that I realized it had been at least a couple of weeks since he'd used any of those wild and crazy vocabulary words. He had been contemplative in a way that wasn't like the Donald I knew. And he hadn't laughed, or poked fun at anyone or anything. And, as if that weren't enough, I knew I had to face the fact that sex had also been different. It had been less frequent, because he kept begging off. And when it happened, it felt as though he were just going through the motions.

I decided to test the waters, just a little. "And here I was thinking we'd go back to my place, make mad, passionate love, shower together, rustle up some dinner, make love again, until we're mere puddles of emotional and physical satiety."

He smiled. It wasn't a rich full smile. It felt almost dismissive. "I think not. But there is something you could do for me. A favor."

I think not? Really? I was too confounded to say anything but, "A favor?"

"There's someone I'd like you to meet."

Immediately my old sense of jealousy stabbed at my chest. Was this why he was drifting away from me? I kept my tone as even as possible. "Oh? An actor friend?"

"No. His name is Robert Karl. And I think you two might have a lot to talk about. He's pretty seriously Christian, as well."

"Not Episcopal, though?"

"Nope. More basic."

"I don't know what that means."

"How about if we have lunch Thursday, and you can ask him yourself. I'll call you with details." He gave me one more empty smile and left. And, once again, I was watching him walk away from me. And despite the warm day, I felt a chill.

Tuesday, at my session with Dr. Connolly, I was a bit of a mess.

"I don't understand what's wrong," I told her. "Are you apprehensive about the upcoming lunch?"

"To say the least. I think if this Robert person were romantic competition, Donald wouldn't be introducing us. If he wanted to do group sex, he wouldn't be so lukewarm with me. So I can't imagine."

"So it seems to you as though something major in Donald's life is shifting?"

"I'm afraid so. I just don't know what."

"Do you think it's related to how church-y he's become?"

"That's what I suspect."

"Why might he be reluctant to talk with you about a major change in his life?"

I shook my head. "No idea."

"Why might you be afraid to ask him more directly than you have?"

"What if I ruin things completely by asking him questions he isn't ready to answer?"

"Spencer, if you can't ask him questions out of your genuine concern for him and for what you have together, then what is it that you have?"

God, but it hurt to hear that. And I think it was at that point that the aching sweetness of spring, which had been changing gradually, transformed completely. Now, it was only ache.

Donald called Wednesday morning with details of when and where to meet. I'd spent hours trying to come up with the best way to ask him what the hell was happening, who this mystery person was, and why I needed to meet him. But somehow, the sound of Donald's voice—definitely his, but somehow devoid of the richness I loved so much—made me hesitate. He was about to hang up, but I wasn't ready to end the call.

I introduced what I thought would be a safe topic. "I'm making good progress in my independent classwork."

Donald's reply baffled me. "That's nice. Of course, you won't stay there. It's like your St. Iggy's priest said, right? There are alternatives to playing a part in a comic book theater."

"Pardon?"

"You know what I mean. All the robes, the colors, the gilt and glitz. Not to mention the rigid script you'd have to follow, in services and also for the rest of your life."

"Well…. But I kind of like the colors." I liked the gilt and glitz, too, even though it seemed unlikely I'd end up in that scene.

"Of course you do." His tone was almost patronizing.

Thursday morning I was a nervous wreck. I'd barely slept, despite two pours of scotch. To try and calm myself down, I played hymns on the piano, singing along with the bass line.

I knew nothing about the restaurant where I was to meet Donald and Robert. I wasn't often in SoHo, and the unfamiliarity increased my foreboding.

I saw Donald immediately, seated at a table for three beside a short man, probably in his early thirties, light brown hair beginning to recede. Robert saw me before Donald did and, somehow, knew me right away. He stood, and his almost-handsome face widened with a broad smile.

Robert held his hand out as I approached. When I offered mine, he clasped it in both of his in an intimate way that made me uncomfortable; it felt like too much friendliness for the occasion.

"I know this will sound clichéd," he said, "but Donald has told me so much about you."

Suddenly I was unafraid of challenging what was going on. I was ready to be confrontational. "Interesting. He's never mentioned you but once. What did he say about me?"

Donald, still seated, watched me with what looked like a guarded expression.

"He says you're bright, talented, Godly, and alone."

I stared at Robert's round face. His beaming smile—I felt certain—hid something. There was a definite agenda to this meeting.

"He's wrong. I'm not alone." As I sat down I looked hard at Donald. "Or I hadn't been." *Was he going to say something? Anything? Or was I on my own, here?*

Donald's eyes dropped to his lap as a waitress appeared to take our order. I asked for a sandwich and glass of water; I didn't want a lot of food in front of me, partly because I had no appetite, but also because I wanted to be able to get up and leave at a moment's notice without wasting a lot of food. Donald followed my lead. Robert ordered a small feast.

"Contributions for the table, for all to share." He beamed as the waitress disappeared. "Spencer, Donald tells me you're on your path get your M. Div."

"At General Theological Seminary, in case you're not familiar with it."

"Oh, but I am. I am. I've never attended, myself, but I've known a few students."

"Candidates."

"Sorry?"

"Most of us are candidates for the priesthood."

"Ah. Of course. Of course. But doesn't that path hold problems for you?"

I glanced at Donald, whose eyes were still down. "What makes you say that?"

"I understand that you've told them you're gay."

I leaned toward Donald and pitched my tone to be cutting. "I might be new to this life, but I know this. You don't out someone else."

Donald glanced up at me and, quickly, back down. I could

tell he was ashamed. I wanted to tell him that was how he *should* feel.

"Please, Spencer," Robert said, his tone placating, "don't be offended." He was about to say something else, but I interrupted him.

"What are we doing here?" I did my best to keep my tone civil, but I was certain nothing good was going to come of this meeting, and I was furious with Donald for dragging me into it.

"I'm hoping we're going to talk about God. I'm hoping we'll examine our respective commitments to Jesus." Robert's face, though it seemed he was going for caring, looked smug.

"And why do you think I would want to engage with you about God?"

He looked surprised, though I was sure it was feigned. "As a priest, wouldn't you want to engage with everyone about God?"

"Not on these terms. Not in an ambush. And I'm not a priest."

Robert shook his head. "I'm so sorry you feel like that. Could we perhaps start over?"

"I can't un-hear anything you've said so far."

"Let me try. Let me tell you a little something about me."

I almost got up at that point; I wanted to know nothing about him. But, angry as I was at Donald, I was concerned. Somehow this man had a hold on him; I didn't like it, and if I left now I'd learn nothing more.

Robert waited until I gave a short nod. Our orders appeared, and as the waitress retreated he said, "I'm a spiritual leader at Risen Christ Church. Have you heard of us?"

Risen Christ. What on earth.... I shook my head.

"We're a first century Christian faith.""Religion."

"Sorry?"

I inhaled, my impatience evident to my own ears. "Faith is belief in something you can't prove. Religion is a system for applying faith. Christianity is a religion."

"A distinction without a difference, no?"

"No. Your average person might use the terms interchangeably with impunity. But if you bill yourself as a spiritual leader, I would expect you to understand the difference."

He gave me one of his broad smiles. "Ah, the coursework from General is showing. Spencer, we're all one in Christ."

"No argument. But that's irrelevant to how you represent yourself."

"I sense so much animosity from you."

"I refer you to my previous comment about being ambushed."

"So if we had met on the street, you would be more open?"

"To what?"

He half smiled and gave his head a shake, as though to summon patience while dealing with a child. "Let me continue, please. By first century, I mean that we strive to live our lives in the manner of the first century Christians, gathering in small groups often and in large groups occasionally. We help each other. We love each other. And we support each other as we strive to live Christ-like lives."

I sat back in my chair, sandwich ignored, and waited for him to continue. I had an idea where this was going, and I liked it less by the minute.

Robert said, "It wasn't my intention to talk in such specifics today. I was hoping to meet you and establish a connection we could build upon. I hoped that you would see Donald's commitment and be inspired by it."

I looked at Donald. "Will you say something? Why are you letting someone else speak for you? And since when are you committed to this—whatever it is?"

His eyes glared at me in a way that almost hurt. "Whatever it is? Really? You know very well that I've missed church. That I've missed being part of a community of believers."

"I don't ever remember hearing you put it like that. And

missing church or not, this—this belief system seems like nothing you'd want to be involved with."

"Perhaps I didn't tell you everything."

Very softly, I said, "Perhaps you didn't."

Robert spoke up. "I'd like to propose that we all take a breath, enjoy our meal. Spencer, I'd like to talk with you more about this, but perhaps now is not the right time."

My head snapped in his direction. "It's the only time. So take your best shot."

He paused, collecting his thoughts perhaps. "We're about love, Spencer. We're about Jesus, and His example for us, the path He wants us to follow. That's what I'm hoping to talk with you about."

"First century," I said, musing. "First century followers of Jesus can barely be said to have been Christians, as we know the meaning of the word. It took quite a while for St. Paul's efforts to bear meaningful fruit in his quest to spread Jesus' message beyond His Jewish audience." My academic training had given me some idea what first century Judea would have looked like. One thing was for sure: They condemned homosexual activity.

Robert said, "Early followers of Jesus met in secret. So we don't know enough about them to say they couldn't be called Christians."

"By the same token, we don't know that they could. We do know that most of them were Jews."

Robert leaned forward, and I got the impression he was beginning to enjoy himself. "We know enough to say that if we follow their example, we are Christians ourselves."

"Do you meet in secret?"

"Well, no. Not now."

"Not now. What else is different, 'now?'"

"What do you mean?"

"Do you cook over open flames? Squat over holes for bodily elimination? Procure life's necessities through barter because you have no way to acquire or secure coinage? Do you make do without doctors and hospitals and public schools and fire departments—"

"You are demonstrating one thing very clearly. We are still the victims of non-believers hurling stones and arrows at us." He wasn't smiling now.

"Non-believers? Is that what I am?"

He leaned toward me, his face intense and, for once, honest. "It doesn't have to be. Come to a service, Spencer. Come see who we are, what we do, how we relate to each other and to God." He held a card toward me. As I took it, I saw his name and some information about The Risen Christ Church.

I'd had enough. There was no point to this conversation. I stood, and without thinking slipped the card into a pocket. I set my napkin gently on the table, left no money there, gave Donald a glance that held both sadness and resignation, and without another word I turned and walked away.

As trying as that meeting had been, I now knew what was different between Donald and me. Whatever this group was, they were trying to pray the gay out of him. It made me shudder to realize how very much like his father they were treating him, and I nearly screamed because he was letting them.

I walked all the way from SoHo to General, to the library, and I looked up everything I could find about Risen Christ Church. I was pouring over an article when someone sat down across the long reading table from me.

Tegan.

She smiled, clearly happy to see me. "Are you back yet?"

I returned the smile. "Not yet." I sat upright. "I've just had a disturbing conversation with someone claiming to be from Risen Christ Church."

Her eyes widened. "Really? They're a pretty radical bunch. How did that come about?"

I closed my eyes briefly in an effort to hide the pain in my heart. "Donald Rainey seems to have fallen under their spell."

Her jaw dropped a tiny bit, and a pretty scowl took over her face. "Oh, no. Oh, Spencer." She paused as if not quite sure she should say more. "It's a cult, you know. They surround you. If a member has dealings with a non-member, it should be for what they call 'witnessing' or non-personal reasons. No friends outside the tribe. They're required to attend multiple meetings every week. They go out on proselytizing missions, in local neighborhoods and to other countries. Members are required to tithe. I could go on. You can bet they'll want to do something about his sexual orientation."

Everything she said agreed with what my impressions and my research were telling me. "You seem to know quite a bit about them."

She closed her eyes briefly and pressed a couple of fingers against her forehead. Then, hands in her lap, she said, "I had a close friend. It was two years ago. She was a lesbian, but something about what she called the purity of this cult compelled her. Our friendship changed. I became a soul to be saved. She chose to fully enter the cult by being baptized, and she insisted she was no longer gay. She moved into a house in Brooklyn with several other baptized women."

I waited while she rubbed her temples. She let out a long breath and spoke again.

"One day she phoned me, desperate, weeping. She'd been caught with another woman in an 'unnatural act,' and she'd been unable to convince them it wouldn't happen again. They shut her out. She told me it was like some heavy, gigantic door had slammed in her face."

Tegan's eyes filled with tears and she paused, clearly in an effort to regain some composure.

"All her friends, she said, were in the church. You see, she had rejected anyone who wouldn't join the cult." She gave a humorless snort. "You can imagine how it felt to have her imply that because I was not in the church, I was not her friend. Anyway, she had no place to stay. I offered her my couch until she could get back on her feet again. She was with me for about a week, inconsolable, weeping. Then one day...."

Tegan closed her eyes again and tears squeezed out of them. She took a shaky breath.

"One day I came home to find her dead. She had ripped up a sheet, braced a thick knot in the upper section of a window, tied the other end around her neck, and leaned or fallen forward until she choked."

I got up and walked around the table where I could sit beside Tegan. I wrapped an arm around her shoulders and she leaned sideways against me, struggling against sobs. Even as I did my best to comfort her, I felt panicked for Donald. Had he allowed himself to be completely taken in? Had he gotten baptized by these charlatans?

After a minute or so Tegan reached into her bag for some tissues. When she could speak she said, "I'm so sorry, Spencer. I know you and Donald are close. Do you think there's any hope?"

"I intend to find out."

At home, I grabbed the keys Donald had given me to his apartment, and I headed down to St. Mark's Place. I didn't ring the bell; I let myself in.

Donald wasn't there. I decided to wait.

I sat in one of his two chairs, wishing I had a book or a newspaper or something to read, because without a distraction I could feel my ire building. Something prevented me from looking around for reading material. Imaginary conversations went through my mind. I replayed them many different ways to decide whether I'd want to say any of it to Donald.

Around four-thirty I heard someone coming up the stairs, and then a key turned in the door. Donald didn't see me right away, but I could see he held a Bible in his hand. When he turned in my direction he gasped.

"Spencer! What are you doing here?"

"Please." I gestured toward the other chair.

"Oh, no. I don't think so. You need to leave."

"Why?"

"I can't be here alone with you. That's too much temptation."

I stood; if he wouldn't sit, fine. "When did this all start, anyway? This thing. With this group?"

"God sent people to me." I shook my head, confused. So he said, "They came to my door one morning. I'd really messed up in a show the night before. Lost my lines. Ended up adlibbing in a way that the other players weren't sure how to follow. I felt horrible. A failure. It was a stupid mistake even a novice wouldn't have made."

"I think you're being too hard on yourself."

"Except that it was the very next morning when two people rang my buzzer. I don't know why I answered. Something told me to. I think now that it was God. I think He made me fail so my heart would be open."

I did my best to ignore the unlikelihood that God would send anyone from The Risen Christ Church after manipulating Donald to ruin his lines. Instead of asking who had told him this bunk, I said, "So this was, what, a few weeks ago?"

He shrugged. "Does it matter?"

"It does to me. You've changed, and I'm trying to understand it."

Something shifted in him, and he assumed what looked like another persona. "*I* have changed. Changed in a moment. That's what Jesus is capable of."

I barked out a dull laugh. "Oh, I agree. You seem different. I can't remember the last time you threw any of your obscure vocabulary words my way. I can't remember the last time you laughed, or shot me an arch look, or kissed me like you meant it. Changed in a moment?"

"Exactly." His tone was defiant. A little too defiant. Trying too hard.

"It strains credibility, Donald. It's not you. You're fun. You're funny. You're sardonic. You're—you're Puck."

His eyes flashed something between fury and fear. "You want to hear some obscure vocabulary? How about this: l'appel du vide. Do you know what that means?" I shook my head. "It's when you're just going about your business and suddenly you're almost irresistibly drawn to throw yourself out of a window, or in front of an oncoming subway train. Literally, it means the call of the void. I feel it all the time, Spencer. All. The. Time."

I shook my head again. "Why didn't you ever tell me?"

He ignored my question. "Puck was a cover. No; that's not quite right. Puck would step between me and that void. I owe him a lot. But I don't want to need him anymore. I want the void to go away. I want to stop hearing that call. But first I must shed everything that holds me to my old life."

"Everything? Including me?"

"Especially you."

"Because I'm gay?"

"Because you're not in the Body, and because you represent temptation."

"The body?"

"The Body of Christ. You should know this. I need to die to the world so that I can become alive again in Christ."

"Baptism."

"Yes. When that happens, I'll be washed clean. Clean of sin. Clean of anything in my past that would prevent me from being saved." He was nearly panting. "I want a family, Spencer! I want a normal life. I want children. I love children!"

I had no words. I was stunned. We stared at each other as the afternoon light grew softer, and the room began to feel gloomy. Then, his voice pleading, almost tearful, he said, "Please, Spencer. Please take this seriously. And please, come to a service. Your soul is at risk. If you stay on the path you're on—"

"Don't do this, Donald. This is a cult. That man, Robert, speaks as if he had a corner on God. Who else spoke like that? Your father?"

"Stop it!" I'd hit a nerve, and he'd shouted. He shook his head, hard. "You haven't been out long enough to know what it feels like, wearing a sign under your clothes that says 'Unclean,' desperately afraid someone will see it. Or shoving wadded tissues into that little bell you have to carry, the one that would warn the Godly of your approach."

"Oh no? Don't I? Maybe I wasn't out at the age of sixteen, but if you think I didn't feel exactly like that, with a father as strict as yours even if he was gentler about it, and a mother whose heart might be broken if she knew what her only child was, you've got your head so far up your own ass you don't know whether it's midnight or high noon."

He took a step toward me. "Then come with me, Spencer! Come with me now. I'm going to a prayer meeting, a Bible study. Come! See for yourself! Robert was right, you know. It is all about love."

"Just not if you're gay."

"But you don't have to be! That's the secret! Anything is possible with Jesus!"

And there it was. "That's bullshit. What did you call it? Deja poo all over again? Can't you see this is just you trying to win back your father?"

"Liar! Satan!"

"Without Satan, Donald, you can't tell the difference between good and evil."

If I stayed I was afraid I would strike him. As I left, I said, "These people are at least as bad as the Missouri Synod. You're not just looking for your father. You're turning into him."

I spent most of my Friday session with Dr. Connolly near tears.

"I don't know what happened," I told her. "One week he was himself. Fun. Teasing. Laughing. Just a few weeks later? He's a different person."

"It seems more likely he's adopted a persona that allows him to fit in with this group."

"But why? You know, I always pictured myself as the stodgy one. He was always full of fun and mischief. He once told me that I was fun, too, that he'd bring it out of me. And he did!" I blew my nose. "He did."

She nodded. "I'm grateful to him for that. I hope you won't hide it again."

"Look, I wasn't expecting we'd spend our lives together. But it seemed we were barely in a really good relationship when— fuck! I don't even know what happened."

"You said he told you he'd missed praying? Missed church? What do you think he really missed?"

"He told me he wants a 'normal' family. Children."

She nodded. "What do you make of that?"

"Isn't it obvious? He wants the family he never had. And he's still looking for his father. And he's confusing that with God the Father."

She nodded again. "Can you tell me why this is so obvious to you?"

I could have sworn someone had struck me in the center of my chest. I barely managed to say, "Because that's what I've been doing."

CHAPTER EIGHTEEN

I barely remember the next few weeks. I called Donald a few times, always leaving messages that felt like scraps of paper in bottles heaved into indifferent waves. "If only," I said to the street as I stared out of the window, "if only I could give up caring."

I considered showing up again at his apartment. I still had his keys. Two things held me back. One was that he'd been clear that being alone there with me was so problematic that he would be on guard, not open to an honest discussion, so another attempt like that was more likely to make matters worse than otherwise. The other was that he might have changed the locks. I could almost certainly get into the building; there were other apartments, and the outside lock wasn't under Donald's control. But I pictured myself outside his door, trying my keys again and again, failing, and growing more angry and more hurt by the minute. The rejection would feel too intense. Too real. Too final.

There were three theaters I knew of where Donald had played, and I spent several hours hanging out at their stage doors. I even wandered backstage in two of them at times when I knew actors were gathering before a show. No one I talked to had seen Donald recently.

I perused every notice I could find about plays and shows all over the city, hoping I'd see Donald's name on one of them. I had found him this way once; maybe it would work again?

It didn't.

I tried to convince myself that it was over, that my very first relationship had ended in some kind of failure I couldn't understand. But having Donald pull away from me like this hurt so much more than I would have anticipated. It left a hole in my chest.

I was grateful for the assignments from my independent study, and I threw myself into the work. I went to Gramercy Park a few times, but that made me think of Donald. This was odd; I'd been there so many times without him and only twice with him. Why would his disappearance from my life affect me here so powerfully?

~

One Wednesday evening in late June I got a call from Ruth Rainey.

"Spencer? Oh thank the Lord you're there. I so hope you can tell me that Donald's all right. I've been trying to reach him for days. Longer, really, but it's only a week or so that I've been in a state."

"Oh, Ruth, I—well, I'm surprised he won't call *you* back."

"You haven't talked to him?"

"Well…not in some time. He seems to have retreated into a religious group in a way that shuts anyone else out."

"No!" I heard a sharp intake of breath. "Oh, he told me he'd found God. I wasn't sure what to make of that."

"I'm so sorry. I don't know how to reach him. I tried. But, Ruth, I met a man from that group who seemed to have some kind of hold over Donald. I argued with him. I argued with Donald. There was no reaching him." Not wanting to repeat what I'd learned, and what Tegan had told me, I felt at a loss for what to say to this sweet woman.

"I'm coming out there. I'm coming to see him. Would you talk to him with me?"

"It isn't that I'm not willing, Ruth. He doesn't want to talk to me."

"We'll see about that."

~

Thursday she called again.

"I'm flying to New York on Friday, landing around five. If he has a show he won't be home, and I can't count on him picking up my messages, but I need a place to stay. He told me he'd given you keys. Do you still have them?"

"I do. Shall I pick you up at the airport?" Maybe I couldn't save her brother, but I would do what I could for Ruth.

~

On the ride from the airport, I told Ruth what I knew about the cult, still leaving out Tegan's story about her friend. I felt she needed to know as much as might help her understand what had happened to her brother.

I had the cab wait at Donald's apartment building. As I opened the street door, Ruth said, "Look."

She pointed to the list of names, tenants in the building. Where once the name Rainey had been, I saw "Morris." Ruth and I exchanged a glance and then hurried up the stairs.

I knocked on what had been Donald's door. No answer. I used the keys in my hand and was surprised when they worked; evidently "Morris" hadn't changed the locks.

Inside there was no trace of what had been Donald's life. The small space didn't allow for much rearranging, but the bed was at a different angle from before, and where Donald's blue-and-green striped bedspread had been was a wild pattern of bright yellow sunflowers. I heard Ruth sob.

I held her while she cried. When she pulled away, she said, "We need to leave."

Without thinking, without asking Ruth what she wanted, I had the cab take us to my house. She went inside with me, too stunned to protest. I sat her down in the living room and took her luggage into Mother's room. Then I poured Ruth a stiff drink. She sipped it absently, her thoughts very far away.

We sat there together in silence, not moving except for when I got up to turn on a couple of lights. I'd wracked my brain as the dark had progressed in the room, trying to figure out how to find Donald so Ruth could talk to him. And as the second lamp broke through the darkness, an idea began to take shape.

In my entry foyer was a table, and on the table was a bowl. In that bowl were a number of little objects that didn't quite have a place anywhere else. One of those objects was the card Robert Karl had given me. It had a phone number on it.

Back in the living room, I shared my idea with Ruth. She agreed enthusiastically. So I set my plan in motion.

"Robert?" I said when he answered. "Thank goodness I've caught you. I—well, I don't quite know how to say this."

"I find one starts at the beginning and keeps going. Seems the best approach."

"Okay. Um...." Had I learned enough about acting to carry this off? Only one way to find out. "I've been thinking about that lunch. When we met. And about how rude I was. I wanted to apologize." *Don't overact, Spencer; don't make him suspicious.*

"Forgiveness is a gift God gives us so that we may give it to others. It's yours."

"Thank you. And thank God."

"Indeed."

I paused, deliberately, wanting to seem unsure of myself. "Well, thanks again. That's a load off my shoulders."

"Thank Lord Jesus for that. He takes all our burdens, if we will but ask Him."

"Indeed. So...."

"Spencer? I wonder if this is a good time for me to repeat my invitation. Come and worship with us Sunday."

"Oh. Oh, well, I don't know.... I had plans."

"No plan is worth putting God aside."

"I was going to go to my church."

He was silent a moment. "That's never a bad idea. But Spencer, if you're going to church anyway, why not come to mine? God is there, too, you know."

"I'll think about it."

"Don't think too hard. Just do it. Let me give you the address where I'll be this Sunday."

Now I just had to hope—pray—that Donald would be at the same service.

He was. Ruth and I were watching the doorway from across the street of a very nice brownstone on East Sixty-third Street, and we saw Donald approach. He was dressed more nicely than I remembered seeing him before. Two other young men walked with him, flanking him on either side.

I had debated whether to watch until I was sure Donald was all the way inside before letting him know we were there, but Ruth was more impatient. She ran across the street and stood right in front of him. I followed more slowly.

"Donnie! Where have you been, you lumpish, fly-bitten pignut?"

It looked to me as though he tried very hard not to smile. In any event, he did not play the game. He did not reply in kind. "Ruth," was all he said.

"Yes, Ruth!" she said, apparently stunned by his lackluster reaction. "Please, sweet brother, tell me what's going on! Why haven't you returned any of my calls? You didn't even tell me that you'd moved!"

I approached them, but from behind Donald so he wouldn't see me right away. I wanted to hear what he had to say to Ruth.

"I wasn't sure how to explain anything."

"Even so, explain. Where are you living now?"

"I've moved in with some brothers."

"Brothers? But—"

"I have brothers in Christ, Ruth. I'm living with them."

"You mean this Risen Christ group?"

"Exactly. Are you here to worship with us?"

She pulled just her head back, a motion implying disbelief.

I moved forward. "Yes. Ruth and I were invited by Robert Karl." I inserted myself between Donald and one of the other men and took hold of one of Donald's arms, and Ruth followed my lead and took the other. "We're all three going in together."

I felt Donald's body stiffen, but he moved forward with us, up the stone steps, through the front door, and into a large room with a high ceiling. Any comfortable furniture had been moved out, replaced by folding chairs in rows, facing the far end of the room, where a table, an impromptu altar, had been set up. Covered with a white cloth, it held a large, freestanding wooden cross, two of what looked like collection plates, and a couple of candlesticks with lit, white candles.

There were maybe twelve people there already, with many more coming in behind us. I tried to scope out the membership, expecting to see families. But no; everyone here seemed to be over twenty. Robert was there, and he headed straight for us. It was hard to tell how sincere his greeting was, but he obviously wanted to seem delighted.

"How wonderful to see you all!" He shook Donald's hand and pulled him gently in a way that moved him away from us. Ruth stretched out an arm as though to hold him, but Robert stepped between them. "Spencer, who is the young lady you've brought with you?"

Ruth spoke up for herself. "I'm Donald's sister. And I want to know if you've discouraged him from being in contact with me."

"Oh, by no means, Ms. Rainey. In fact, I'm very glad to see you here. You can experience the closeness we have with each other and with Jesus, first-hand." He turned slightly and caught the attention of a young woman. "Beverly," he said to her, "I'd like you to meet Ms. Rainey, who's with us for the first time today."

Before I realized what was happening, Beverly led Ruth in one direction, and Robert attempted to steer me in another. When I didn't move with him, he gestured toward a row of chairs near the front.

"Let's sit up here, where you can experience everything up close."

I scoured the room with my eyes but couldn't see where Donald had gone. Many people were standing, and if he had taken a seat he'd be hidden from view. "I think I'd prefer to sit with Ms. Rainey."

"Oh, she'll be just fine. Beverly will take care of her."

"That's what I'm afraid of." I walked away from Robert and took a seat in the row behind Ruth, tapping her shoulder as I sat to let her know I was there. Beverly was asking Ruth questions and getting only curt answers in as few words as possible.

Ruth turned around toward me. "I don't see Donnie anywhere! Is he still here?"

I stood and managed to locate him. "He's over on the other side, surrounded by people. No seats are open over there."

Despite Beverly's attempt to discourage her, Ruth stood and

left the row she was in to take the one empty seat in my row, on my right. "Don't let them separate us."

"I won't. Not again."

Beverly turned and, thwarted by the lack of seating near Ruth, continued to try and engage her until Ruth had had enough.

"Will you please turn around? I'm not here for you."

I nearly laughed. I hadn't pictured Ruth as someone who would be so bold. But perhaps her courage came from concern for her brother.

A man I didn't recognize stood in front of the alter/table and smiled benevolently at what I supposed must be called a congregation. He raised one hand and held it out to the side, and all talking ceased.

"I offer you greetings in the name of Jesus Christ, our Lord and Savior."

The crowd responded, "Amen."

"For those who don't know me, I'm Brother Ken Stoddard. And I want to welcome all of you, but especially those who are here with us for the first time."

I nearly giggled. It was *Rocky Horror* all over again.

He held up his other arm too, holding both out in an apparently benevolent gesture that would send blessings out into the room. He looked for all the world as though he were nailed to a cross. The crowd responded, "Welcome!"

Brother Ken addressed the room so enthusiastically that I could almost see the capital letters appearing in the air as he spoke. He talked about the Wonders of being with Christ, about being Saved, about how Blessed it is to Help Others find their Way to Jesus and His Love.

At one point Ruth leaned close to me and whispered, "I almost feel as though I'm in a revivalist tent."

"Yes. That's it, exactly."

Ken went on at some length before introducing another man,

Barry Keen, evidently recently returned from a missionary trip to Japan to see about setting up a church there.

"I had a fascinating talk with a Buddhist," he told the crowd. "I was asking him about Buddha and telling him all about Jesus." He paused briefly for effect, and I couldn't help but see the actor in him. I glanced at Donald, who was watching Barry intently.

"It became clear in no time," Barry continued, "that—well, there was just no comparison between the man he revered and the Savior of Mankind. Everything he told me was like lukewarm water beside what Jesus is, what Jesus offers, what Jesus promises. And the final blow," again he paused and gazed around the room.

Again I nearly giggled, because it reminded me of when Dr. Frank N Furter had leered at his frightened, accidental guests and said, "I see you shiver with anticip……" his eyes and nostrils flare "….pation."

Barry Keen was no Tim Curry, but he was making an effort. "The final blow was when I told him that God brought Jesus back to life! He brought Him back from the dead! The Buddhist was so stunned he had nothing else to say."

I muttered to Ruth, "The Buddhist was probably wondering what Jesus had done to deserve such punishment."

Ruth covered her mouth, but her laughing snort was heard by many people all around us. It brought Barry's rant to a halt. He looked our way, and his eyes fell directly on me.

"I see we have something humorous happening. Would you care to share the fun?"

I wasn't there to speak. I wasn't there to challenge these people. But I also wasn't going to cringe in my chair like a child chastised for passing notes in class. I was a priest in training. I was unafraid of addressing rooms full of people. And I was disgusted by what this man was saying and by his inexcusable ignorance. As I stood, I saw Donald's face turn toward me, his expression unreadable.

"The spirit of Siddhartha Gautama, the Buddha, had already lived many lives and had been reincarnated—brought back to life—many times," I said directly to Barry. "When he died as the Buddha, his time on the wheel of life was over. He had achieved the state called enlightenment, and he passed into Nirvana, where unhappiness and the attachment it causes would no longer trouble him."

I looked around at the room before I continued.

"If the man you spoke to in Japan was speechless when you said God had brought Jesus back from the dead, he was either waiting for you to come to the point, or he was wondering what Jesus had done that was so horrible as to make God punish him in that way. I hope you'll revisit that exchange in your mind and come to a greater understanding of Buddhism."

I looked down at Ruth. "Shall we go?"

She stood. "Yes. It seems there's nothing here worth staying for."

As we made our way out of the row, Barry said, "Such a common misunderstanding. I wish you would stay so that Jesus can help us bring you to His Love and save your souls!"

Safely outside on the sidewalk, Ruth and I stared at each other in a kind of fugue state. Finally she broke the spell. "Well. They were not expecting *that!*"

"No. And yet that Barry character knew just what to say. He never gets off-message."

She heaved a sigh and looked back up at the doorway. "But what can we do about Donnie?"

I shook my head; there was nothing I could offer. "I don't think there's anything we can do. There are deprogrammers, but typically they're hired for under-age people. Teens, mostly. And we don't know where Donald lives."

"A private detective could find him."

"Yes. And then what?"

Ruth's eyes filled with tears. "I don't know! I don't know. I just can't leave him like this! I can't, Spencer! There has to be something."

We walked to a nearby restaurant for breakfast, though we didn't talk much. As she held her nearly-empty coffee cup in both hands, Ruth closed her eyes. "I'm picturing the view from the balcony at The Cloisters. That gorgeous expanse of water and forest, and in the distance, the city of Manhattan." She opened her eyes. "Did I tell you that Daddy had died?"

"No." I almost offered the typical, banal expression of sympathy, but I reminded myself in time that there was no love lost there. "Does Donald know?"

"I didn't want to leave that information in a voice message. The executor tried to reach him and failed. So unless he was notified by someone else—no." She heaved a long sigh that I couldn't interpret. "Our family had always lived very frugally. Donnie and I assumed there wasn't much money. But it turns out that Mom had brought quite a bit of wealth to the marriage, wealth Daddy wouldn't touch and wouldn't let her touch."

She emptied her cup before continuing.

"I think you know Daddy kicked Donnie out of the house, and out of his life. The will specifies that nothing goes to Donnie. It all comes to me. We're not talking millions, here, but close to one million, anyway. So I'm selling that house, not that it's worth much. I'm getting rid of almost everything in it. And I've decided—just this minute, actually—that I'm going to move to New York. I don't know what I'll do here yet, but I should think the possibilities are endless. And I can keep looking for Donnie." She grinned at the surprise on my face.

"Wow. Well, that's news, to be sure."

"Turns out Daddy was good for something."

"When will you start living here, do you think?"

She shrugged. "I suppose I should go back briefly to salvage a few things, though the executor put me in touch with an estate agent who'll pretty much take care of everything on my behalf. I could go back when the house is sold or give the executor power of attorney to handle it for me. Truly, if I never see that place again I'll be happier for it."

I ordered another round of coffee for each of us, working through some thoughts while we waited. And then I told Ruth the idea that had taken me all of five seconds to hatch.

"If you like, you're welcome to live in my house as long as it suits you. I expect you'd want your own place eventually, but there's no need to rush. Would you like to take your time and look around before jumping into anything?"

Her smile had sunshine in it. "That would be marvelous, Spencer. I won't impose on you any longer than I need to, but it would be a big help not to have to figure everything out at once."

And, just like that, it felt like I had a sister. Perhaps Donald had left me behind, but Ruth—this delightful, energetic, remarkable young woman—had adopted me.

Ruth and I had just arrived back at my house when the phone rang. I picked it up in the kitchen where I was heating water for tea. It was Donald.

I said his name loudly enough for Ruth, in the living room, to hear, and as I'd hoped, she picked up the extension there.

His voice shook with emotion, though I could tell he was trying not to let that show. "All I want to say to you is to stay away from me. If you find yourself drawn to The Risen Christ, ask Robert to point you toward another house church."

"What's a house church?"

"We were in one today."

"Why must I stay away from you?"

"Spencer! You know very well why! You represent temptation. You embody everything about my old life I need to leave behind."

"So you still want me?"

"Stop it! Please! Satan is testing my faith."

"How?"

He was nearly shouting by now. "Don't pretend! Don't patronize me! If my faith is strong enough, I can put you and the life I had behind me. But until I'm stronger, it would be too easy to fail."

I wracked my brain for something that might get through to him. "You know, I didn't see any families in your house church."

"They were in another room."

"What?"

"For every service, some people are assigned nursery duty. And one day, my kids will be in there. I'll have a family. You can't offer me anything better than that."

Words would not form in my head.

Ruth had words that took Donald in a different direction. "Donnie, you're wrong. About the test."

If it surprised Donald that his sister was with me at home, he gave no indication. "I'm not! This is a test!"

"There's a test. Yes. But you misunderstand. Jesus is about love. He's not giving gay people a test of faith. He's giving everyone a test of love."

"You don't know what you're talking about. Go home. Go back to Dad."

"He's dead, Donnie. And I do know what I'm talking about."

Apparently the mention of his father's death was enough of a shock that Donald didn't speak, which gave Ruth a chance to say something I'll never forget.

"The test for people like Robert and Barry is to love you no matter how uncomfortable it makes them that God made you gay. And your test," she stopped briefly to take a breath, "your test is to love them even when they fail."

The line was silent for several seconds. Then Ruth said, "They're failing their test, Donnie. That's what's going on here."

Donald's voice sounded strangled. "Go away." And he hung up.

CHAPTER NINETEEN

Ruth and I had a long talk about Donald. She sat across from me, in the chair Donald had used so many times. I asked her if she thought this turn of events was something that might have been predicted.

Ruth asked, "Did Donnie ever tell you he talked about becoming a minister? This was years ago, of course."

"Yes. But he made it sound like something he said to placate your father. Though he also said he missed church."

"How much do you know about the Missouri Synod?"

I gave a snort. "Enough to know I don't want anything to do with it. Oh, sorry; I hope that wasn't offensive."

She laughed. "You can't say enough bad things about it to offend me. But back to your question…. I just don't know. On one hand I was horrified when you told me what had happened. On the other, though, it seemed like not really much of a surprise."

"He asked me to take him to different services. That is, before he disappeared into this cult."

She nodded. "Did you two go to a UU service?"

I shook my head. "No. Unitarian Universalist wasn't on his

list. Thinking back, I'm wondering whether it wasn't quite Christian enough for him."

"Daddy didn't know this, but for about four years I've been going to UU services almost every week."

"Really? What, specifically, appeals to you about UU?"

"Well, for one thing, they have a great sense of humor about themselves. There's a saying that instead of a cross or a star of David or anything else, the UU symbol is a question mark."

That made me chuckle. "What else?"

"How about the joke that an angel with beautiful wings appeared before a Universalist, and he threw bread at it."

That made me laugh.

"Or the idea that when dogs go to heaven and get to chase squirrels, it's actually also squirrel hell."

I groaned appreciatively.

"Or the UU family who got tired of shoveling snow from their driveway and hired Moses."

"Moses?"

"To part the white sea. And then there's how bad we are at singing hymns. We discuss everything to a fare-thee-well and seldom agree on very much. So when we're singing, everyone has to read ahead to see if they agree with the next verse."

"Okay, that's quite enough." I grinned broadly.

Ruth laughed. "Okay, but you asked. It can be frustrating, because there are so many different ideas in play all at the same time in any UU group, and nobody wants to offend anybody else by actually disagreeing with them. But it's also great fun, partly for the same reason, and partly because we really care about each other. We're a real community. And we don't care how you see God, or whether you see God at all."

"Will you find a UU congregation once you move to New York?"

"I'm sure of it. You should come see for yourself what it's

like, for perspective if nothing else." She smiled, a warm smile that made me feel better than I'd felt in a while.

Ruth went into Mother's room to rest for a while, though when I asked if the piano would bother her she insisted it would not. So I went to the keyboard. I needed balance—the kind of balance that exists for me between the clear, logical pattern of the black and white keys and the subjective beauty of the music they produce.

Later, Ruth made a soup and some biscuits, and we called it dinner.

"I've decided to go back to Cedar Rapids tomorrow," she told me. "I'll put some things in order, sign over my power of attorney, and put that place behind me for good. I hope to be back here by Friday, if that's all right with you."

"Perfectly."

I felt my heart sink a little when she announced her departure, but it was lightened again at the thought of her return. There was something calming, even tranquil about Ruth, and I was sure she felt as comfortable with me as I did with her. I stopped myself in time, before I said what was in my mind: that Donald was insane to do anything that shut her out of his life. I didn't know if Ruth would want to hear that, or if it would be rubbing salt into the wound he'd made in her generous heart.

Something else I didn't say aloud was something that troubled me about the current situation. That is that Ruth was, once again, devoting her life to the service of another family member. Her father was gone, and now she felt she had to reclaim her brother. She was either a saint or a martyr. But I guess those roles are not mutually exclusive.

I rode with Ruth to the airport Monday afternoon. As I lifted her luggage out of the trunk and set it on the ground, she hugged me.

"See you in a few days, you bawdy, dizzy-eyed bugbear." As I watched her walk into the terminal, my heart swelled with a soft warmth that slowly moved through my whole being. It was wonderful, but it was tinged with sorrow for what both Ruth and Donald might lose if she couldn't bring him back.

~

Tuesday's session with Dr. Connolly included a watershed moment, if a quiet one. Of course we had talked in previous sessions about Donald's disappearance into the cult, but Tuesday Dr. Connolly asked me this question for the first time:

"Are you ready to say that your relationship with Donald is behind you?"

The question was surprising, and it wasn't. Because although for some time it had seemed unavoidable that I would need to release any lingering hope for the relationship, the reality of the separation had not quite registered with me.

I told her, "I'm not sure. I have so many memories of him. His humor. His wit. His joy, which I suspect now might have been a cover. And, of course, I miss the intimacy."

"You will always have those memories, though like most memories they will probably fade over time. Are you saying they're still too fresh?"

"It still hurts. He changed so quickly. And then he disappeared so—God, so inexorably." I rubbed my face. "I almost wonder if my own struggles with my faith, with my vocation, sucked him into a spiritual vortex that resulted in… you know."

"Spencer, the only role you could have played would have been that of a catalyst. Whatever caused Donald to move his life in this direction came from inside him. And as for how quickly things changed, I can tell you that it's not uncommon, with something like this, for the change to happen quite rapidly.

Consider the level of desperation someone must feel in order to take this step."

"But that's just it. I didn't see anything like desperation in him. I didn't see it coming at all."

"Then consider this: You might have delayed it. Didn't you tell me he approached you initially after he learned of your calling?"

My smile was humorless. "Yes. That, and that he loved my voice."

"Which is deep and masculine." I thought she might have been about to say something else, but I also thought I knew what it was.

I said it for her. "A father figure."

"We've touched on this subject many times in the past months, in relation to Donald and also to you. What I see in Donald's withdrawal into the cult is your failure to substitute for his father. And while I don't think he was a substitute for yours, I'll ask you this: Do you have a clear understanding of the difference between seeking your own father's approval and serving God?"

This time, my smile was genuine. "You know, I think I do. Or, at least I know what to watch for in terms of confusing the two." I chuckled. "That part of my subconscious is not so 'sub' anymore."

"What did Donald represent for you, if not your father?"

Wow. That made me sit back in my chair. "What did he represent," I echoed, stalling for time. Dr. Connolly waited as I took nearly half a minute to search through my mind and feelings for an answer.

Finally, I nodded and said, "I think he represented escape. Being with him, allowing myself to let go of at least some of the rigidity of that—that carapace I'd grown to deal with my parents —was profoundly freeing. He was fun. He saw fun in me I'd never suspected. And it was being with him that helped me see how I want to live my life. Or, rather, how I don't."

"How is that?"

"Repressed. Hidden. Hiding. Lying."

We regarded each other for a moment before she asked, "Will you be able to carry this freedom forward without him?"

"Yes."

"Are you ready to put the relationship behind you?"

I hesitated for a few seconds. "Yes." And I meant it.

"That's our time for today. I'll see you Friday. And between now and then, give some thought to whether you're ready to meet once a week instead of twice."

I had just enough to keep me busy while I waited for Ruth's return. My assignments from General were more challenging than the standard coursework, because they were meant to help me make up for lost time. I appreciated the independent tutoring I received; it made me work harder, and it kept me on track.

Friday I told Dr. Connolly that I thought once a week was a good idea. We discussed whether continuing at all was necessary, and in the end we both agreed it would be beneficial. I had to admit, at least to myself, that I still had some digging to do, more excavation on my way out from under years of pretense I hadn't been altogether aware of even as I'd lived it.

Ruth gave me a big hug when she saw me at the airport. And later, over dinner, I was unable to avoid agreeing to go with her to a UU service on Sunday. In fact, I didn't even try.

So go we did. There were not many UU services in Manhattan to choose from, but Ruth had done her research and had landed on one she thought sounded very much like the sort of parish she'd want to belong to.

The church itself, sitting primly on the corner of Lexington and Eightieth, looked as though it could have been transplanted from some Revolutionary Era New England town. Huddled amidst more typical New York City buildings, its location reminded me of St. Ignatius. Inside very much matched the exterior: simple white pews; not much in the way of opulent ornamentation; spare and pure.

Ruth took my arm as we walked into the nave. "Isn't this exciting?" she whispered. "I can't wait to hear the sermon."

I nodded agreement but said nothing; I didn't feel her excitement, but I wouldn't have dimmed hers for all the world.

The choir did a commendable job. I didn't expect them to match that of a larger church or a cathedral, and they didn't. But they were well-trained, the music was interesting if not the standard Episcopal fare, and their expression was sincere. I couldn't fault it.

The pastor, a Dr. Stein, took the pulpit and smiled out at the congregation, waiting for them to settle. Into the relative silence, she greeted the gathering.

"Welcome," she opened. "Welcome Muslims. Welcome Pagans. Welcome Jews. Welcome women. Welcome men. Welcome children and grandparents and aunts and uncles. Welcome gays and lesbians. Welcome Buddhists. Welcome atheists. Welcome Zoroastrians. Welcome agnostics."

She stopped, her smile still warm, and then she laughed quietly. "Oh, I almost forgot. Welcome Christians."

The congregation, far from being insulted, laughed with some abandon. And as the service went on, I felt a down-to-earth quality about the entire experience.

Dr. Stein's sermon started out on a somber note. Evidently, someone in the congregation, someone very well known, had recently died unexpectedly. It wasn't clear to me what had taken them, but the loss was evidently felt keenly by many people around us.

"The famous poet, Emily Dickinson, is often quoted. So much of what she felt is expressed universally in her work. Today I give you, first, these two lines from her poem called 'They say that time assuages'. She wrote, 'Time is a test of trouble, but not a remedy.'

"Now, we need to be clear. This is not a test of the sufferer, but a test of the trouble itself. Dickinson is saying that rather than healing all wounds, which—by virtue of not being a remedy it will not do—time tells us whether the trouble is still troubling us as much, or at all, after enough time as passed.

"Those lines appear in the poem after another set that reads: 'An actual suffering strengthens, as sinews do, with age.' These lines tell us that if a trouble is real, if it is troubling us deeply, if it has legs as the saying goes, then over the course of time we will be stronger because of it. The body strengthens with strain. Muscles increase *after* we push them to the point of tearing.

"Think of the forging of steel. The metal that is not yet steel must go through flames, through intense heat that refines it rather than destroys it. But first it must go through the flames."

Dr. Stein paused and gazed down at what I assumed were her notes, although rather than reading, it appeared she was gathering her thoughts. Then she looked up again and continued.

"Let's consider the five stages of grief outlined by Elizabeth Kübler-Ross in her book, *On Death And Dying*. These stages are denial, anger, bargaining, depression, and acceptance. I will not argue with Kübler-Ross about these stages. But I will advise anyone who is suffering to keep a few things in mind.

"First, don't expect to go through them quickly. And because we're suffering, time might seem to go very slowly indeed. The key is not to give up, not to lose hope that the suffering will change and become less overwhelming.

"Second, don't expect that the stages will behave themselves and move smoothly from one to the next. Rather, it often happens that bargaining, for example, might slip backward into anger if the bargaining doesn't seem to be getting us anywhere.

"Third, there's no rule about the length of time any one stage might take. Or, rather, the rule is that there's no predicting it.

"As we move together through our suffering, we need to remember that two individuals, both suffering from the same event, might in fact go through these stages. But they will not necessarily go through them at the same time or in the same way. Understanding the individual nature of suffering allows us to be kind and even empathetic toward someone whose outward expressions of grief don't match our own."

There was more, but I confess my mind got locked onto the suffering of losing Donald. The length of time I had known him was much less important than the depth of feeling I had for him, much less important than the effect he had on my life. And his willful removal from my life had the effect on me of something so close to his death that it was hard for me to think of it in any other way. In fact, if I didn't think of it as death, it was likely I'd hold onto a vain hope that he would leave the cult and be once again the Donald I knew. Even if he came back, he would be changed. And if I held onto any hope, that hope would hamper me from moving forward with my life.

Ruth, on the other hand, was determined to push forward toward recovering her twin brother. Over breakfast just this morning, she had talked about finding a private detective to locate Donald, and she'd already identified a deprogrammer specializing in recovering people from cults. So while I couldn't have said that I'd passed through the first four grief stages, I was closing in on acceptance. Ruth was still in denial. And I had to allow her that.

~

Ruth and I went for lunch after the service. She was over the moon.

"Spencer, wasn't that beautiful? I like Dr. Stein so much. I felt like she really cared. And the closeness of the congregation —couldn't you feel it?"

"They did seem sincere," I admitted.

"What was your favorite part?"

Almost against my will, I smiled. "I'm not sure whether it was 'Welcome gays and lesbians' or 'Welcome Christians.'"

Ruth clapped her hands, clearly gleeful. "Oh, I know! Wasn't that marvelous?"

I shrugged. "As a Christian, I'm not entirely sure I like being treated as an afterthought."

"Of course you don't. Who would? But consider that in this country, Christians have always been at the head of the line, and everyone else was an afterthought. When you've been in a position of privilege, seeing the non-privileged rise can feel like you're losing something."

I gave Ruth an assessing glance. "Have you ever thought of becoming a minister?"

I thought she would laugh. At least chuckle. But she leaned forward on the table.

Her voice low and intense, she said, "Have you ever thought of becoming a Unitarian Universalist minister?"

It was a busy week for Ruth. She met with at least three private detective and two deprogrammers. She also looked at several places where she might live, and I was selfishly glad she didn't find anything. Not yet. I enjoyed her company too much.

I was busy as well, even with only one therapy session that week. Since the UU service, I had felt more clear-headed than I could remember feeling in a long time. I found myself digging into some of Dr. Stein's points as I worked on my private studies for General.

And I found myself coming back to Ruth's question, not frequently but often enough to notice. The possibility of being a Unitarian Universalist minister was now as firmly lodged in my brain as was any other possibility, once I had earned my M. Div. from General.

On Thursday afternoon, a beautiful summer day when the sky was a clear blue and there was just enough breeze to keep the sun from feeling too hot, I picked up my Gramercy Park key and went for a walk. Ruth was out looking at an apartment, and the house felt empty.

As I approached the gate, I saw there was a young woman with two small children at the entrance, looking into the park. The woman's hair was almost black, pulled back into a ponytail. Her clothes were neat but obviously inexpensive. The boy with her was about six, the girl perhaps eight or nine. They didn't see me right away, so I overheard some of their conversation.

"Diego, no. We can't go in. The fence is locked, and I don't have a key." The slight lilt in her accent made me think she came from somewhere south of the border, as the expression goes, as did the dark tan color of her skin.

Diego stomped his foot. "But why? Why is it locked?"

The girl had her own ideas. "Because, estúpido, it's for rich white people. They don't let people like us inside."

"But why?" Diego's plaintive whine got to me.

"I have a key," I said. All three of them turned quickly toward me. To the woman I said, "Would you like to go inside?"

"You would not get into trouble?"

I smiled. "I would not. Here." And I moved forward and unlocked the gate. "I was planning to go in, anyway."

The two children ran ahead, and I said to the woman, "My name is Spencer Hill." I held my hand out.

"Marta Ortiz." She smiled as we shook hands. "Thank you. Thank you very much."

"My pleasure. We'll need to be sure to leave at the same time, so I can secure the gate again."

"Of course."

We walked forward together and, of course, ended up at the bench I associated with Donald. She sat, and I asked, "Do you mind if I join you?" She waved at the bench beside her, and we watched the children chase each other around Edwin Booth's statue.

"They're your children?" I asked.

"Sí. Yes. Juanita and Diego."

"Do you live close by?" Not everyone in the area had keys, and I didn't want to presume.

"Not far. But not so grand." She paused in a way that made me think she had more to say. But she shook her head quickly two or three times.

"Are Juanita and Diego enjoying their summer vacation from school?" I couldn't have said why, but something about this woman—a vulnerability, perhaps, or a need she wanted to hide— made me want to know whether I could help her in any way, so I wanted her to feel comfortable talking about herself.

"I suppose. I wish—" Again, she paused and shook her head.

As gently as I could, I asked, "What is it you wish?"

She sighed. "I wish they had better places to play. Like this. We go to other parks, but the subway, it is expensive for me, and the children don't understand how it can be dangerous."

I nodded. "That sounds challenging. Is there no one who can go with you? Another adult?"

"Not now." Something hard descended over her, a barrier between us, and I knew she didn't want to say more about that.

I decided it might put her more at ease if I spoke about myself. "I'm studying at a seminary, a little west of here."

"You are a priest?"

"Not yet." Maybe never, but she didn't need complicated explanations.

"Catholic?"

"Episcopalian."

"I am Catholic." She called out to Diego not to run so fast. Then, "It is important, no? To have faith?"

"I think so, yes. Especially in times of trouble. When we're struggling, emotionally or with the expenses we must meet."

"Yes." Again, the barrier.

Tread carefully, Spencer. "I think it helps to remember that God has always been there for the people who need Him most. The Bible is full of examples of when He came to the aid of people in trouble." I gave a slight chuckle. "It's funny how often people in control of worldly things think God is on their side. But, really, God favors those who are on His side, not the other way around."

I stopped talking. Let her have a chance to say whatever she wanted to, or not to speak at all. We watched the children for a couple of minutes. And then Marta spoke again.

"I hope God will favor us soon."

"Why is that?"

"I need my—how do you say, the man I will marry—to come back. I was born here, but he was sent back to Guatemala."

"Your fiancé is not with you? Will he be able to come back soon?"

She shook her head again. "I don't know. He is in danger. His brother wants him to work with him, but it is illegal."

"Illegal?" I wasn't sure I should say it, but I added, "Do you mean drugs?"

"Yes. Esteban will not do it. So he is in danger."

"Marta, I'm so sorry to hear that. He sounds like a good man."

"He is. Juanita and Diego? They are not his children. But he would take care of all of us." I had no idea how to respond. Then she added, "And I am almost lost my job." She seemed ready to cry.

Well, Spencer, I told myself, *you wanted her to open up. Be careful what you wish for.*

I waited for her to calm herself and then asked, "What kind of work are you doing?"

"I'm a housekeeper. The family have two children. I help take care of them. Today they are on Long Island with their parents. But the family moves soon to California."

"How discouraging for you." I had to ask, "Do you live with them, or do you have your own place to live?"

"We are in our apartment. It is small, but it is enough. But soon I cannot afford to pay the rent."

I wracked my brain. Surely, there was something I could do to help this young family. I couldn't exactly fire my current housekeeper and hire Marta. I tried to bring to mind anyone else who might be in the market for a housekeeper, and I drew nothing but blanks.

And then I had a brainstorm.

"Mrs. Ortiz, if you would be willing to give me a way to contact you, I will ask people I know if they might need someone like you. Is that too forward of me?"

She lifted one hand to her throat. "You would do this?"

"I'd be happy to ask. I can't promise, but I would like to help if I can."

She dug in her bag and pulled out a pen and a scrap of paper, on which she wrote a number. "My telephone." She smiled, but her eyes watered. "You are so kind. You will be a good priest."

"I hope so, Mrs. Ortiz."

We watched the children for another several minutes, our

comments limited to the weather and a few other superficial topics. It seemed to me her mood had lifted, and I hoped fervently that I had not given her false hope.

As soon as I had locked the gate and had bid farewell to the Ortiz family, I headed toward General, walking quickly.

Dr. Dunfee was not in his office, but I tracked him down in the library. After I described my meeting with Mrs. Ortiz, I told him my idea.

"I was hoping there might be something for her here. She has experience in child care. I know there's child care here for students and staff, so when her kids are not in school they could come here."

"It's an interesting idea, Spencer, but I'm not—"

"She's from Guatemala, I think, but her English is very good. Maybe she could even teach the children Spanish."

He laughed. "Slow down! I hear you. I'm not the person to speak to. But I will put you in touch with someone who is."

Late Friday afternoon I heard back from the administrative office. I called Marta immediately.

"Would you be able to go to an interview on Monday morning?" I told her a little about the job, which was pretty much exactly as I had described to Dr. Dunfee.

"I will need permission," Marta said, "but I am sure they will let me. They are sorry to let me go."

"Then they will give you good references. That's perfect."

I had done it! Of course, she didn't have the job yet, but I felt really hopeful that everything would work out for her. I could barely sit still and finally gave up on classwork for the day. I expected Ruth to be back soon, and I wanted to take her out for a fine dinner.

I went to the piano, but I was too distracted even for that.

Something Marta had said had been echoing in my brain: *You will be a good priest.*

Yes. I will. The title might not be "priest," but meeting with Marta, being able to help her, renewed my commitment. It gave me joy. It reminded me what my calling was, what my vocation needed to be.

Donald had once said to me that while being loved was wonderful, the real joy comes from loving. And something Father Fleming had said to me was that God does not necessarily speak directly to those who ask Him questions. More often, He speaks through someone in our lives.

God had spoken to Marta through me. And when God used me in that way, it wasn't about me. It wasn't about the messenger. It was about the message.

And the message was Love.

ACKNOWLEDGEMENT

I lived in Manhattan between 1980 and 1983. One of my closest friends during this period was Reid Farrell. At that point in his life, he was studying for the Episcopal priesthood at Manhattan's General Theological Seminary, the same institution as my protagonist, Spencer Hill. Reid was graduated from the seminary and has had a successful and fulfilling vocation.

Like Spencer, Reid had to face the Episcopal Church's evolving attitudes and acceptance of priests who were homosexual. Acceptance was granted or denied according to the diocese in question, and even acceptance was qualified in different ways.

As I worked on *For Love Of God*, Reid was very generous with his time, his insights, and his personal experience, helping me understand what life would be like for Spencer, as a gay man who feels called to the priesthood. It was only during the last few months of writing this story that I became aware of the tremendous strength of character, courage, and determination Reid showed in refusing to turn away from his calling or to betray his personal truth.

Reid Farrell refused to lie. He also knew that living a life that denied who he was would not only be less authentic for his parishioners, but also it would feel like slapping God in the face. He was the perfect advisor to help me represent Spencer honestly and realistically.

So I thank Reid for his help and support. But even more, I admire him. And while the denigration of queer people continues to be a problem that affects and sometimes ruins lives, the *Blessed Be* series is my latest effort to help bring respectful acceptance to the queer community.

FOR LOVE OF GOD

(Blessed Be Series, Book 1)

Robin Reardon

About This Guide

The suggested questions are included to enhance your group's
reading of Robin Reardon's novel, *FOR LOVE OF GOD*,
Book 1 of the *BLESSED BE* series.

DISCUSSION QUESTIONS

Note: The questions in this guide contain spoiler information. It is recommended that you finish the book before reading the questions.

1. How would you describe the relationship between Spencer and his father? Between Spencer and his mother? Between his two parents?
2. How do you think Spencer's father would have reacted to the news that Spencer was gay? What about his mother's response?
3. Donald tells Spencer, "People always play games. We might be trying to avoid admitting that our behavior matters. We might want to lord it over the loser. We might want to validate our own feelings of superiority by fooling someone else. But in the end? In the end the game is real. So is it still a game?" If you had to answer Donald's question, what would you say?
4. On the terrace at The Cloisters, Donald accuses Spencer of avoidance. In fact, there are several points

in the story where Spencer avoids one thing or another. Can you name some of them?

5. What do you think of Tegan? Consider her first date with Spencer, her sympathetic and sensitive response to his mother's death, her acceptance of his orientation, and the ways in which she tries to convince Spencer to continue his studies. Is Donald's conclusion that she's a fag hag correct, or is her relationship with Spencer more complicated than that?

6. Donald tells Spencer that while it's great to be loved, true joy comes from loving. Do you agree with Donald? If so, why? If not, why not?

7. There are a few places in the story where we see that children are important to Donald. In fact, he tells Spencer that having a family is one reason he joined The Risen Christ group. Given that the story takes place in the mid-1980s, can you understand how the gap between being gay and having children of one's own might be at least part of what would drive someone to do what Donald did?

8. Think back to the scene where Spencer confronts Donald about joining The Risen Christ. Donald accuses Spencer of not knowing what it's like to wear the sign "Unclean" beneath his clothing. Spencer insists he does know. This sign implies a warning to others. But hidden beneath clothing, isn't the wearer its audience? In what ways are the two men's responses to this message different from each other?

9. In what ways do you think Donald helped Spencer move forward in his life, aside from the obvious way of showing him how to love a man?

10. One thing that troubles Spencer as he considers whether to continue in his chosen vocation is how

important it is to him that the Episcopal Church often includes what Donald considers theatrics. Do you think Spencer will be able to choose a path that doesn't include the colors and the pageantry, or will his familiarity with and fondness for this pageantry be too powerful?

11. Have you ever experienced anything like Spencer's first conversation with Robert Karl, or like the service Spencer and Ruth attended? Has anyone ever tried to convince you that they held the answer to life? If so, how did you respond?

12. What do you think will happen to Donald? Is his conversion genuine? Is it just one more acting job for him? Or is it something else?

AUTHOR'S NOTE

While I do not follow any institutionalized religion, I was raised in the Episcopal Church. Having studied various religious traditions over the years, both deist and non-deist, it seems to me that humans everywhere are looking for Love—capital L.

I was moved by what novelist Ian McEwan, whom I consider to be a devout atheist, had to say about Love. In September of two thousand and two, the series Frontline (Public Broadcasting Service) released "Faith And Doubt At Ground Zero." In the full transcript of McEwan's interview for the program, he talked about how someone's last words were once known only if that someone were among "the grand and the great." Technology has changed this inequity.

Paraphrasing McEwan: Because of technology and because of the events of September 11, 2001, we know what teachers and plumbers and stock brokers and security guards and office workers will do when they see that their personal deaths are imminent. They will respond to a basic human instinct. They will reach for communication devices, they will contact someone they love, and they will say, "I love you."

From agnostic to Zoroastrian, from Jew to Christian to Muslim, it seems to me that Love is humanity's primary driver and motivator. Its lack takes us to dark areas. Its presence, or our belief in its existence, leads us to the light. Belief in an un-created creator is not necessary.

I do not identify with Spencer's calling. But I believe his calling can help others to find Love.

If you enjoyed this book, please consider posting a review on the online sites of your choice. This is the best way to ensure that more titles by this author will become available.

If you would like to be notified with news about this author's work, including when new titles are released, you can sign up for Robin's mailing list at robinreardon.com/contact.

ABOUT THE AUTHOR

Robin Reardon is an inveterate observer of human nature, and her primary writing goal is to create stories about all kinds of people whose destinies should not be determined solely by their sexual orientation or gender identity. Her secondary writing goal is to introduce readers to concepts or information they might not know very much about.

Robin's motto is this: The only thing wrong with being queer is how some people treat you when they find out.

Interests outside of writing include singing, nature photography, and the study of comparative religions. Robin writes in a butter yellow study with a view of the Boston, Massachusetts skyline.

Robin blogs (And now, this) about various subjects that influence her writing, as well as about the writing process itself, on her website.

Other Works by Robin Reardon

Novels

ON CHOCORUA (Book 1 of the *Trailblazer* series)
ON THE KALALAU TRAIL (Book 2 of the *Trailblazer* series)
ON THE PRECIPICE (Book 3 of the *Trailblazer* series)
AND IF I FALL
WAITING FOR WALKER
THROWING STONES
(Published by **IAM Books**)
EDUCATING SIMON
THE EVOLUTION OF ETHAN POE
A QUESTION OF MANHOOD
THINKING STRAIGHT
A SECRET EDGE
(Published by Kensington Publishing Corp.)

Short Stories

GIUSEPPE AND ME
A LINE IN THE SAND
(Published by **IAM Books**)

~

Essay
THE CASE FOR ACCEPTANCE: AN OPEN LETTER TO
HUMANITY
(Published by **IAM Books**)